# DEDICATION

*Carolyn Bruce Porter*

*1933-2020*

*I Love and Miss You Mom*

## PRAISE FOR *HERE THEY COME*

"With *Here They Come*, Scott Porter takes his place in the line of writers such as Tim O'Brien and Philip Caputo who have translated the horrors of war to a personal level. Porter draws the reader into the ethnic tensions that exploded into the war in Kosovo through characters who are well drawn, complex and all too human. His precise and focused writing exposes the true costs of a war in a distant European corner that took its toll not only in blood but more so in the spirits of those who fought it, and those caught in its crossfire."

—Greg Fields, author of *Arc of the Comet*, 2018 nominee, Kindle Book of the Year in Literary Fiction

"In taking readers into how real historical events impact the lives of civilians and combatants, Scott Porter combines the best of historical fiction in his riveting novel, *Here They Come*. The author weaves a story of war, love and comradeship amidst the brutality of not only the battles, but also the ethnic cleansing in Kosovo. The story never lags as the characters wrestle with conflicted loyalties of the heart, friendships forged in battle, and powerful identities rooted in history. A great read from start to finish."

—James Ballard, Author of *Poisoned Jungle*

"Fantastic read! Scott captures the tribulations felt by thousands of frightened citizens during the Kosovo War in the story of *Here They Come*. Scott depicts this time with such historical and cultural detail you feel like you could be their neighbor. The intensity of the military missions, portrayal of soldier comradery, mixed with the humanism expressed by those surviving and fighting, is illustrated in a most profound manner."

—Master Sergeant Nathan Aguinaga, (USA, Ret.), Author of *Division: Life on Ardennes Street, Roster Number Five Zero,* and *Wake Up, You're Having Another Nightmare*

"Simply put, one of the best war novels that I have read in the last ten years! Combat veteran Scott Porter provides a vivid and moving account of the 1999 war in Kosovo and the men and women who found themselves on opposing sides, engaged in the defense of their homeland or convinced that the elimination of Kosovo and its people must be accomplished at all costs. The reader will find themselves in the ranks of the Kosovo Liberation Army, assisting in the evacuation of Kosovar towns and villages, and engaged in close combat with units from the invading Yugoslavian Army, supported by Special Police and paramilitary units, intent on eliminating the Kosovar population through ethnic cleansing. An authentic, exciting, and 'you are there' account that makes for great storytelling."

—Lieutenant Colonel Thomas G. Bradbeer (USA, Ret.), PhD in History

*Here They Come*

by Scott A. Porter

Published by

 köehlerbooks ™

3705 Shore Drive
Virginia Beach, VA 23455
800-435-4811
www.koehlerbooks.com

# HERE THEY COME

A NOVEL

SCOTT A. PORTER

VIRGINIA BEACH
CAPE CHARLES

*If you're going through hell, keep going.*
Winston Churchill

The Kosovo War lasted from February 1998 to June 1999. The Yugoslavian Army (Vojska Jugoslavije or VJ), Serbian Special Police and paramilitaries facilitated a systematic campaign of terror, including ethnic cleansing using mass murder, expulsions, rape, torture, and the complete destruction of Albanian Kosovar and minority villages. Over 90 percent of Albanian Kosovars were displaced during the war. Albanian Kosovars and volunteers from other countries fought back. Numbering over 20,000, the Kosovo Liberation Army (KLA) aggressively engaged the Serbian forces. With air support from the North Atlantic Treaty Organization (NATO) starting on 24 March 1999, the war grew in intensity and devastation. Over 1,000 NATO aircraft and 30 warships and submarines supported the KLA. The following story is based upon real and imagined events. All characters are imagined.

# CAST OF CHARACTERS

## (IN ORDER OF APPEARANCE)

**Agim Shala**: Father of Julianna Shala

**Julianna Shala**: Albanian Kosovar from Drenica

**Miroslav Cadikovski**: Serb from Klina

**Mirjeta Shala**: Mother of Julianna Shala

**Josif Shala**: Brother of Julianna Shala and Kosovo Liberation Army 3rd Brigade commander

**Niko Radic**: The man arrested at the Montenegro border crossing

**Lieutenant Colonel John Phillips**: British SAS officer

**Lieutenant Colonel Travis Savage**: US Army Special Forces officer

**Trooper**: Lieutenant Colonel Travis Savage's military working dog

**Lieutenant Prek Luga**: Kosovo Liberation Army Special Forces platoon leader

**General Arsim Gashi**: Kosovo Liberation Army commander

**Deidra Aliti**: Roma refugee

**Shabin Aliti**: Deidra Aliti's four-year-old son

**Bekim Mali**: Kosovo Liberation Army deputy to 3rd Brigade commander

**Major Borozan**: Serb political officer

**Colonel Dragan Cadikovski**: Yugoslav Army commander of the Guards Brigade and older brother of Miroslav Cadikovski

**Sergeant Luka Kovac**: Miro Cadikovski's Yugoslav Army supply sergeant

**Filip, Suzana, and Ana Marin**: Family in Mitrovice where Miroslav Cadikovski was housed

**Sergeant Bogdana "Bog" Komazec**: Miro Cadikovski's Yugoslav Army platoon sergeant

**Corporal Vuk Kovac**: Miro Cadikovski's squad leader

**Lieutenant Aleksandra "Alex" Buha**: Miro Cadikovski's American Yugoslav army platoon leader

# 01: ELOPE

**IN KOSOVO NO DAY** is like what came before. A large white banner adorned with red lettering reading *Dita e Veres*, meaning "Summer Day" in Albanian, hangs over a dirt road leading into Drenica, Kosovo. Young boys laugh and taunt each other as they kick a worn-out soccer ball under the midday sun. Shish-kabob smoke, mixed with the smell of bread baking in clay ovens, fills the light breeze with tantalizing aromas. A few hundred people, mainly women, eat and drink the local red wine while enjoying the exotic sounds of Albanian Kosovar folk music and dance. At times the crowd claps enthusiastically while the patriotic "Rapsodi" is played by a small ensemble of older men with long-tailed wooden string instruments.

One of those men, Agim Shala, stands off to the left side of the ensemble playing a handmade wooden flute. He is a short man in his fifties with a wrinkled leathery face and a long, gray, drooping mustache. He wears traditional Albanian Kosovar clothing consisting of brown *opinga* shoes, white baggy pants, white shirt with a red vest, and a brimless, white felt *plis* cap. Agim

Shala sets the pace for the string musicians and dancers to follow. Most of the time he sets a lively fast pace, such as in the "Rapsodi."

Close to the ensemble are twelve women dancers dressed in traditional ethnic attire: white scarves, blouses adorned with hand-embroidered red and yellow flora, skirts with aprons, knee-high thick socks and flat slippers. Their skirts, long earrings, necklaces and bracelets whirl as they dance to the rhythm.

Typically, male dancers would likewise be dressed in traditional Kosovar clothing, but this year there are no men. There are no young men in the crowd either, just boys and older men. No one can recall a Summer Day celebration without young men. But the young men of Drenica are in the hills, armed and watchful, ready to pounce on any Serb paramilitary force that comes close to their village.

The festivities end late in the afternoon, and one of the young dancers, Julianna, the daughter of Agim Shala, dashes over to him. Breathing hard, she gives her father a tight hug, a kiss on his left cheek, then whispers something in his ear. His red, droopy eyes moisten. She is in a hurry and hastily scurries away. Agim Shala solemnly watches her until she disappears toward the edge of the village.

Already winded from hours of dancing, Julianna leaves the main road and runs down a rough goat path leading into the nearby woods. Careful to avoid the numerous stones jutting out of the trail, she keeps her eyes down to avoid being bitten by a sharp rock. She has been down this rocky path many times before, mainly during her childhood to play with children from the nearby village of Klina.

She is running to meet with one of those childhood friends. Dashing around a left turn on the trail, she collides head-on with a man stepping out from behind a tree. Startled at first, Julianna is ecstatic as the two embrace, then kiss passionately. The man holds her at arm's length, admiring her splendor.

With a jumbo smile he gasps, "You look so beautiful today, Julianna. I wish I could have seen you dance like in the old days."

She gazes at him and thinks his is the most handsome face she has ever seen. His piercing blue eyes, long, sandy-colored hair, and that big smile make her melt. She has known him all her life, played with him as a child, and eventually fell in love with him when they were teenagers. He adores Julianna just as much as she does him. Her beautiful tan skin, long, flowing black hair, and big brown eyes highlight her bright-white teeth behind sensual lips. As an accomplished gymnast, she possesses an incredible athletic physique. She is stronger and faster than some men, and Julianna has caught the attention of many a young man in the past.

However, this young man is her future husband, Miroslav Cadikovski, a Serb.

Julianna reaches into her right blouse pocket and pulls out a red-and-white braided bracelet. She gently places it around his left wrist. Miroslav knows what it means: the Summer Day *Verore*, a bracelet symbolizing love and commitment. With the Albanian Kosovar men's absence at today's festival, it is ironic that a Serb will be the only man to be presented a *Verore* on this day. Miroslav cherishes it more than anything given to him before. It is a tender moment, and they hold each other quietly.

With tears rolling down her cheeks, Julianna glances up at his face and whispers, "I love you more than ever, Miro."

That jumbo smile lights up again before her entrancing eyes.

Miro says, "We will be together starting tonight, my love. I will be in front of your house at seven sharp. Let's quickly say goodbye to your parents and then be off. I want it to be that simple, not drawn out and painful. Besides, we have no time to waste. We must cross the border tonight." He pauses briefly, then softly says, "Tonight will be the most important night of our lives."

Julianna relaxes and looks softly at Miro. "I am sorry we have to leave so late, but today was also so important to me. You know what Papa means to me."

Miro nods approval, realizing it might be her last *Dita e Veres* for a long time, if ever. The last time she might ever see her father play his flute.

The two briefly hug once more, then dart off in different directions, Miro toward his Serbian village of Klina, and Julianna back to Drenica. Walking at a fast pace and perspiring heavily, Julianna dreads saying goodbye to her parents. She loves them dearly, as she has all of her nineteen years. It will be difficult to part with them, but she knows it is imperative to leave. During these difficult times of ethnic strife in Kosovo, it is just too dangerous for a Serb and Albanian Kosovar to marry, much less even be seen together.

Returning to Drenica, Julianna tries to catch her breath as she walks down the roads lined with small brick homes. Drenica is a typical village in the Balkans—winding dirt roads, small family-owned shops, and spotty electricity. She turns down a side street and waves to her neighbors sitting on their front steps. Finally, she enters a small square home composed of large, red, hollow bricks and a light-brown tile roof. Stepping inside, she sees her parents glumly sitting in the front room.

Julianna stops and looks at them with tearful eyes. "Hello, Mamma and Papa. It is almost that time." Neither of her parents look at her or say anything. It is an uncomfortable and awkward silence.

Julianna steps softly to the back of the house. "I must wash and finish packing. It won't take me long."

Still without a word, her mother, Mirjeta, puts her hands over her eyes. She wears a long, dark dress, typical women's attire for anywhere in the Balkans. Like Julianna, she has long black hair and brown eyes, now swollen from crying. She stayed home that day from the festivities, unable to enjoy what might be one of the saddest days of her life: the day she loses her daughter. She glances at Agim, who stares into space and says nothing while tightly grasping his flute.

Julianna lowers herself into a hot bath. Still preoccupied with saying goodbye to her parents, an intense anxiety starts to control her thoughts. Emotionally, it will be the most difficult part of her upcoming trip. As she washes, she wonders what life will be like away from the safety, comfort and love of her parents for the first time in her life. Although she has waited what seems like an eternity to elope with Miro, now it seems everything is moving too fast. She hastily finishes bathing, wraps herself in a towel, and shuffles just a few feet into her small bedroom.

Her mind moves like a hummingbird's wings, to a point where she is unable to think clearly. Julianna randomly throws her few belongings into a large blue canvas bag, but she leaves one thing behind: on her bed is the traditional Kosovar dress she wore that day. Her mother once wore it, as well as her grandmother and great-grandmother.

Julianna gazes at the cherished dress in a trance-like state, coming to terms with the reality that she is about to leave almost everything she values behind: her family, village, and way of life.

After dressing in jeans and a soft woolen sweater, Julianna ambles back into the front room. Her mother meets her as she comes from the kitchen holding a basket of food covered by a small white towel. Julianna manages a smile, but lowers her head as she contritely takes the food basket. She tries as hard as she can to keep from falling to pieces.

A man's loud voice breaks the silence. "Aren't you going to kiss me before you leave?"

Startled, Julianna jumps, then nervously spurts out, "Josif, I didn't hear you come in!"

Her twenty-five-year-old brother stands in a corner of the front room, his usual charming self, grinning from ear to ear.

"I just arrived while you were packing. Papa sent word you were leaving, and I had to say goodbye, because . . . well, you are my favorite person in the world!"

Josif laughs and holds out his arms. She runs up and gives her brother a long hug, kissing him gently on both cheeks. Julianna has admired Josif her entire life. While growing up, he was the big brother who always protected her and won her fights. Seemingly larger than life, he is a head taller than most Kosovars, and has a muscular build from his years as a prized soccer player in Yugoslavia.

Josif has remained away from home for several weeks. He fights as a soldier in the Kosovo Liberation Army, or KLA. The KLA started as a guerilla army but has formed into a dedicated force of thousands to protect all Kosovar minorities from Serbian aggression. He wears a US Army camouflage uniform and black boots, but instead of American insignia he wears a red KLA patch on his left arm. Under his command are the men of Drenica, along with Albanian Kosovar men from the surrounding villages.

Julianna looks up to him with a faint smile. "I *am* happy you came to say goodbye. I have no idea where you are from day to day, and I always worry about you. I really wish you would not be a freedom fighter. If the Serbs find you, they will . . . well, it will be awful. I am going to miss you so much, big brother."

With that, she buries her face in his chest, wondering if she will see him again—alive. Tears flow down her checks onto his uniform. Josif is touched. He kisses his sister on the top of her head.

They hear a car drive up. The brakes squeal, and the engine turns off. A car door slams followed by a light knock on the door, arousing everyone's attention. Josif grabs a pistol from his shoulder holster, but Agim tells him to put it down. Agim knows who it is, and with his flute in one hand, he opens the door with the other. Miro stands in the doorway, jittery and pale. Agim motions him to hurriedly enter. Instead, Miro walks in hesitantly, awkward like a teenage boy meeting the parents of a first date. But this is no first date; he is eloping with their daughter. Miro becomes even more uncomfortable once he sees Josif. He knows Josif well from their childhood days, and they have both been protective of Julianna. Now here is Josif, in battle uniform to fight against his people, the Serbs.

Miro and Josif have not seen each other since ethnic hostilities blew wide open after the wars in Bosnia and Croatia. Miro has never even seen a member of the KLA. Josif, sensing Miro's discomfort, approaches him with an extended hand. Miro eagerly accepts, tightly shaking Josif's much larger hand.

"We have known each other all our lives, Miro. There are a few good Serbs, and you are one of them. The KLA will not harm you, my friend. Besides, you know I can still kick your ass in soccer."

Miro manages a chuckle, but remains speechless.

Taking a step closer to Miro, Josif continues, "These are difficult times between our peoples, Miro. I wouldn't let Julianna leave if I had any doubt she didn't love you. So, let me get to the point. You must promise me now to take care of her, no matter what." Josif looks sternly at Miro, as if seeing right into his soul. "*No matter what.* Never for a moment think that your Serb roots are more important than her. If you run out on her to join the Yugoslav army, or turn your back on any Kosovars to save your own skin, well, you better think about the consequences. Take her out of Kosovo, but bring her back once it is safe."

Miro breaks into a weak smile, then gulps loudly. He glances at Julianna, then back to Josif. He stands straight, and in a firm voice he states, "I will, Josif. I promise my life on it. You know I love her with all of my heart. I hope everyone here thinks our departure is the right thing to do. If I stayed here, I would be forced into the Yugoslav army. To me, that is unthinkable. I could never fire a shot in anger at anyone unless it was to save Julianna."

Mirjeta, relieved that Josif and Miro seem to be on amiable terms, breaks the tenseness by inviting everyone to sit for hot tea. Josif sits across from Miro and queries him if his car parked outside has Serb license plates. Miro, still uncomfortable in front of Julianna's family, anxiously blurts out he took them off temporarily, knowing with the current hostilities a parked car in Drenica with Serb plates would most likely be targeted for vigilantism, or worse.

Mirjeta serves the customary hot tea in shot-style glasses. As the sugar is passed around, Agim looks at Miro, with his distinctive light-brown hair and blue eyes, so different from that of Kosovars.

Agim asks, "What do your parents think of you eloping with Julianna?"

Miro, stirring his tea, suddenly stops and looks sheepishly at Agim. "They don't know."

Everyone but Julianna is shocked. They all gaze at Agim to hear his response. Agim slightly raises his voice. "They don't know? What did you tell them?"

At first hesitant to speak again, Miro has the look of a child caught doing something terribly wrong.

"I told them I was leaving to join the Yugoslav army, as instructed by my father and by the government conscription act. If my father knew what I was really doing, he would have the police arrest me before we could get away."

The room becomes silent. Miro continues, "There has been a mandatory call-up of all Serbian men living in Kosovo between the ages of eighteen and thirty-five to go to Belgrade by next week to enlist. That is why we are leaving for Montenegro tonight."

Josif asks Miro why the enlistment order was given. Miro looks down, clears his throat, then makes eye contact with Josif.

"I think President Milosevic is going to attack you, the KLA, with everything he can. He will need troops for that, especially troops that live in Kosovo and speak Albanian, as they will also know the Kosovar villages and the ground."

Astonished, Josif puts his tea down. Everyone present knows what this means.

Atrocities by the Serb paramilitaries against Kosovars have steady increased in the last year. Hundreds of Kosovars, including men, women and children, have been murdered by Serbian paramilitary thugs. The resistance, the KLA, grew quickly in numbers to combat the paramilitaries, and now, apparently, Milosevic will attack them with a larger conventional Yugoslav army, the Vojska Jugoslavije or *VJ*.

Anxiously, Miro says, "Listen, a very dangerous time is coming soon. Agim and Mirjeta, please come with Julianna and I. There is plenty of room. Josif, come with us also. If you don't, you must go immediately into hiding."

Josif, in a low and serious voice, speaks and looks hard at his parents. "Since Milosevic became president, Kosovar rights have been eroding. No longer can we send children to school, vote, or even speak our own language in public. We the KLA have a sworn duty to protect our people in our land, and our ranks are swelling higher each time the Serbs commit another crime."

Like Miro, Julianna senses bad times are approaching, and once again begs her parents and Josif to come with them. But, like numerous times before, they state they cannot leave their ancestral home and give up everything. Josif says he will protect them, and explains that is why he is in the KLA—to ensure what happened in Drenica a year ago will not happen again. Serb paramilitary forces murdered an entire Kosovar family and other villagers because of their support of the KLA. Josif states he will not back down; too much blood has already been spilled to quit now.

Miro is not backing down either, and he tries his best to convince Josif and Julianna's parents that Milosevic is planning the total annihilation of the KLA by using overwhelming conventional forces. No matter how hard the KLA fights, they will be outmanned by at least ten to one. After that, the entire Kosovar population will be murdered or driven away.

With his eyebrows clenched down, Agim looks intensely at Miro. "Does your brother know what you are doing?"

Miro responds hesitantly. He is embarrassed. "I don't think Dragan knows anything about Julianna and I. He has been gone for years in the VJ, is a colonel now, and he only comes home to visit our parents from time to time. You know we have never really gotten along. My father worships him but thinks little of me because I am just a struggling electrician. To my father, it is all about Serb nationalism, and the rightful Serbian claim to Kosovo."

Julianna leans her head on Miro's shoulder. The room is uncomfortably quiet once again, with a profound sense of sadness and dread of what might happen to Kosovo.

Josif breaks the silence. "If things get too bad—I mean, if the VJ are going to attack Drenica—we will evacuate the village and send families south into Macedonia. But the KLA will stay and fight, to the bitter end if necessary."

Again, stony silence; awkwardness. Somberly, everyone rises from the table. Hugs and handshakes are traded with gloomy faces. Without a word, Miro and Josif look into each other's eyes and trade confident stares. They shake hands tightly. Agim sits down with his face in his hands, silently crying.

Mirjeta looks into Julianna's face, with both of her hands clutching Julianna's cheeks. She can only mutter, "Please never forget us."

"*Never*," Julianna promises.

Josif opens the front door for Miro as he quickly packs Julianna's bag and the basket of food into his dirty white two-door Crvena Zastava. He opens the passenger door for Julianna, then hastily trots around the back of the car and hops into the driver's seat. As he starts the car a large blast of black exhaust pours out of the tailpipe, and the two begin their long-awaited dream.

Miro and Julianna drive slowly out of Drenica and travel north, still leaving the Serb license plates off because of several Kosovar neighborhoods along the way. The last thing Miro wants is to be stopped at a KLA checkpoint with a beautiful Kosovar lady. That would turn ugly, fast.

Once out of town, Miro drives as fast as he can, but like all failing public services in Kosovo, the few remaining paved roads are in disrepair. Miro constantly jerks the steering wheel back and forth as Julianna bounces about and hangs on the best she can. After an hour and a half of avoiding potholes, they turn west toward the Montenegro border. It is getting dark, and few cars are on the road. Miro stops on a side road and put his plates back on. It is not an easy task in the dark, especially because Miro is so nervous and shaky. He is that way for a good reason. To get across the border into Montenegro, they have to get past a Serb and Montenegrin border police checkpoint.

The couple drive west for another hour, then back north straight toward the Rozaje border crossing into Montenegro. In the valley ahead, Miro can see the lights at the crossing from miles away. At first the lights are white dots shining through a thick evening fog, but as they drive closer the lights grow in size and intensity, mesmerizing Miro. His driving becomes haphazard. He hits one pothole after another, and his tight grip on the steering wheel only slightly loosens when Julianna gently places her left hand on top of his right. He glances at her and sees a confident smile. It makes him feel better, and he discerns it is time to gather his composure. Miro tries his best to relax, but his anxiety climbs once again upon seeing the ghostly outline of cars waiting in line at the crossing site. It is just before 11 PM, and about a dozen cars are stopped, awaiting their turn to cross. No vehicles are coming into Kosovo, but that is no surprise considering the impending increase in hostilities.

They pull behind the last car in line and wait. Each vehicle seems like it takes forever to get through the crossing. Miro notices the VJ are manning the crossing instead of the Serb or Montenegrin border police. Even worse, once a car gets to the station, he sees VJ soldiers forcing all occupants out of their vehicle.

"Damn!" Miro blurts out, frightening Julianna.

"What is wrong? What happened?"

Miro sinks into his seat and sighs, explaining the situation to Julianna. This is an unexpected and alarming situation, as Miro knows what they are looking for: Serb men living in Kosovo escaping from the mandatory military call-up. Julianna reaches over and gives him a gentle kiss on his lips. They look into each other's eyes, knowing what lies ahead is going to be difficult.

One by one, the occupants and cars are inspected and pass through the border into Montenegro. Just one car remains in front of them. Miro and Julianna gently roll down their windows to hear what the soldiers say to the driver.

"Name?"

"Nicholas Radic."

"License!"

Miro can see the driver hand over his license, but Julianna, straining to see, cannot from the passenger's seat. She can only hear. Miro watches the soldier compare the driver's license to a paper on a clipboard. After examining the license and whatever is on the clipboard, the soldier glances at the other soldiers, as if silently communicating with them.

"Get out!"

The driver hesitates for a second, maybe two, just long enough for another solder to quickly open the door and grab him by the collar, pulling him violently onto the concrete. Three soldiers grab the man and flex-cuff him so efficiently it is apparent they have done it many times before.

The driver stands up and begins to protest, but to his own detriment. Without hesitation, a soldier smashes him in the face with the butt-stock of an AK-47, immediately collapsing him to the ground. The two other soldiers drag the limp body and dump it on the curb next to the border-crossing station. Another soldier jumps in the man's car and drives it to a lot full of other cars, many of them full of bullet holes. Soldiers begin searching the car in earnest, throwing everything on the ground.

It has all happened so fast, and now they are next. Julianna is perfectly cool, sitting calmly as if it were something she did every day. Police can pick up on nervousness, and Julianna knows it. Miro is in a different state. His anxiety is getting the best of him, but he knows he must gather himself to act his role. There is no margin for mistakes.

The soldier with a clipboard quickly approaches, along with three more armed with AK-47s. Miro notices that the soldier with the clipboard is a senior sergeant by his collar insignia, and obviously very much in charge. The sergeant suddenly stops in front of Miro's car, apparently writing down information from the license plate. Dropping the clipboard to his left side, he puts his right hand on a holstered pistol on his hip and walks to Miro's open window, glancing inside.

"Names?"

Miro keeps a straight face. "Miroslav and Julianna Cadikovski."

"License!"

Miro hands over his license, trying his best to not shake. The sergeant studies the license and compares Miro to the picture.

"You are from Klina. Where are you going?"

Miro, confidently speaking in his native Serb, says, "To Berane to visit family before I go into the army. I have worked all day, and we are driving tonight so I can visit tomorrow and then drive the next day from Berane to Belgrade for enlistment. My brother is Colonel Cadikovski, commander of the Guards Brigade."

The sergeant is about to speak, hesitates, then sternly says, "Wait here."

He walks to the border station, entering the small hut and standing erect as if his spine were made of hard oak. He must be speaking to a person of authority. After a few minutes the sergeant walks back to the car in a military quickstep.

This time in a much friendlier tone, he says, "Please get out and stand over there," pointing to the rear of the car.

Miro and Julianna immediately comply and calmly stand behind their car. They observe three soldiers thoroughly searching their car, including inside their bags. Finally, a soldier reports to the sergeant that no contraband has been found, and the sergeant approaches Miro with his clipboard.

"Sign this and take it with you. You have seventy-two hours to cross the border back into Serbia before you are considered a fugitive. When you reenter, be sure you give this to the sergeant at the border crossing. You are lucky Colonel Cadikovski is your brother. *That is all.*"

With their windows still down, Miro and Julianna drive slowly through the crossing. They remain composed as armed soldiers stare ominously at them. Although outwardly tranquil, Miro and Julianna are elated. They are on their way to freedom.

This elation quickly subsides as they notice the flex-cuffed prisoner now sitting on the curb, bleeding from his nose and mouth. As they pass the bleeding man, he looks up at Miro with the hollow eyes of a doomed man. Miro can't help but make eye contact, and his gut instinct is to save the man. He thinks that maybe he can stop and throw the man in the back seat. It would just take seconds. Miro continues to drive slowly past the bleeding man. He is concerned that even hitting his brakes might alert the guards. Miro swallows deeply, stares straight ahead, and begins to pick up speed. The lights behind them fade as they drive through the pass and into the winding Mokra Gora mountains.

It is a strenuous night of driving on a dark and dangerous winding road. Their car barely makes it up the steep hills, and going down is not any better. Even while downshifting to slow the engine speed, the brakes overheat with a burning metallic smell, making them both nauseous. The muffler falls off and the car sounds like a tank. They thunder over expansive bridges that traverse 1,000-foot ravines. Hairpin curves are frequent, with no shoulder between them and seemingly bottomless canyons.

By early morning Miro and Julianna are thrilled to finally arrive at the small Bosniak mountain village of Rozaje. Miro stops his embarrassingly loud car for gas and oil while Julianna retrieves bread and grapes from her mother's gift basket. After gassing up, Miro pulls the car off to the side of the service station. They eat and discuss the next step of their plan, to reach Berane by noon and be married by two. It is not the wedding either wanted, but considering the circumstances, it is miraculous that it is happening at all.

They drive on, paying no attention to the disgraceful sound of the car and their weariness. Their long-awaited wedding is just hours away. The roads are much better, and they arrive in Berane within an hour and a half. Traffic is light, and unlike in Kosovo, people go about their day with a sense of normalcy. Except, that is, that people stare at the loud obnoxious car driving by. Miro drives straight to the town center and quickly finds the courthouse. Like all government buildings, it is an old Yugoslavian communist-style architecture of cement and simplicity, nothing remotely fancy.

Berane, a multiethnic and multireligious city living in harmony, is a blessing. Miro and Julianna can be married without any underlying ethnic tensions. The justice of the peace turns out to be a middle-aged, short, bald Bosniak man. He hardly even glances at them, being more interested in quickly filling out the paperwork and getting his money—with a fat tip, of course. The bureaucratic process is over in fifteen minutes, and they hold back their emotions inside the quiet, ugly government building.

Once outside, they both cry in each other's arms. They are married.

Too early to get a hotel room, they buy lamb sausage, cheese, bread and red wine for a picnic on the lush green grass at the beautiful Limski Park on the Lim River. It is the most striking city and park either has seen. Cradled in a valley surrounded by snow-covered mountain peaks, it is a magnificent early-spring day. The fast-moving waters of the Lim, along with the birds singing in a bright-blue sky, make it a dreamlike moment. They stay all afternoon, eating, laughing, but mostly cradling each other. They speak of their childhoods together and all of the funny things that have happened over the years, such as the numerous times Julianna tried to tutor Miro in his English lessons—oh, what a disaster that was. Then there was the time Drenica played Klina in soccer, and Julianna was thrilled when Miro scored the winning goal. In Tito's communist era, people didn't even think of ethnic divides. With Tito's death, the communist era passed. Those times of peace and ethnic harmony, despite the wrath of communism, are sadly long gone.

Eventually the conversation turns to those they left behind in Drenica. Even in this beautiful spot, Julianna already misses her family, and feels awful she couldn't convince her parents to leave Drenica. After the hostilities are over, she and Miro will return, have children, and be a united family once again. But first, their plan must continue. Tomorrow they will drive 180 kilometers to Podgorica and catch a flight to Germany as political refugees. They simply can't stay in Montenegro, as the Serb Special Police will track Miro down within days.

That night they stay in a quaint hotel, complete with restaurant and small cozy room. At dinner they sit so close together they are always touching. Nibbling on the typical Balkan grill fare of various meats and vegetables, they speak mostly of their upcoming journey. Together.

Afterwards they ascend the stairs to their room and bathe separately. Both are excitedly uneasy. They have never made love, or even seen each other nude. As is custom in Kosovo, women do not have intercourse until they are married. Julianna takes her bath first and sits timidly on the bed, nude. She splashes perfume behind her ears and waits for Miro to finish his bath.

Miro comes out with his towel on. He stops in his tracks once he sees Julianna sitting on the bed. She eyes Miro as he drops his towel. Julianna slowly rises and they kiss naked, their hearts thundering with primal exhilaration. Their breathing increases dramatically. They fall into bed connected as one, absorbing each other's beating hearts and unbridled passions. They give themselves to each other for who knows how long, each bathing in the sweat of the other. Making love fills them with joy and brings out an uninhibited lust that has been secreted in their hearts for years. Eventually, they both collapse from exhaustion, falling asleep in each other's arms. Tomorrow will be another day of uncertainty.

Podgorica is home to Montenegro's international airport. Small in comparison to anything in Europe, it has one flight at 10:30 each morning directly to Frankfurt, Germany. Miro has two tickets for March 16, and passports Miro acquired for both of them a year previous, anticipating their possible departure from Kosovo.

Everything is set. They arrive at the small airport and quickly find their terminal. Miro parks the car in a crowded parking lot. He takes off the license plates and throws them in the trunk. Julianna has their bags, and hands one to Miro as he closes the trunk. Heading toward the terminal, they stop halfway to rest. They turn around for one last look at the dirty car that they have enjoyed for years. He thinks about how amazing it is the damned thing made it this far without breaking down. Julianna looks at the car and thinks of all the good times they have spent in it together. They pick up their bags and head toward the terminal. It is a rather hot day, and the walk seems to take forever.

As they enter the terminal they are both surprised at the throngs of Kosovars waiting to get out of the Balkans. Miro and Julianna make their way through the packed crowds and stand in line for check-in. People are pushing, trying to get ahead in line. The stench of body odor and stale cigarette smoke is repulsive. An hour later at the counter, the clerk is happy they have tickets. Most who are there are waiting have no tickets and little money. The plane is booked with over 300 people on the waiting list.

The newlyweds have to pass one more stressful hurdle—making it through security. Again, it is a long, tiresome wait in line. Montenegrin customs officials and VJ soldiers are carefully checking passports. Once their turn comes, Miro feels the cold stares from the officials, and senses they know what he is: *a Serb deserter*. It seems like an eternity as their paperwork is carefully examined. Finally, the customs official stamps their passports, and they are on their way into the waiting area. Miro and Julianna, hand in hand, find seats in a corner of the room so they can keep watch. Relieved to sit down, they clench each other's hands, looking about nervously for any sign of trouble. What trouble they can't say, but they sense something bad can still happen—until takeoff.

Miro notices a newspaper on the seat next to him. He reads the large-print headlines before he even picks it up: *Serb Forces Attack into Kosovo, Thousands of Kosovars Flee*. He grabs the paper and shares it with Julianna. Thousands of VJ soldiers and special police have launched a massive invasion, forcing Kosovars from their villages and driving them toward Albania and Macedonia. Deaths have occurred in Kosovo, but the paper doesn't state the numbers.

Miro is astonished, and Julianna is overtaken with grief. She weeps for her family, grabbing Miro's arms and asking if they can go back to save them. Miro holds her tight as she loses all composure, crying hysterically on his shoulder. Miro realizes this is a dilemma that requires a decision, a fast decision. Josif did say he would evacuate his parents in case of a full-scale invasion, but how will they know for sure? If they fly to Germany, Julianna will live with feelings of guilt and constantly worry about her family, but to go back will be at great peril. Serb men living in Kosovo are expected to be in the VJ, not married to ethnic Albanian Kosovars. Miro holds Julianna in his arms and looks deep into her tearful eyes.

"We will go back and make sure your parents and Josif are safe."

Julianna clutches Miro's arms tightly, then gives him a big, tearful hug. It is a difficult decision, but Miro knows there is really no choice. He lets go of Julianna and turns to pick up his bag. In doing so he is face-to-face with a man in a dark-blue uniform, a Serb Special Police sergeant. Another special policeman is just behind the sergeant, with a scowl on his face.

The sergeant holds his right hand out. "Passport."

Miro pulls it out of his shirt pocket and hands it over. The sergeant glances at it to make sure he has found the right man.

"Your brother, Colonel Cadikovski, is right. You are here to run away from your duties in the VJ. *You are under arrest.*"

# 02: SOMETHING INTHE AIR

**FLYING AT NIGHT WITHOUT** lights, an American Air Force C130J coasts at 25,000 feet above the Korab Mountain Range in Albania. The plane's hydraulic rear ramp lowers as the bitter cold rushes into the back of the aircraft and onto two men staring into the windy darkness. Each man is wearing an oxygen mask and a pair of night vision goggles on their helmets. The goggles give off a bright, illuminating green glow around their eyes. They carry an enormous amount of gear: main parachute, reserve parachute, weapons, oxygen apparatus, rucksack, communications equipment, food, water and ammunition. One man has a Belgian Malinois tethered to him on top of his ruck. The dog is fitted with a special oxygen mask and canister to avoid hypoxia.

A red light by the ramp turns to green, and both men shuffle toward the black wilderness. The man without the dog jumps off the ramp first, and is swallowed into infinity. Without hesitation the second parachutist mimics the first man's exit. They keep their arms straight to their sides and soar over 100 miles per hour into the unknown.

Through the night vision googles, the men see bright green instead of darkness. Below them, sharp granite mountain peaks covered in snow are the first discernable feature they see for their mission into Kosovo. The men glide through the skies for almost thirty minutes before their chutes open at 9,000 feet. The landing zone is just inside Kosovo. They both pull down as hard as they can on the parachutes' risers, slowing their approach to the ground. The lead man is able to steer his parachute into what he thinks is a nice flat green field, but night vision goggles do not adequately display depth or grade. The first man lands on his feet, albeit at a fast run down a steep hill. The second man notices the first jumper's contact with the steep grade and tries to adjust his landing. Upon contact with the ground, he immediately unhooks his dog successfully. He then tumbles backwards down the hill in a repeating sequence of feet, ass, and back of head. As he rolls, the nylon risers and silk parachute wrap around his body and rucksack, forming a cocoon-type entombment. He lands upside down at the bottom of a ravine between two trees, unable to escape the tightly-spun womb.

The dog runs up to the trapped man and whines as he investigates his master's predicament. The lead parachutist unhooks his parachute, then his ruck and weapons case. Once free of his equipment, he grabs his AK-47 from the weapons case and runs down the hill to untangle his fellow jumper upside down in the ravine.

"Are you okay, mate?"

"Everything is fine except my pride," comes a weak response from the cocoon.

"Just hold on, I'll get you out as fast as I can."

He puts his AK down and pulls a sharp knife from his boot. He slices through parachute cord and silk, and within a few minutes the trapped jumper is free.

Each man grabs his AK-47 and lies prone, facing away from each other and listening intently. It is a clear night, and their goggles enable the men to see clearly down the ravine and up the hill. The dog patrols the area, returns, and lies down; all is clear. The parachutists gather up their chutes and toss them, along with the oxygen equipment, into the ravine. From their rucks, they unfold entrenching tools and hastily bury the equipment tossed into the ravine. Within five minutes they toss their rucks on their backs and run into the nearest tree line for better concealment.

Once in the woods, they take a knee. One of the men is on security while the other opens his ruck and takes the mic from his satellite radio.

"Pine Tree, this is Razorback, over."

"This is Pine Tree. SITREP, over."

"On LZ. No issues."

"Roger, Charlie Mike; good luck, out."

The men recheck their bearings using GPS and plan their route by examining a 1:25,000 map. The man on security quickly puts a tactical vest on the dog. They lead the way, constantly checking their location while the other man follows twenty yards behind, holding his AK-47 at the ready and keeping a keen lookout in all directions. Every thirty minutes or so they halt, take a knee and verify their location and surrounding terrain. On the third halt they determine the linkup point with the KLA is just two miles distant. Everything is going to plan, so far.

Both men know it is risky business to link up with someone in hostile territory they have never met. They wonder if the KLA will show up at the right time and place, or an enemy Serb force that knows about the plan. With only two men and a dog, the risk has to be mitigated as much as possible.

One mile from the linkup, the dog's handler rolls up a message and inserts it inside a small tube. He attaches the tube to the dog's collar and gives the command, "Seek."

The dog dashes off in the direction they are walking. Within ten minutes he makes contact with a group of men. One of the men takes the tube off the dog's collar, reads it, writes a response and sends back a reply. The dog runs back at full speed, too fast for a person to follow. The two paratroopers are concealed in tall grass when the dog returns. The handler takes the message out of the tube and gives a faint smile to his cohort.

Both men carefully creep toward the linkup site but halt fifty feet away. One of them pulls out a clicker and clicks it three times. Seconds later they hear five clicks coming from the linkup point.

All the passwords and signals are correct, but the moment of truth awaits. The handler and dog go forward. The other paratrooper covers them. A few moments later a short man stands up in front of the man and dog.

In a soft voice he says in English, "I am the KLA platoon leader, Lieutenant Prek Luga."

The dog handler takes off his night vision goggles and replies in a low voice, "I am Travis Savage, lieutenant colonel, US Army Special Forces."

The second man comes forward and quietly introduces himself to the small man. "I am British SAS lieutenant colonel John Phillips."

After handshakes, Lieutenant Prek Luga murmurs, "We must hurry before daylight comes. You will be in the middle of the patrol."

At that moment nineteen other men simultaneously, but slowly, rise from the long grass, each carrying an AK-47. The hair on the American and British officers' necks stand up, and the skin on their heads tingle. It is an eerie welcome.

Travis whispers to John, "Thank God they are on *our* side."

"You got that right, mate," John whispers back.

Three KLA scouts bound ahead, followed by the rest of the patrol five minutes later. Their destination is the KLA's headquarters, five miles distant on the top of Mount Pastrik. The KLA scouts move fast, racing to beat the morning's rising sun. Before daylight the scouts make contact with the KLA defenses at the bottom of Mount Pastrik. They coordinate to dispatch an old blue Yugo car and two old Yugoslavian green army trucks to pick up the NATO officers and Prek's men.

When the vehicles reach the patrol, Prek Luga directs the NATO officers to load their packs into the trunk. Then they sit in the back of the car while the rest of the patrol mounts the truck beds. Prek jumps in the front passenger side, and the dog jumps on his lap, happily licking his face. Travis can't help but laugh. John is annoyed.

Travis claps his hands and calls, "Trooper, here." The dog jumps over the seat and into the back, sitting in between the NATO officers.

"Sorry about that, Prek. Trooper loves to ride in the front seat," exclaims Travis.

John looks over at Travis. "I thought you trained that mutt; he has no manners!"

The spontaneous laughter from the officers breaks the ice with Prek, who has never seen an American or British officer. Prek wipes his face with his right sleeve and laughs along. It is the first time he has laughed in a long time. It feels good. Having NATO allies feels even better.

The ride up Mount Pastrik is long and snaky. The car weaves through the gaps in the midst of triple-strand concertina wire that is formed in long coils. Along the way Travis and John notice numerous KLA fighting positions, all occupied with at least two soldiers. They all have stern, hard looks, carefully keeping an eye out in front of their positions. On top of the mountain is a heavily sandbagged concrete bunker with multiple antenna wires whipping in the wind on top.

A dozen or so KLA soldiers serve as an honor guard into the front entrance. At the end of the honor guard stands the KLA's commander, General Arsim Gashi. Soldiers open the back doors for the officers, and the honor guard raises their AKs to salute them. Gashi strolls forward with a giant smile lighting up his face. He firmly shakes each officer's hand and invites them inside the bunker. Gashi is a big man with gray, piercing eyes. The type of eyes that can look at you and read your mind. Middle-aged and balding, he once served in the Yugoslavian Army as a major. When Milosevic took power, he ridded the army of all Albanian Kosovars. Gashi joined the Croatian Army and fought in Bosnia against the Serbs. When the Yugoslavian Serbs began atrocities in Kosovo, he left the Croatian Army and became the commander of the KLA. He remains the center of gravity for the KLA movement, and is anxious to build a coalition with NATO.

As they enter the bunker, a steep flight of stairs leads them down into an underground command post. Trooper, still outside, begins to whine.

"Can Trooper come, too?" asks Travis.

General Gashi lets out a short laugh and says, "Sure, no problem."

As they enter through a curtain, KLA staff officers are busy talking on the radios and plotting KLA and enemy positions on a large map affixed to a wall. Gashi motions with his right hand, inviting the officers into a different room.

Once inside he closes the door and asks them to take a seat around a large, round, wooden table. Trooper lies at Travis's feet as Gashi opens the door and yells something in Albanian. Within seconds a soldier arrives and serves hot tea in small shot glasses, along with a glass bowl of sugar and small spoons. A glass of tea is placed at an empty seat, and the NATO officers wonder who is to join the meeting. Gashi profusely thanks the officers for risking their lives by meeting him at his headquarters.

Travis and John glance at each other, and John says, "I think I can speak for both of us, General; we volunteered."

The general smiles once again from ear to ear. Then Travis adds, "Hell, General, it beats having a desk job in Washington!"

All three laugh as the door opens. In steps Prek Luga, apologizing to the general for being late.

"No problem, Prek. I think you have met these friends of ours." Both NATO officers stand out of respect. Gashi asks them all to sit down as he places a map on the table.

A customary silence fills the room as Gashi pours a huge amount of sugar in his hot tea and stirs it for a few minutes.

Travis grows impatient and downs his tea in one swallow.

John angrily whispers to Travis, "It's not booze, you uncivilized Yankee. Wait for the general, then sip it slowly."

Prek overhears John and chuckles to himself.

General Gashi finally finishes stirring his tea and starts the conversation by pointing at the map. "Here we are in southern Kosovo at Mount Pastrik, and here are our five operational zones."

"Yes sir, we are aware of those. We were given an in-depth briefing before we came," states John.

Gashi takes a sip and says in a very clear, serious voice, "I understand that NATO air strikes are to begin soon. Is that why you are here?"

Travis makes direct eye contact with Gashi and simply responds, "Yes sir."

John nods.

Gashi asks for more details about the NATO officers' mission.

Travis continues, "Here's our mission, General: first to provide intelligence on Yugoslav—well, actually in reality Serb—units and movements, report anti-aircraft sites, and any other essential information, like Serb paramilitary units. Our second priority is to coordinate with you and your units to call in and observe air strikes on Serb units and vehicles. Our third priority is reporting war crimes and humanitarian crises."

"So, how are you going to do that on Mount Pastrik?"

Once again, Travis is first to respond. "We hump to contact points, link up with designated KLA forces, then execute a movement to contact to develop the situation, primarily using NATO air assets, then Charlie Mike until given an on-order change of mission."

John interjects. "General Gashi . . . in Queen's English that means we must move about within your various KLA units, gathering intelligence and calling in air strikes. In other words, we will not remain on Pastrik, but will track enemy movements and operations. As mentioned, when possible, we will call in air strikes to break up their tactical formations and degrade their combat capabilities. The KLA will be the ground force and we coordinate the air."

General Gashi sits silently, processing the information.

John continues, "Sir, we will need some protection. We humbly request a platoon from your KLA special forces company. Your best platoon, um, please, sir."

Gashi breaks out of his train of thought and responds, "That is why Prek is here, gentlemen. I have already designated him and his KLA special forces platoon—the ones that met you in the woods last night. He speaks good English and knows his way around. He works for you now, and he and his men are the best in the KLA. However, I am staying here on Pastrik to command and control all my forces in Kosovo."

John adds, "We will stay in contact with you by means of radio or runner."

General Gashi leans forward. "Yes, thank you, but I am still a little concerned we will lose contact with each other. We must be able to talk, to share intelligence and coordinate our efforts."

John responds, "We will stay in communication daily by way of our secure satellite communications, what we call SATCOMs. Both Travis and I have one. We will also communicate with our higher headquarters, *Pine Tree* in Albania."

"Yes, we have contact with Pine Tree here. That's how we knew you were coming. Prek has two radios also, but if we lose radio contact for more than a day, Prek, I want you to send a messenger to me."

"Yes sir!" Prek quickly responds.

This seems to comfort the KLA general to some degree, but Gashi realizes more detailed planning needs to be coordinated to maintain command and control with all his ground forces and the NATO officers' mission.

The next few days are busy with packing equipment, ammunition and food while also rehearsing actions on contact with Prek's platoon. John Phillips and Travis Savage are experienced officers who worked closely together in Bosnia tracking down Serbian war criminals from 1995 to 1998. John, an imposing, large bald man of six foot four inches, is a principled, follow-the-rules type of man from humble beginnings. He grew up in Birmingham in a large, lower income–class family. His father worked hard but also drank hard, and at the age of twelve John was fatherless. Admiring the SAS soldiers stationed in Birmingham, John yearned to escape the industrial slums to become *one of them*. Through his own diligence and perseverance, he advanced well in school, eventually attending and graduating first in his class at the Royal Military Academy Sandhurst. After commissioning in the British Army he served a short stint as a junior officer in the Parachute Regiment before volunteering to attend the British Army's Special Air Service Course, or SAS.

Upon graduation from the difficult course in 1984, John progressed quickly through the ranks, and in his personal life as well. Married in 1989, he and his wife, Carolyn, have two sons. Most of their postings are back and forth between Birmingham and Germany. Even though John is gone often from home on various missions, he still volunteers for the hardest jobs. When he heard Travis had volunteered for the Kosovo mission, he immediately threw his name in the hat to go with his American colleague.

Like his counterpart, Travis Savage is fit and muscular, but much shorter at five foot ten inches. With light-brown hair and an attractive bronzed face, Travis is the product of a military family. His father, a Vietnam War veteran, retired after twenty-two years in the Army. During those years Travis's family moved every few years, mostly around the States and Europe. The saying "Home is where the Army sends you" sums up Travis's life. Married only to the Army, all Travis wants in life is to be a Green Beret. An ROTC graduate from the University of Arkansas, he was commissioned infantry in 1978.

Volunteering for and graduating from the Special Forces Qualification Course in 1980, he has remained deployed most of his career. Travis, a little on the *smart-ass* side of life, will most likely never be promoted to colonel, but he is fine with that. At thirty-eight, his greatest fear is manning a desk until retirement. Travis is at his best in the field, working with allies and indigenous armies to make a difference in people's lives. He takes to heart the US Army Special Forces motto *DE OPPRESSO LIBER*—"To Free the Oppressed." Travis volunteered within his special forces group to head the mission into Kosovo. He realizes it will be a challenge, and maybe even the biggest of his career, as it will be a dangerous and covert mission deep inside enemy territory.

On March 23 John and Travis will hold a final coordination meeting with General Gashi, his staff, and Prek. First on the agenda is to share a combined intelligence briefing John and Travis received from the CIA, SOF, and SAS.

John begins, looking at General Gashi, "Most of the information has come from signal interception of Serb communications within the last two weeks. From this information, the intelligence officers have pieced together, then analyzed, numerous bits of information to determine Serb army and air force dispositions and intentions within Kosovo. The Serbs' plan, called *Operation Horseshoe*, is a detailed plan to expel ethnic Albanian Kosovars and minorities from Kosovo.

The VJ's tactical plan is to storm across Kosovo in a horseshoe design, first securing the Montenegro and Macedonian borders, followed by the main invading force oriented toward the heart of Kosovo. This will include the capital, Pristina, followed by the Drenica Valley area, and then continuing south and west to Peje and Prizren, and finally here at Mount Pastrik near the Albanian border. As anticipated, based upon this intelligence, the NATO air war is estimated to begin within the next . . . twenty-four hours."

General Gashi is surprised the air war will start so soon. He sits forward in his chair and starts writing on a notepad.

"Once the air war starts, within two days we think NATO will gain limited air superiority by destroying anti-aircraft systems such as the SA-3 launchers, along with most Serb MiG-29s in the air and on the ground. This doesn't mean air supremacy; there will still be MiGs throughout the conflict when they see an opportunity to use them. By the third day a strategic bombing campaign consisting of multiple NATO countries, but primarily US and British, will strike pre-planned and targets of opportunity. Primary targets will first be any surviving Serb anti-aircraft systems, then various key strategic targets within Serbia and tactical Serb army formations, specifically armored forces within Kosovo."

Travis stands up to brief his part. "John and I will be the forward air controllers within Kosovo. Of course, we do not expect to provide all, or even most, of the targets for the entire air campaign, but we do need to find and direct air strikes on certain critical targets. Here is the priority target list."

John hands a list to General Gashi, then gives him a few minutes to look it over.

"I see some interesting targets on your list, such as some Serb paramilitary units."

Travis continues, "Yes sir, that's right. Once we identify any, we will destroy them. They will most likely be in Kosovar villages, so it will be a direct-action fight.

"What is direct action?"

John simply remarks, "We will kill them ourselves."

Prek grins and adds, "It would be an honor to assist."

"That's why I am sending you!" Gashi quips with a short laugh.

John continues, "Most of these targets will require us to get close to the enemy in order to identify them. We will most likely be moving about Kosovo to find these targets. That's why it is imperative we move with not only Prek's men, but with other larger KLA formations, the one and only allied ground force in Kosovo. Remember, sir, this is a top-secret operation. If this gets out to either the Serbs or the press that John and I are on the ground in Kosovo, then the operation is compromised."

"And what will happen then?" asks the general.

Neither Travis nor John answers. After an uncomfortable few moments, John finally admits, "We don't know, sir. Maybe we would be extracted."

General Gashi responds in perfect English, "You must remember the KLA and Serb paramilitary forces in Kosovo have been fighting for over two years. The only difference now is that the greater part of the Yugoslav army, the VJ, is now attacking over the Serbian border into Kosovo. NATO air support combined with the KLA ground forces is the only way to defeat tanks, artillery, and other conventional forces. If you guys get extracted, we would lose coordination with NATO."

Travis pets Trooper's head, then looks straight at the general. "That's why we are here, sir. John and I are that critical link between NATO airpower and your KLA forces. And we mean to do *exactly* that."

General Gashi sits back in his chair and claps his big hands together, elated that the two NATO officers have formally recognized the KLA as the legitimate ground force for part of a NATO mission. He has sought international recognition for the KLA for years. At the beginning of hostilities, many nations considered the KLA as a terrorist organization, when in truth they were fighting for the survival of the Albanian Kosovars and other minorities in Kosovo. Serbian propaganda against the KLA was effective for only so long, especially once Serb atrocities began to leak out to the free press.

Gashi thinks for a while, then explains, "Right now I need you where the VJ is aiming for, the Drenica Valley. Drenica is the main village, but others also exist in the valley. The Serb paramilitary has attacked Drenica before, but now the VJ will want to capture this area as it is the heart of the KLA movement. It is where our resistance started, because of the atrocities by paramilitary groups. Prek will link you up with the 3rd Brigade commander, Colonel Josif Shala. He is the best commander I have, and he is about to feel the full brunt of the VJ. He will desperately need air strikes to keep the large VJ formations and vehicles from running him over."

John has done his homework. He responds by describing the Drenica Valley precisely, including the terrain, villages, and even the enemy's most likely plans for attacking. "Obviously we agree with you, sir, that the Drencia Valley is a decisive piece of terrain. NATO knows it is both symbolic to the Kosovars, as you said already, sir, and a crossroads to the western part of Kosovo."

*Boom!*

The entire underground headquarters shakes. General Gashi falls out of his chair, and the NATO officers jump on the floor with Travis on top of Trooper. Prek falls briefly, but runs out through the curtain and continues until he is outside the bunker.

General Gashi yells, "I hope NATO is not bombing us by mistake!"

John responds, "Sir, that was a MiG."

Prek runs back down into the bunker and sticks his head in the room. "General, you need to come see this!"

General Gashi takes off toward the top while the NATO officers follow. Once outside, they all marvel at the sight. It looks like the skies are full of supersonic dragonflies, all flying in different directions trying to get in the best position to make a strike against one another. Travis calls Pine Tree to get information.

A MiG explodes several kilometers away on the horizon; then another erupts into a fireball closer to the mountain. An American F14 Tomcat from the USS *Theodore Roosevelt* flies past the hill traveling over 1,000 mph, firing a missile and striking a MiG in the far distance. The explosion echoes through the hills. KLA soldiers jump with joy out of their foxholes, trying to wave at the American pilots as they continue to thunder by.

Travis puts his mic down and looks up. "Day 1 air war."

# 03: DRENICA

**MIRO TRIES TO SLIP** away from the two special policemen by sprinting past them. He hopes to disappear into the crowd, and save Julianna from the brutes. One of the police brandishes a blackjack and slaps him on the back of the head, knocking Miro out cold. As the two policemen pick Miro up off the floor, Julianna goes into hyperdrive. She takes hold of Miro around his waist, trying to pull him from their grasp. Her strength surprises the two men. One of the police lets go of Miro and puts Julianna in a choke hold. To avoid passing out, she lets go of Miro, but she isn't giving up that easy. Julianna jumps on the back of the policeman who is holding up Miro, clawing at his eyes and face.

She has angered both police, and they are not going to tolerate her defiance any longer. The one who put her in a choke hold pulls her off the other policeman's back and shoves her hard against the wall. He slaps her twice on her face; open, then backhand. Knocked senseless, she slides down the wall onto the floor.

Julianna can make out Miro being whisked away, but this time she can't react. She sits on the floor trying to regain her senses while a crowd gathers around her. An elderly lady kneels down and offers Julianna a drink of cool water. She takes the cup and tries to drink, but her face is so numb she can't feel the cup on her lips. Some of the water spills down her chin onto her T-shirt. Warm blood from the inside of her mouth mixes with the cool water, resulting in an awful taste. Something in her mouth is bleeding, but she can't tell what. She tries to stand up and momentarily loses her balance, leaning against the wall. Julianna remains there for a few minutes, trying to regain enough balance and strength to walk. In the meantime, blood drips from her mouth onto the tile floor.

With a groan, Julianna straightens, picks up both bags, and hurries down the hall and out of the airport doors, shoving her way through crowds trying to make their way inside. Once outside, and on the verge of hyperventilating, she silently prays that their car is still in the parking lot. After all, they intentionally left the keys in it for someone to make use of it.

There are a lot more people and cars outside than when they arrived, and she can't remember the aisle where they parked. She rushes down one lane after another, occasionally bumping into people or hitting them accidentally with one of the bags. She finally collapses and flops on a curb, shaking and sobbing uncontrollably. She cries over Miro being taken away, but she also is worried sick about her parents. Disheartened, she has never felt so helpless, and she blames herself for being selfish. She feels she should have just stayed home and cared more about her family than herself and Miro.

After a long cry, Julianna wipes her bloody mouth on her sleeve, picks up her bags and starts plodding along. She has some money for food and gas, but not much more. Delirious, Julianna looks down at the ground while dragging the bags behind her, not knowing which direction to go. After several hundred feet, Julianna bumps into a parked car, and without giving it much thought, starts to go around it. She notices the color of the paint out of the corner of her eye. There the car is, just where they left it.

It dawns on Julianna she must have run out a different set of doors at the airport than those they had entered. She drops both bags and puts both arms on the roof of the car, as if hugging it. She tries to open the back door on the driver's side, but the door handle button is stuck once she pushes it in. Agitated, Julianna pushes the button and pulls as hard as she can on the handle. The door flings open and knocks her to the ground. She is mad as a hornet and screams out a long sentence of obscenities.

Julianna tosses the bags into the back seat, kicks the door shut, then hurriedly opens the driver's door and plops behind the wheel. She reaches for the key in the ignition. It is not there. She cocks her head to look on the floorboard. She does not see the key. Panic, again. She jumps out of the car, gets on her knees and desperately feels for the key. Her mouth is bleeding again but she hardly notices, especially when she finds the key under the gas pedal. Julianna hustles back into the driver's seat, anxiously inserts the key in the ignition, and the engine turns over with a roar followed by a large plume of black smoke belching out the back. When she places her hand on the gearshift, she sees herself in the rearview mirror. Her lower lip is swollen and still leaks blood. She lets out a silly laugh as tears flow from her swollen eyes. Her stomach feels queasy, and she belches up a stomach full of water and blood out the window.

"Fuck it, it's time to go home."

On the way back Julianna stops in beautiful Berane, the village in the mountains where they were married the day before. She goes to the toilet to clean up her face, then buys gas and a loaf of bread. She is back on the road in no time, driving as fast as she can. Unstoppable—as long as the car doesn't break down. In a trance, Julianna puts her brain on automatic pilot and races through the winding mountain roads all night. The Zastava's loud engine coughs, sputters and smokes the entire way, but Julianna is unconcerned; she just keeps pushing the old car to its limits.

Arriving at the crossing into Kosovo in the early morning, a seemingly disinterested old man in a VJ uniform holds up his arm for her to stop. She hits the brakes, and the pedal goes all the way to the floor. The car comes to a grinding stop. The guard motions her by twisting his wrist to turn off the ghastly engine. Once she does, he sticks his head into her open window and coughs a cigarette hack while looking inside. He stinks like stale cigarettes, and his teeth are dark yellow.

"You are Albanian Kosovar?"

"Yes sir."

"Why are you driving a car with Klina plates?

"The car was abandoned because it is a wreck. I am going into Kosovo to bring out more Kosovars."

"Pop your trunk."

He strolls to the back of the car and glances into an empty trunk. He slams it shut and slaps the side of her car, indicating she can pass through. As she crosses the border back into Kosovo, she sees hundreds of refugees trying to enter Montenegro, some with cars, but most with donkey carts piled high with worldly possessions. The worse-off are pushing wheelbarrows containing the elderly or sick. It is a graver human disaster than at the airport. And they are all *her people*, Albanian Kosovars desperately trying to save their families from Serbia's wrath.

On she drives toward Drenica. Reaching the outskirts of the village, her worst fears come true. The entire village is void of anyone. Homes are ransacked, and some completely burned to the ground. Pulling up to her parents' home, the front door is ajar, and household items are spread throughout the yard. She quickly parks and dashes inside. She yells as loud as she can. No one answers. Julianna, panting, is so weak and shaky she can hardly remain standing. She shuffles around the front room, looking for any clues of what happened. Her head swims with questions. Are her parents okay, and if so, where did they go?

How is she going to find them? It is hard for her to think clearly, as she catastrophizes her parents' whereabouts and safety. She has no idea which direction they may have gone, but she pictures them in a long column of refugees just like she saw coming home.

Julianna works up enough courage to walk through the house, her heart stuck in her throat. Seeing her loving childhood home in this condition is surreal. Items are scattered everywhere, obviously by looters looking for something of value. In her room she notices her traditional dress she left on her bed is gone. Julianna picks up one of her childhood dolls off the floor, holding it close to her, as if in some small way it will provide her comfort.

She wanders into her parents' room and stops cold, looking at her family's photo on the floor with the frame and glass broken. Julianna gets on her knees and slowly picks it up, gently pulling the frame and glass off. She places the photo in her pocket and starts to leave the house. Suddenly it dawns on her to see if the two suitcases her parents own are gone. She runs back into her parents' room and looks in the closet; no suitcases. That is good news. She assumes her parents packed their suitcases and left in a hurry. At least they must still be alive, but she wants more assurance.

Julianna wanders around Drenica. Livestock and pets lie dead. Flies are everywhere, and the smell of death lingers. She recognizes a German shepherd that belonged to her neighbors. The dog's name was Loti, and Julianna played with her as a pup. Now she lies in her neighbors' front yard, shot multiple times. She assumes poor Loti died defending her masters against the Serb soldiers. "Loyal to the end," she whispers to herself. Julianna reaches down and pets her head for the last time. Her fur feels soothing. She scratches behind Loti's ears; Loti always liked that, and then she would roll over to get her belly rubbed. This time Loti does not move. Julianna gazes at Loti with deep sorrow, placing her hand on the dog's chest.

As she continues her walk Julianna sees bodies—a line of dead in the village square, exactly where her father played his flute just days earlier during the *Dita e Veres* festival. From a distance, all she can see are the soles of their shoes; men's shoes. She hesitates, terrified of who they are. She knows everyone in the village. To see her brother or father dead would be unbearable. Julianna feels her stomach twist and churn, and her knees weaken. She faces away from them, paralyzed with fear. She doesn't know what to do, so she runs into a nearby house to escape the horror.

As Julianna runs through the doorway, she trips over something large and falls forward onto the floor. She tries to see through her watery eyes. Just inches away, a dead man's face stares at her. She recognizes him as one of the musicians in her father's band. He was a kindly older man who would never hurt a fly. Why he was killed she will never know. Julianna cannot imagine the heart of the man who fired the shot that killed him, he whose only crime was his ethnicity. But there he lies, shot in the chest, eyes wide open. Nauseated and trembling, Julianna sits in the nearest chair, trying to muster enough emotional strength to carry on.

She eventually walks out of the house and slowly approaches the men's shoes. What if one or more are still alive? She walks faster toward them, concentrating on looking for possible signs of life.

Julianna is sadly disappointed. All were lined up and shot. No Josif or Papa, but that does not make her feel any better. She knows them all, and has all her life. She stares at each, remembering them as living people, not murdered corpses. None of them were in the KLA, but perhaps they had protested the Serbs' action. Maybe the Serbs were shooting all males. She feels a profound sense of sadness, wondering what else she will discover in the ruins of her village.

She slowly rambles through the streets and searches inside homes, finding damage but no people, dead or alive. Just as she starts to backtrack to her car, she notices something unnatural at the forest's edge in a grassy field; more bodies. As she draws closer, she notices three men, all KLA wearing camouflage American battle dress uniforms, or BDUs. Her heart sinks once again, thinking one might be her brother. This time she does not hesitate to run toward them.

Still, no Josif. But again, she recognizes them. All are from Drenica and her brother's close friends. Apparently they were not lined up and shot like the men in the village square, but killed while fighting. Their AK-47s are gone, and their pockets turned inside out from being searched. As Julianna turns the dead on their backs, she notices a pistol under one. She picks it up and examines it; a Browning semi-automatic 9mm. She takes the pistol belt, holster and ammunition off the corpse. Julianna straps it on and tightens it around her slim waist. When she places the pistol in the holster, it feels heavy and awkward. She has never worn a gun, but Josif has taught her how to shoot. He was a shooting instructor, and from time to time took her to the shooting range. At the time it was fun to shoot.

Julianna walks back to her car and sits in the driver's seat with the door open. She takes the pistol out of her holster and pulls the slide back to ensure it is loaded. Contemplating what to do next, she thinks through her options.

She reasons it would take a long time to bury all the dead, although that is what she wants to do. It is the right thing to do, and the thought of leaving her friends to rot in the sun is disturbing. However, looking for her parents and Josif must be the priority. What direction to go?

Only two options are plausible: northwest back toward Montenegro or south to Macedonia. She did not recognize anyone on her way back home from Montenegro, so most likely everyone from Drenica went south. She decides to drive toward Macedonia with hopes of finding them, or at least finding someone that can tell her something about her family.

Julianna's stomach is still upset, and she has not eaten since devouring the bread while driving the night before. She searches several homes and finds a loaf of stale bread, canned goods and water to take with her. She has a little money left, and half a tank of gas.

Juliana looks back over the village from a distance, regarding the fall of light and realizing she will never see it the same way again, no matter what happens.

Driving out of the village she has an idea. Maybe Miro's parents can tell her something about his whereabouts. She turns around and heads toward Klina, a Serb enclave. Twenty minutes later as Julianna approaches the town, what she sees is disheartening. Ahead is a VJ checkpoint on the road, manned by armed soldiers.

Beyond the checkpoint she can make out many military vehicles, including tanks. Julianna knows they are likely the ones who destroyed Drenica, drove away the inhabitants and murdered innocent people. She steps on the squealing brakes and quickly turns the car around and speeds in the direction she came from. She realizes escaping the VJ is paramount, but she needs fuel. She drives toward a Kosovar-owned station west of Drenica.

Arriving at the station, Julianna pulls alongside a gas pump. She cuts off the engine and slides her stiff body out of the car. No one is in sight. Grabbing the pump's hose, she opens the gas cap and shoves the nozzle in. No gas, not even a drop. She has less than half a tank, and that is not going to get her very far.

Julianna walks into the station, hoping to find some gas in liter containers, a common way to buy gas throughout the Balkans. Inside the station is the attendant, lying facedown in a pool of blood. She has known Mr. Lute for years. He was an older man who had a good sense of humor and had worked on Miro's car many times. She places her hand on his shoulder. Letting out a long, sad sigh, she notes the station has been looted, so she turns around to go back to her car.

She hears voices speaking in Serbian coming from an attached garage. Julianna nervously pulls her pistol out of the holster and waits. Speaking casually to each other, three VJ soldiers appear with AKs slung over their shoulders. At first they do not notice Julianna because she is standing so still. When the one on the right finally notices her, he holds his arm out for the others to stop. All three freeze.

Julianna aims her pistol using both hands, waving it back and forth between the three of them. None of them flinch. In Serbian, the one on the right asks who she is. She responds in Albanian, proudly stating her name and where she is from. When they do not understand her, she knows they are not Serbs from Kosovo.

The men continue to stand still. Julianna's arms start to get heavy, then shake. It is a matter of time before she has muscle failure and lowers the pistol, giving the soldiers time to unsling their weapons.

In Serbian, the soldier on the right again speaks, telling the one on the left to start moving to Julianna's left, while he will move to her right. He thinks Julianna does not understand Serbian, but she does. Fluently. They are going to surround her, and she will be unable to hold the gun on all three. She is in a tight situation, and has to do something fast. Real fast.

She levels her gun on the soldier in the middle.

She yells in Serb, "If one more person moves, even a little, I shoot."

Surprised she speaks Serbian, the two soldiers stop walking. The soldier Julianna is aiming at drops his weapon, striking the concrete with a loud clatter. No one moves for what seems like hours, but in reality is only minutes.

Julianna's hands shake more and more as they grow numb. She starts switching her hands out, holding the pistol with just one shaky hand. She contemplates what to do. If she shoots the one in the middle, the other two will have time to shoot her. The Serb on her right, the one that spoke, grins confidently at her. The soldier in the middle, very young and scared to death, now holds his hands up. The soldier on the left is nervous and sweating profusely. Something has to give.

Julianna remembers Josif instructing her to always shoot the most dangerous target first, and always aim center of mass. She works up her courage, holds her breath, turns to her right and shoots the grinning soldier in the chest. She swivels around as fast as she can, loses her balance, and falls on her left side. Lying on the ground she sees the man on the left unsling his AK-47. He raises it as Julianna shoots three shots hastily before hitting the soldier in the groin with at least one round. The soldier shoots a burst over her head, then collapses to the ground screaming in pain. The bullets come so close Julianna feels the air swooshing by her head.

Still on the ground, she turns to look at the young soldier in the middle. He has picked up his AK-47 and is pointing the muzzle directly at her. He shakes like a leaf, barely able to hold his weapon. Julianna throws her pistol away and stands up slowly. She looks the soldier in the eye for a few seconds, then turns around and walks back toward her car, expecting to be shot at any moment.

The soldier shot in the groin is holding his intestines, trying to keep them from spilling out. In agony he screams at the soldier holding the AK-47, "Shoot the fucking bitch, now."

Julianna keeps walking. Once she reaches her car, she opens the driver's door and quickly gets in. For some reason she looks at the soldier, who is still pointing his AK toward her. She starts the car and drives off.

Julianna continues south, slowing down every time she sees refugees, hoping she will recognize someone. About sixteen kilometers further she spots a lady with a young boy. It is hot and they are barely able to walk. Though short on gas, Julianna feels she should give them a ride for as far as possible. She slows down and parks in front of them. Julianna swings out and limps toward the lady and boy. She approaches the woman very calmly so as not to scare her.

"Come on, I will give you a ride as far as I can. Please get in the back and try to relax."

The lady and boy say nothing; neither even makes eye contact with Julianna. Julianna picks up the boy and places him in the back seat. The lady reluctantly climbs in and puts the little boy on her lap. Julianna starts the car and begins to drive slowly so she can look at her passengers in the rearview mirror.

"What's your name and where are you from?" queries Julianna in a gentle voice.

"I am Deidra and I am from a small Roma village about seventeen kilometers north of Drenica. I have nothing; I had to escape with Shabin as quick as I could. We have been walking south for two days toward Macedonia, without any food or water."

Julianna pulls the car over to the side of the road, grabs the food and water she took at Drenica from the front floorboard, and hands it to them.

"Thank you, you are very kind."

As she drives, Julianna feels good about helping Deidra and her son as they eat and drink. It is the first thing she has felt good about in a long time, although she knows without gas the ride will be over within a couple of hours.

An hour and a half down the road, rounding a tight curve Julianna is surprised to see a road checkpoint manned with two soldiers in BDUs, both holding AK-47s. Her first thought is that they are VJ looking for her, and once more her stomach turns into a knot. But they are not VJ. They are KLA, and as she drives closer she recognizes a huge bearded man as a good friend of Josif's:

Bekim Mali. She stops by Bekim and presents her swollen smile.

"What has happened to you, Julianna? How did you get bloody puffy lips? You need help!"

Before she can get a word in, he points toward a side road and tells her to park amongst the bushes. She follows his instructions, and parks in the shade.

They bring water and speak quietly to her. "We have set up a checkpoint to ambush VJ."

He points to the woods on the left and right, where more KLA are armed with heavy machine guns.

Julianna can't wait to ask, "Is Josif safe? Do you know his whereabouts?

Bekim takes a few steps closer to her. "He is just twenty kilometers away, in a location safe from the Serbs."

"What about my parents? Have you heard anything about them?"

The men look at each other, but no one can recall anything Josif mentioned about them.

Bekim looks at Deidra and her son. "Who are they? I have not seen them before."

Julianna tells him the story about seeing them on the side of the road. Bekim opens the door and picks up the little boy, hugging him and kissing his cheeks. The little boy clings on tight, smiling from ear to ear.

Bekim asks the boy his name. "Shabin, and I am this old," the boy says, holding up four fingers.

Bekim places Shabin down and tells them all to come with him. He leads Julianna, Deidra and her son down a long path to three cars hidden in the woods. Bekim recommends to Julianna it will be best to be driven to see her brother.

Julianna hands over her car key to Bekim, stating, "Better to just leave it—it's had it."

"I was wondering where you got this heap. Did you know it has Klina plates?"

Julianna acts surprised. "I found it in a parking lot."

Bekim shrugs it off and approaches a KLA driver and orders him to take the women and boy to the KLA 3rd Brigade headquarters at Skanderbeg Farm.

Julianna sits in the front passenger's seat while Deidra and Shabin sit in the back. To Julianna, in a hurry to unite with Josif, the ride seems unnecessarily long. The driver takes endless back roads, often on donkey-cart trails that wind through dense forests. Finally, she sees two men standing by a barn. As the car approaches, the men open the barn door, and they drive inside. The driver asks for everyone to get out of the car. A guide will lead them out of the barn and along a trail into the woods.

Another KLA soldier appears and leads them past three armed men at a checkpoint along the trail. No one says a word while Julianna carries Shabin and Deidra shuffles along. They keep walking, this time down a steep ravine. They finally come upon another barn and a large house with armed guards. Entering the house, the escort tells them to wait in the front room. He then disappears through a door. Julianna can hear men talking but can't make out the words.

Abruptly, Josif opens the door and sees Julianna's condition. Stunned at her swollen lips, he still does not hesitate to embrace his younger sister. Tears run down his face as Julianna joyfully buries her head in his chest. *Nothing* has ever felt this good to her before; for once, she cries tears of happiness.

Inside the house Josif uses a hot cloth to clean Julianna's lips. She forgets the stinging when Josif says, "Mama and Papa are safe in Macedonia."

Julianna puts her hands over her mouth and nose, closing her eyes. What have thus far been the worst days of her life now turn to relief, and maybe a sliver of hope.

Josif continues, "I put them on a bus with older people and children from Drenica, just before the Serbs sacked it. They are living with an Albanian family in Tetovo, a village in northwestern Macedonia. I will surprise them and send word that you will be with them shortly. We still have buses going back and forth, and the Serbs are more than happy to see Kosovars leave. I will put all of you on the next bus. I think it will be in a couple of days."

Deidra hears what Josif says and hugs Shabin, elated they are finally headed for safety.

Julianna looks at Josif with concern. "My plight is complicated."

Josif quickly responds, "What is so complicated about getting on a bus?"

Julianna tells Josif her experiences from the time she and Miro left home until running into the KLA checkpoint.

Josif seems amazed, stating, "I cannot put you on the bus knowing the VJ will be looking for you. After shooting two of them, they will be searching every vehicle crossing the borders. Besides, your presence on the bus would jeopardize the lives of everyone riding with you."

Julianna asks her brother what she should do.

Josif thinks for a while, then says, "You must stay with us. There is no other option."

Julianna smiles. "I will go where you go, Josif."

They hug once more, and Josif kisses Julianna softly on her cheeks. "It is so good to see you again, little sister, even under these circumstances. You have had such a difficult time. Try to get some rest."

Julianna hesitates, then asks, "I want to hear what happened in Drenica. I told you who I saw . . . dead. I know it is painful, but please tell me."

Josif takes Julianna's hands and says, "Okay, you have a right to know. Well, three days ago the VJ attacked much sooner and more violently than we expected. They first fired artillery into the village, then attacked with tanks and infantry. Their objective was not only to attack us, the KLA, but to terrorize all Kosovars. For the most part they let the very old and young leave, but shot anyone who resisted leaving or posed a threat to them, especially fighting-aged males. They didn't know who was in the KLA, so they just shot who they suspected. Of course we counterattacked, but they were too strong. We tried flanking them rather than having a head-on fight, but they outmanned and outgunned us. You saw the three KLA killed; they were an RPG team trying to sneak up on a tank to get a good shot. Before they could get into position, the tank crew saw them and killed them with a machine gun. We had to retreat, and couldn't even bury our dead. It is still too dangerous to go back there because of the VJ battalion in Klina."

Julianna looks sadly at her brother and asks, "So what is next? What can we do?"

Josif responds quickly, "Reinforcements are coming. Right now as we speak thousands of KLA are coming from Albania and through Peje to join us. We will form larger and more capable units. From what I hear, NATO has started an air campaign. We will be the sole ground force unless NATO sends in troops also. So, we just need to hang on for now."

Julianna is skeptical. "I wish it were so, Josif, but I just don't believe anything anymore. It is not that I don't trust you; of course I do. But I . . . I just have this terrible feeling that we will lose Kosovo. We have already lost our home and village. What is left for us?"

"Plenty is!" Josif said. "We will not surrender to evil. We must prevail. We will prevail!" Josif then smiles, kisses Julianna on her forehead and steps out of the room.

Julianna sits by Deidra and her child in a bedroom. She tries to speak to Deidra, but she and her son are silent and solemn. They seem to be traumatized from the last few days' events and are numb to their surroundings.

Julianna speaks. "Come on, Shabin. It is time to take a bath." She grabs his tiny hand, and the little boy instantly rises and follows Julianna into the bathroom. As she scrubs Shabin, Julianna can't help but wonder why such an innocent child has to endure such horrible hardship.

As Julianna tries to hold back tears, Shabin innocently stares at her. "Where is Papa?

Julianna is shaken by the question, assuming the answer is not something Shabin needs to hear.

"I don't know, Shabin, but your mother is here and waiting on you in the other room."

Julianna dries Shabin's thin body, then helps him don his filthy clothes. Julianna changes her mind and takes his clothes back off, wrapping the little boy in a towel. She holds his hand and they walk back to where Deidra sits solemnly on the bed. Julianna puts Shabin in the bed, then takes Deidra's limp hand and leads her to the bath.

Deidra seems almost catatonic, so Julianna undresses her and helps her into the bathtub. Julianna, with dried blood on her clothes, undresses. She gently scrubs Deidra with a soft cloth. After a calming washing and rinse, Juliann dries Deidra off, trying to stimulate her back into reality. Just like her son, Deidra speaks a few words, thanking Julianna for her help. This pleases Julianna, knowing that Deidra is coming back around. They hug each other, and Julianna grabs Deidra's hand once more, leading her to the warm bed where Shabin is already fast asleep.

Julianna saunters back to the tub, exhausted. She empties, then starts filling the tub with delightful hot water. As she puts her hand under the spout to feel the temperature, she gazes into the pouring water. She worries about Miro, wondering about his plight. She even contemplates whether he is still among the living. She turns the water off just before the tub is full. Stepping carefully into the full tub, she enjoys her own first hot bath in four days.

Once evening arrives, no lights are allowed on inside or outside the house for security reasons. After such a long and difficult day, Julianna, Deidra and Shabin lie peacefully in bed. Julianna and Deidra face one another, and Julianna runs her fingers through Deidra's silky black hair. Shabin lies behind his mother with his arms around her, fast asleep. The women speak softly to each other about their situation. Julianna is hesitant to ask Deidra what happened to her, especially concerning her husband. The women are quiet for a few minutes, just looking softly at each other.

Deidra says, "I think I have something to tell you. I heard your story today when you were speaking to your brother. Now I want to tell you mine. You are the first person I have told, as I am very ashamed."

Julianna gazes at her with empathy but says nothing.

"My son is named after my husband, Shabin. He, myself and my son were eating breakfast at home when we first heard it . . . a loud explosion somewhere close. More explosions followed, then it became quiet for a few minutes. We all ran into a closet and sat down huddled together. Soon we heard tanks rumble by, shots fired, and people screaming. We heard our front door kicked in, and a few minutes later a VJ soldier found us in the closet. He pointed his gun at us and I thought we were all going to die. Instead of shooting, the soldier told my husband to get out of the closet. Once he did, the soldier pointed his gun at his back. I quickly stood up and ran out of the closet and begged the soldier to leave him alone, and told him my husband was only a cobbler, not in the KLA. I even grabbed the soldier, but he pushed me down and threatened to kill me. In that instant my husband turned around and tried to wrestle the gun from the soldier, but another soldier must have heard the commotion and rushed into the room."

Deidra paused, and her big brown eyes moistened. "It was so terrible. The soldier that came into the room shot my husband in the back, and he fell to the floor. His eyes were still open, looking at me. The VJ then dragged me out of my house, with my son following. They took turns raping me right there in the street. After they were done, they left me there, with my son crying at my side. If it were not for my son, I would have killed myself. Instead, we just started walking, to where I did not know. We just walked."

Julianna's self-pity evaporates. She realizes she is not alone in her misery. She pulls Deidra closer to her, embracing her warm body.

Early the next morning Julianna awakens to the sound of men yelling. Still in Deidra's arms, at first she thinks the other woman is Miro. But she isn't. Julianna doesn't even know where she is. She slept so hard she has difficulty getting her bearings. Once fully awake, she notices that Deidra and Shabin are still fast asleep. Julianna slides out of bed and sees a set of American BDUs on a chair. Josif must have placed them there for her. She puts the uniform on slowly, inspecting each piece. Julianna feels strange as she has never worn a military uniform. In a way she likes it. It makes her feel part of the liberation movement, part of something much bigger than herself.

After lacing up her combat boots, she opens the bedroom door and walks quickly down the hall toward the sounds of the men's voices, entering a large room full of men toasting with the high-octane drink *rakija*. Josif approaches her and grabs both of her shoulders, smiling at her.

"NATO has started the air campaign in the Drenica Valley! Isn't it wonderful?"

Julianna is a bit taken aback. She asks Josif, "So what is going to happen? What does it really mean?"

Josif answers, "It is the beginning of the end for the VJ. They can't hide from jets, much less continue on the offense."

Julianna takes his hands from her shoulders and holds them tight. "But how do you know these jets are here? I don't hear anything."

Josif states, "We have gotten numerous reports from the field. So far we know of at least three Serb MiGs shot down by American F-16s. After NATO gets control of the skies, they will start bombing. You will hear that! These murderers will get what is coming to them. I hope they all die."

Josif suddenly remembers something. He pulls Julianna aside and leads her into the hallway. In a low voice Josif becomes very serious. "Do not tell anyone, and I mean anyone, that you are married *to a Serb.*"

Julianna quickly responds, "I don't think of Miro as a Serb, but my husband."

Josif takes a deep breath and exhales. "You must put him out of your head. He may not even be alive. The VJ probably shot him for cowardice."

Julianna is shaken by Josif's words, but also annoyed. "He is still alive. No matter where Miro is, he will run away and find me, you will see."

# 04: INDOC

**AFTER HIS CAPTURE AT** the airport, Miro is interrogated and beaten by the special police at a military prison in Podgorica. He eventually signs a legal document stating that he was trying to skip out of the war. By the time the special police throw him into a cement cell, he is only half conscious.

The smell in the cell is putrid. He hears mice skittering about but can't see them. His head throbs and his eyes are so swollen he can hardly make out anything, but he does sense another person in the cell. Someone breathing, shifting about. Miro lies on the concrete for several hours until a guard brings him a thin soup with small pieces of what resemble meat and potatoes. He swallows a few sips but becomes violently ill, vomiting on himself and the hard, filthy concrete.

"If you want mine, you can have it."

In the dimly lit cell Miro tries to focus on the source of the voice. A man is leaning his left shoulder against a wall, holding his tin bowl of soup out with his right hand.

"I'm good. I think I already ate too much," Miro cynically responds as he struggles to sit up against a wall.

"Remember me, friend? I'm the guy you abandoned at the border checkpoint while you and your girl drove away. Well, what do you know, here you are again, but this time with me—sharing a jail cell!"

The man pitches his soup on Miro face. Luckily it is cold.

Miro just sits against the wall, not caring about getting a face full of soup. He wipes it off with his sleeve.

"What is your name?" asks Miro.

Surprised at Miro's calm demeanor, the man answers, "Radic, Niko Radic."

"Well, Niko, let's just say I did stop to pick you up. Since your hands were tied behind your back, I would have had to jump out, grab you, and throw you in the back seat. By the time I would have driven away, how many bullets do you think would have already been shot at us? Even if we had made our escape, the VJ would have easily caught up to my old car in no time at all. We would have been shot on the spot. And worst of all, we would not be enjoying ourselves here in good conversation with free food and lodging."

Niko Radic sits down against the wall opposite Miro, not uttering a word. The two men sit in silence. Miro's eyes clear enough to notice his cellmate is badly beaten also. Had they fought after Niko threw the soup on Miro, it would have been a ridiculous spectacle. Both men can hardly move.

Breaking the silence after several minutes, Miro says, "I am Miroslav Cadikovski, from Klina."

"Trying to escape the call-up?"

"Yes. After we last saw you at the crossing point, we had plans to get to Germany. I had passports, tickets, everything. I was nabbed right before we boarded."

"Where is your wife?"

"I don't know," Miro says under his breath.

There is another bout of silence.

"So, what's next for us I wonder?" asks Niko.

Miro looks around the dingy cell as he answers, "Well, there are several things. They can shoot us, assign us into some kind of a labor unit, or just let us rot right here."

"The VJ need us. Any Serb from Kosovo is useful for information."

"What do you mean?"

"Most Serbs don't know much about Kosovo, like the language, or where the Albanian Kosovar enclaves and villages are."

"Where are you from?" asks Miro.

"Just outside of Pristina. I am proud to be Serb, but not to the point of murdering innocent people. Especially people who have been my neighbors all my life."

"I know what you mean," Miro reflectively responds.

The following morning both men have diarrhea. They use a corner of the cell to shit, puke and piss. About 7 AM three secret police enter their cell and handcuff them. They are led outside and put on a bus full of other weary men in handcuffs. After eight hours traversing Montenegro and into Serbia, Miro begins to recognize the buildings of Belgrade. He is somewhat familiar with the city because he attended the electrical engineering school here after high school, and grew fond of the big city because of all of its entertainment venues and cultural features. He knows this trip will be drastically different.

Entering the military complex of Belgrade, Miro and Niko watch with displeasure as the bus drives by numerous military unit buildings. They notice a sign, *Penal Battalion*, on a building ahead and assume that is their final destination. The bus stops in front of the building, and a VJ sergeant gets on the bus with a roster in his hand.

"The following traitors will get off the bus."

The sergeant begins to read aloud last and first names. Both expect their name to be read as others dismount. Surprisingly, after more than thirty names are called, neither Miro's nor Niko's name is announced. The sergeant jumps off, the driver closes the door, and the bus continues.

It is not long before the bus stops again. They see a sign: *Indoctrination Battalion*. Again, a VJ sergeant gets on the bus.

Instead of calling names off a roster he screams, "Get off the bus!"

The sergeant dismounts the bus while Miro and about twenty other men lethargically shuffle off. Once outside, Miro and Niko stand with the other men.

As the last man steps off the bus, a VJ soldier violently whips the man on the head, face, and legs with a rubber hose. In agony, the unsuspecting man withers and collapses to the ground.

The VJ sergeant who initially got on the bus screams, "When I tell you to move, I fucking mean move! Get back on the bus!"

In a rush the men scramble to get back on, using their elbows to shove others out of the way as best they can while handcuffed. Niko is one of the first to get aboard, and Miro makes it on toward the end, but is not last. Again, the last man is grabbed just before he gets on and unmercifully whipped with the rubber hose.

The VJ sergeant once again jumps on the bus, and from the front screams, "Get off the bus!"

The sergeant smartly jumps off the bus as men dart as fast as they can toward the front door. Once again, the last man is whipped. This same process is repeated three more times; the last time, Miro is last and suffers the excruciating sting of the rubber hose.

The VJ sergeant glares at the men. "Get in line and stand at attention! Do not say a word unless asked a question."

Miro picks himself off the ground and stands in line, still wincing from the painful beating.

The sergeant walks up and down the line shouting, "You are here because you are a coward. Instead of fulfilling your duty to

Serbia, you ran away. We had to go find you, then bring you back. If it was up to me, you would all be shot right now. But because Serbia is a merciful country, I must give you one more chance. That's right, one more damn chance. If you live to graduate from the indoctrination battalion, or indoc, you will serve as a private in the VJ. That is, if you live."

A VJ soldier starts walking down the line unlocking handcuffs and pitching them in a box. Niko starts to massage his sore wrists, only to experience the sting of a rubber hose on his back.

"I told you to stand at attention. Did you not fucking hear me?"

Niko, still in pain from the hose's wrath, looks at the sergeant with contempt, saying nothing.

"Did you or did you not hear me tell you to stand at attention?"

Niko grimaces as he responds with, "Yes, sir."

The sergeant approaches Niko and screams in his face. "I am not a sir; I am a sergeant. Officers are *sir*, you idiot!" The sergeant struts in front of the men and bellows, "Count off beginning with one. From now on you will be addressed as coward and then your number." He points at the first man in the line. "Count off!"

Each man then counts off by numbers, with Miro being number thirteen and Niko fourteen. In all there are twenty-two.

"Throw any contents in your pockets on the ground!"

As other VJ soldiers gather up all the personal belongings in a box, the sergeant orders the men to strip and throw their clothes in a pile. Niko complies with lightning speed while Miro hastily strips, but clenches the red-and-white bracelet Julianna gave him in his left hand. The sergeant, watching the men like a hawk, takes quick note of Miro's hand.

The sergeant slaps Miro's hand with the rubber hose. Miro holds it even tighter. The sergeant takes a step back and stares at Miro in disbelief. He slowly takes a silver lighter out of his right trouser pocket, swings open the top and holds it close to Miro's face. Miro looks straight forward and does not react in any way.

The sergeant thumbs the lighter and turns up the fire. He lowers it, holding it under Miro's hand. After three long seconds Miro opens his fist and the bracelet falls out. The sergeant picks it up and places it in front of Miro's face, swinging it back and forth.

"What in the fuck is this?"

Miro remains silent, thankful that the sergeant doesn't know the bracelet is a sign of commitment in the Albanian Kosovar tradition. That might earn him a bullet.

With Miro staring straight ahead without expression, the sergeant screams in Miro's face, "Looks like you have a problem opening your mouth and talking. *Open your fucking mouth, coward.*"

Miro slowly opens his mouth, still gazing forward. The sergeant stuffs the bracelet into Miro's mouth, followed by a hard punch to his face. Miro once again collapses to the ground, with blood pouring out of his nose. He quickly pulls himself together and stands at attention. Miro still has the bracelet in his mouth.

A VJ soldier pours gasoline on the pile of clothes, strikes a match and ignites the heap into a fireball. The naked men still stand at attention, staring as the fire burns the last remaining vestiges of their personal lives. Except for Miro's bracelet.

"Okay, smart guys, let's see who drops first," the sergeant declares, smiling at the sweating men.

It is sunny and burning hot. The sergeant joins two of his VJ subordinates sitting in the shade smoking and laughing. An hour lapses, then another. The VJ soldiers drink cold water and wager on who will drop first.

"Look, there is one wobbling now," laughs one of the soldiers.

Another soldier gleefully bellows as he points. "There is another one about to take a dive!"

It will be another twenty-two minutes until one of the men falls straight down on his face, hitting the hard ground with a loud, sickening thud. The soldiers exchange money and vulgar comments on who they had wagered on.

"How do you always know who will drop first, Sergeant? This makes the third time in a row you have won," grumbles one of the soldiers.

The sergeant folds the money and stuffs it in his shirt pocket. He grabs a plastic water jug and walks up to the man on the right end of the line. "Take two gulps and pass it on."

When it is Niko's turn, he takes two quick drinks and passes the jug to Miro. He takes one drink, careful to not swallow his bracelet. He pours the second allocated swallow on his nose, wiping off the blood.

A VJ soldier saunters up to the man on the ground and pours an entire jug of water on him. The man manages to make it back to his knees. The soldier lets him take a few swallows of water, then barks at him to stand up. He clumsily stands while gasping for air and shaking violently.

The sergeant glances at the man and cruelly snickers. Turning toward the rest of the men he shouts, "Stay in line and march double-time into that building," gesturing toward a large warehouse. The cowards shuffle out of step but in line toward the warehouse.

Once inside the warehouse the cowards are instructed by VJ soldiers to hold their arms out straight. Walking down an assembly line, each man is issued a blanket, two sets of military uniforms, a pair of boots, and various equipment. Once finished, with the men still in one line, the sergeant leads them a couple hundred meters and stops in front of an old wooden barracks.

The naked men hold all their issued gear in the hot sun. None of them dare move.

The sergeant scowls at them, then bellows, "When I count down to one, you will run inside the barracks and stand at attention in front of a bunk. Five, four, three, two . . . one!"

Twenty-two men sprint through one open door into the

barracks. By the time the sergeant walks inside the large room, he sees all twenty-two standing at attention in front of their bunks. Each man still holds out their issued items. The sergeant walks up and down the line slowly, staring at each man. Miro and Niko stand next to each other, sore and sick, but not wavering a bit.

"Who is missing a boot?" the sergeant calmly asks while holding up a typical combat boot.

No one moves. To even flinch means punishment. The dilemma for each of them is whether to risk looking at their bundle, or not look. If they look and they are not missing a boot, they will be hit for moving while at attention. If they do not look, and it ends up being their boot, well, there will be hell to pay.

The sergeant yells in a whimsical way, "Well, let's see here, looks to be a size twelve. Someone with big feet!"

Miro and Niko and all but two of the men let out a shallow breath.

"If you *DO NOT* wear size-twelve boots, get dressed and start putting your gear away."

Miro, Niko and eighteen other men start to dress and stow their gear. Two are still standing at attention holding out their gear, naked. The sergeant walks up to each, inspecting their equipment. With a shit-eating grin on his face, he seems to relish the moment.

"I know which one it is," the sergeant joyfully announces.

He struts up to one of the men and sticks the boot in his face. "Get dressed and stow your shit away."

The sergeant walks up to the last man. "Drop your gear and get outside, *NOW*!"

Outside, three VJ soldiers are waiting for their prey. The naked man runs out of the barracks.

The three soldiers scream at him to perform various drills. "Get up, get down, get up, get down, do push-ups, more, more. You fucking pussy, crab-crawl like the coward piece of shit you are . . ."

Inside, the sergeant continues to issue orders. "This is your holding area until you go to war. Each one of you cowards is privileged to have a bed and a locker. Once I leave this room you have eight minutes to finish getting dressed, make your bed, stow your equipment and line up in your assigned coward number. Anyone that takes longer than eight minutes will be awarded extra motivation, like our big-footed friend outside."

At this point, no man needs motivation. The humiliated man from outside comes limping in, and everyone helps him get dressed and stow away his gear. All twenty-two are lined up outside within seven minutes.

The VJ sergeant briefs them on the rules and length of their stay. "If you survive fourteen days and prove you are committed to Serbia, then you will be placed in VJ infantry units for combat into Kosovo. To prove your commitment, you will have to run everywhere. You must also recite the VJ Creed before getting fed, stand at attention whenever a soldier approaches, and be thoroughly educated on Serbian nationalism by the political officer. If you have shown compliance but quit in the two weeks, you will serve in the penal battalion, providing labor for the good of the war effort to liberate Kosovo from terrorists. The third group will be those of you who do not make the fourteen days. Men from the penal battalion will bury them in a pauper's grave."

After a few seconds' break, the sergeant announces, "Your training and education starts at four tomorrow morning, so be ready." He saunters away from the twenty-two men still standing at attention in the sun.

Exactly one hour later a VJ soldier marches the men to get haircuts. Five men from the penal battalion shave each man bald. Within fifteen minutes the task is complete and the men stand in the sun once again, this time for half an hour. VJ soldiers stand in front of the men and study each man for signs of weakness. Some men start shaking and sweating profusely, but Miro, or

Coward 13, and Niko, Coward 14, hold their own.

Suddenly, a VJ soldier yells, "Hit the Devil's Playground," pointing toward an obstacle course a few hundred yards away. Obviously, training will not wait until tomorrow morning.

For the next two hours four VJ soldiers run the cowards through an obstacle course that tests every man's endurance and perseverance. Rope climbs, horizontal and vertical bars, low-crawling through mud, clawing their way out of deep muddy trenches while being sprayed with water, jumping over obstacles, climbing up cliffs, crab-crawling over rocks, and all the while running from one obstacle to the next. Miro and Niko stay together as a team, helping and encouraging one other. They know if a coward falls too far behind or quits, he will instantly be whipped to *motivate* him. Several of them do, and Miro and Niko can hear their pathetic cries of pain. At the end of the course, the men are once again lined up at attention.

A VJ soldier points toward the mess hall and gives the men fifteen minutes to eat and return to the line. Miro and Niko run with the pack, exhausted but realizing they have to eat to survive. One by one the men file into the mess hall, grabbing a tray and moving quickly through the serving line. Penal battalion men looking like walking skeletons serve the food, slopping cold hash and withered vegetables on trays as fast as they can. The cowards sit at long tables and stuff their mouths while a soldier screams at them to hurry. It is the fastest Miro has ever eaten, but in an odd way it is enjoyable compared to anything else he has experienced thus far. Niko doesn't even taste his food. He just swallows it without chewing.

After dinner the men are given half an hour to shower and put on clean uniforms. Afterwards they form a line and are marched to a nearby building. Each sits at a desk inside a large room. Miro and Niko, sitting together, wonder what it is all about, but it doesn't take long to find out.

A soldier in the back of the room announces, "Attention!"

Everyone jumps to attention while a squat man struts quickly from the back to the front of the room. He stands on stage staring coldly at the men.

"Sit!" he shrieks. As Miro and his fellow cowards sit, they notice the man on stage is a VJ major, the first VJ officer they have seen.

The VJ major stands with his legs spread shoulder-width apart. He holds a swagger stick horizontally in his hands and wears a visor cap and knee-high black shiny boots. A closely cropped mustache is dominated by a large, crooked, fat nose. Miro thinks this is the ugliest man he has ever seen, and feels like laughing. This feeling evaporates quickly as the major stares at him with steely gray eyes.

"I am Major Borozan, your political officer and the highest-ranking person in this camp. My job is to turn cowards into brave patriots who will fight and win for Serbia. Quit feeling sorry for yourselves or you won't make it. The first week here, called Hell Week, will test your resolve as a man. If you make it past this week, you will start learning combat skills while also learning to be aggressive. Most important is that you become a comrade, someone who truly believes in your country and is willing to die for her. It is I who decides if you are committed or not."

As Major Borozan speaks, a soldier places a small pocket-sized book on each desk. Miro looks quickly at the book and reads the title, *Serbia, Land of the Slavs: A Warrior's Handbook.*

Miro quickly looks back up as the major continues.

"You will memorize this book, everything in it. Most importantly you will remember the VJ Warrior's Creed. If you do not *exactly* repeat it going into the chow hall, you will not eat. Carry this book with you everywhere you go. A rubber bag is now being placed on your desk to keep it in. But for now you will listen to me."

Pacing back and forth on stage, the political officer starts to lecture. He uses no notes, and obviously has given the lecture countless times before. He speaks of Serbia's glorious history, how the Ottoman Empire invaded and brought deviants to their land, deviants that remain still to this day, especially in Kosovo. The First World War brought invaders, causing great hardship on the native Slavs, but of course ultimately the brave Slav people prevailed and destroyed the enemy. In the Second World War, the criminal Albanians living in the Drenica Valley in Kosovo formed the *Skanderbeg Division* and fought for the Nazis, murdering countless Slavs. By war's end, the patriotic Slavs of Serbia prevailed, with the aid of their Slav cousins from the Soviet Union. Now the ethnic Albanian criminals in Kosovo are once again becoming violent, and they are the direct descendants of those who fought for the Nazis. They are the Kosovo Liberation Army. It is time for the brave Slavs of Serbia to unite once more, to not only destroy the KLA, but to finally solve the *problem* by expelling all the criminals from the sacred land of Kosovo.

Major Borozan is just getting started. He becomes more emotional as he bellows his fiery political rhetoric.

"It is your duty to stop the criminals, to save Serbia as your fathers, grandfathers, and their fathers before them. Wake up and arise to the challenge! You should be proud to be a Serbian Slav, not a coward who runs away from evil. Kosovo is our sacred land, and you will be part of saving her."

Niko sits still, looking seriously at the political officer but thinking he is a moron. Next to Niko, Miro's head is bobbing. A soldier taps on Miro's shoulder and motions him to get up and stand in the back of the room. Miro fears he will be beaten as an example. Instead, the soldier gives Miro a large stone to hold for the rest of the lecture.

"You won't fall asleep now, *Coward 13.*"

That evening Miro and Niko help each other memorize the

book, especially the ridiculously long and rambling VJ Warrior's Creed. Miro is still quivering from holding the large stone in class, and Niko's body aches all over. After studying with Niko, Miro lies in his bunk and thinks about Julianna. Miro realizes graduating from the indoctrination battalion would be his first step to being united with Julianna, and that will be his real motivation to make it through. Somewhere she is *out there*. He thinks she most likely went back to Kosovo to reunite with her parents. He envisions her on some godforsaken road with thousands of others trying to flee toward Macedonia. He is anxious about her safety. With her looks she would be prime for raping by some Serbian paramilitary group. Miro's mind wanders even more. Maybe she was too late in getting back to find her parents, and instead has found Josif. She might be in the KLA.

The next four days are worse than the first. Every evening there are two hours of Major Borozan's lectures, including reciting passages from the *VJ Warrior's Handbook*. Otherwise, constant harassment, painful exercises, and long runs are the norm. Again, any coward that falls behind receives *motivation*.

They get two meals a day, but any slip on sounding off with the creed, or even any hesitation on a line, will result in a missed meal. The coward is forced to drop out of the food line and undergo a painful series of exercises while his fellow cowards shove food in their mouths. Fortunately, neither Miro nor Niko fail to exhibit false motivation, and they sound off loudly with the creed. Although the food is awful, their bodies receive the nourishment needed to persevere.

On the third night Miro finds Coward 2 while getting up to go to the bathroom. The man lies dead in a pool of blood between two toilets. He used a razor to cut lengthwise down his left arm. Miro uses the restroom and returns to bed. He reasons there is nothing he can do at this point but get more rest.

On the fourth day, Coward 18 sneaks up behind a VJ soldier and grabs his pistol from the holster. As the soldier turns, Coward 18 shoots him point-blank in the face and runs toward the front gate. Once at the gate he points the pistol at the guard to open the lock, which he gladly obliges. Coward 18 dashes out of the compound, crossing the street and a parking lot. Meanwhile, whistles blow throughout the compound, and most soldiers hunt the escapee. Two soldiers remain behind, pointing their weapons at the remaining men, ordering them to lie facedown on the ground. All Miro and Niko can do is remain still on the ground and look at the two soldiers, hoping they will not open fire. Both soldiers hold their guns nervously, looking around and wondering if the man's escape might be the beginning of a larger breakout attempt.

A few minutes later Miro and Niko hear an exchange of gunfire. It isn't long until the soldiers file back into the compound, two of them caring Coward 18's lifeless body. They toss the body on the ground, and several soldiers cuss and kick the corpse. The remaining cowards lie on the ground until the body is taken away. In a way, Miro admires the dead man. After all, he was no coward.

After the incident on the fourth day, the last three days are especially brutal. This is when most collapse, some passing out unconscious. Right when Miro thinks it can't get any worse, it always does. He is amazed that a human body, his body, can endure so much physical punishment. Besides hustling as hard as he can, he fully realizes staying healthy is a must. To sprain an ankle or suffer a back injury would mean five years of hard labor in the penal battalion.

From early morning until dinner they endure numerous exercises, runs, harassment, and the dreaded Devil's Playground obstacle course. Miro thinks maybe it was a blessing to be whipped the first day, as it left an indelible imprint on his psyche to avoid a whipping at all costs.

But desperation brings about the best and worst in people. In four days Miro and Niko support each other whenever possible, but both have turned into animals, shoving and pushing others aside, eating like starving dogs, and even pleased to see others getting the thrashing instead of them. Other men merely capitulate, allowing others to always get ahead of them. They accept their punishment without reservation, passively absorbing the lashings as if they were an act of fate. These men Miro would later admire, as he isn't proud of himself. He learns a lot about himself that he does not like. But at least he and Niko are surviving, and that is what matters to him right now.

The first week finally does end. Miro, Niko and nine others remain from the original twenty-two. Most physically or mentally collapsed, and were sent to serve a humiliating and labor-intensive five years in the penal battalion. After the nightly political officer lecture, Miro falls in bed and sleeps soundly. In the morning after breakfast, Miro is surprised to be granted one hour to write a letter. Of course, it must be to their families, and thus addressed to someone with their same last name. Niko takes the hour to sleep. Miro hesitates to write his parents. He lies on his bed daydreaming, mostly about Julianna. What could have been, and might still be. Someday.

Miro decides to write his parents after all. Maybe, just maybe, his mother will send word to Mr. Shala, the flutist, to let him know he is okay. As far as he knows, his parents have no idea what has happened to him, even his marriage to Julianna. So, if he can phrase the letter the right way, to ask his mother to notify many of his Serb friends, someone might also notify Mr. Shala. It is unlikely, since he is a Kosovar, but still possible. He writes the letter as vaguely as he can, telling his parents he is now serving proudly as a VJ soldier in Belgrade. The gist of the letter is that he is doing well, and he will write again, soon. In the meantime, his mother is to tell everyone she knows he is okay.

After signing his name, he licks the envelope and tosses it in the basket for mailing. That is that. A shot in the dark at somehow reaching Julianna. He relaxes back on his bed and dreams of Julianna being told where he is. She would know he is alive, and understand he was a forced into service.

Twenty minutes later Miro and Niko stand at attention in line with the remaining men. After just one week instead of the standard two-week indoctrination course, the VJ sergeant tells them they are being amalgamated into VJ combat units. The cowards are instructed to quickly grab their bedding, clothing, and equipment to move into another barracks.

Amazingly, the last man out with his belongings is not whipped.

This is a new precedent, and Miro feels optimistic for the first time since his capture. Instead of running, the sergeant marches them to their new barracks for cohabiting with other recruits. The sergeant, in a calm voice, gives them thirty minutes to make their beds and put away their equipment.

Miro quickly makes his bunk and stows his equipment in a metal locker. He fears it is some type of cruel trick by the sergeant. He has never been so lenient before, much less spoken with a calm voice. Miro runs outside and stands in line within eight minutes. Three others are already there. The sergeant approaches them.

*Here it comes*, Miro assumes.

The sergeant, again in a calm voice, states, "Go back inside until I call you."

At first all remain at attention.

"Go on, go on," states the sergeant.

The sergeant walks away and joins a conversation with other soldiers at the end of the building, out of hearing range. All the cowards break ranks and skeptically amble back into the barracks.

"Something is going on," Niko says.

Once inside, Miro gazes out the window at the sergeant. "I

agree, but I think it has nothing to do with us. Something has happened in the war. They want us to join the units—*now*."

Suddenly, a loud, piercing whistle startles the men, and everyone in the barracks runs outside. Miro's bunk is toward the back of the room, and he has to push and shove to keep from being last. Once outside and in a line, he is delighted to note no one is whipped. Even more surprising is who stands in front of the line—Major Borozan, the political officer.

Major Borozan walks the line, staring coldly at each man. He slowly returns to the front, standing erect and motionless. "We are at war. NATO is determined to deprive us of our rightful land—Kosovo. Have no doubt, we will prevail. You will prevail. In a few days every one of you will go to your new units. You will have plenty to eat, and will once again be respected as upright citizens of Serbia. You have proven your strength and determination. It is now time to rise to the occasion for our Slav race, fight for our beloved nation, and preserve our way of life. Do not misinterpret me. If you show weakness, or any sign of cowardliness once again, this time you go straight to the penal battalion, where you will stay—indefinitely."

Borozan stands silent once again, studying each man as if he can see straight through their souls.

# 05: ARRIVAL AT
# SKANDERBEG

**AS A GUERILLA ARMY,** the KLA has always been on the move, including General Gashi's headquarters. In their transition from guerilla force to an organized army, for the first time a stationary defensive strong point is essential to communicate with the KLA brigades. Mount Pastrik is suitable for this, as its dominating height provides radio communications with the five KLA brigades throughout Kosovo.

The downside of a headquarters on Mount Pastrik is its vulnerability to Serb artillery and aircraft fires, as evidenced by the MiG bombing. If threatened to the point of evacuating, Gashi's only option is withdrawing toward the Albanian border to the south. He realizes how strategically important Mount Pastrik is, as securing this entire area means maintaining resupply routes from Albania, a must for all KLA units in Kosovo to survive.

Travis and John instruct the KLA on methods to maximize cover and concealment of the headquarters and the fighting positions. The NATO officers instruct Gashi's men that every position needs to be at least six feet deep with good interlocking fields of fire. Grenade sumps are dug inside the positions, and mines and razor wire strewn down ravines. A minimum of twenty-four inches of overhead cover on top of each position will provide protection from artillery. For this, the NATO officers build an example by laying steel pickets over a position, then placing sandbags in three layers on top of the steel. Next, they put thick wooden beams on top of the sandbags to absorb the initial impact of an artillery shell. The spoil from digging the position is scattered about with fresh foliage covering everything.

The KLA get to work, but quickly discover digging adequate fighting positions into the rocky soil on Mount Pastrik is a difficult undertaking. So, everyone pitches in, including the NATO officers, Prek's special forces platoon, and even General Gashi and his staff. It doesn't take long to divide responsibilities—improving the existing holes, delivering and placing the steel pickets, cutting and delivering wooden beams, and gathering foliage. John and Travis help the KLA soldiers sight in their weapons on the best killing zones.

To Travis, the work pace and organization of tasks resembles an ant colony. Everyone has a designated task and are moving as rapidly as they possibly can. Their lives will depend on it. Within nine hours the fighting positions meet the minimal requirements for survival. John reminds them that improving their positions every day will increase their chance of warding off any attacking enemy.

Mount Pastrik is finally the KLA headquarters' new home: bleak, windy, and isolated. However, it will serve as the one and only command-and-control and communications link for prosecuting the entire resistance movement to stop the genocide of the Kosovar population. On Mount Pastrik, every KLA soldier understands the importance of the headquarters mission, and are determined to be part of what they hope will free their country and save their families.

Priorities of work continue, with soldiers cleaning their

weapons, mortar men sighting in their tubes, medics setting up an aid station, cooks preparing food, and staff officers becoming more proficient in communicating with KLA brigades throughout Kosovo.

Before departing, John and Travis train Prek and his KLA special forces platoon on basic tactics, like conducting reconnaissance, sniping skills, clearing a building, fighting the enemy, and conducting an ambush. The NATO officers are pleased that most of Prek's men already know most of the tactics, and are excellent marksmen. Employing standard operating procedures is just as important, such as hand and arm signals, code words, radio protocols, and casualty evacuation. The KLA special operators catch on quick, as they are already experienced in their own fighting methods and survival skills. Best of all, they are hardened fighters in top physical condition and highly motivated to liberate Kosovo.

For General Gashi and the NATO officers, planning and coordinating future operations is paramount to defeating the Serbs. Travis and John are the linchpin between KLA ground operations and the NATO air campaign. Because the KLA lack heavy weapons, such as tanks and artillery, their success means the integration of NATO airpower. Conversely, airpower alone will not defeat the Serbs. Ground troops are essential to take and hold ground. It is a partnership of mutual support, each one dependent on the other.

Some targets will be more important than others, so a prioritized target list from NATO headquarters is key to striking the right targets at the right time. For security purposes, the NATO officers have memorized the target list. Likewise, the primary and alternate routes to the first linkup with a KLA unit are memorized. It will be with the KLA 3rd Brigade headquarters at code name *Skanderbeg* in the Drenica Valley. The commander of the KLA 3rd Brigade is Colonel Josif Shala.

The NATO officers and Prek's KLA special forces platoon will initially begin using eight cars, spread out in intervals of ten minutes. Each car will take a different route and drop off the men at different points. The eight small groups will rally at a predetermined rendezvous point. If that point is unsafe, an alternate point is planned.

Once at this point, the NATO officers and Prek's men will move in a column formation at night along the primary route. Travis and Trooper, along with a point man from the special forces platoon, will lead 100 meters in front, looking for any signs of danger or impediments to movement. Every KLA special forces soldier will carry a heavy backpack and be armed to the teeth. Most have AK-47s, semi-automatic pistols, K-bar knives, and demolitions. Two have US M60 machine guns with ammunition belts crisscrossed over their shoulders. Two more are armed with Dragunov sniper rifles. The NATO officers have their favorite knives, 9mm pistols, and Yugoslav AK-47s.

On the night of their departure, a spring thunderstorm rages in torrents. For the KLA soldiers on Mount Pastrik, they spend the night in misery soaked to the bone while bailing water from their newly dug fighting positions. The overhead cover helps, but the rain blows in sideways. To the NATO officers and their KLA platoon, the storm provides a limited amount of cover from the VJ.

All eight cars leave on time but hit numerous potholes because of limited vision caused by the storm. After the torturous ride, drivers drop off the soldiers and Trooper. In the lashing rain they slither through the woods undetected. Trooper has the time of his life while soaked men follow close behind.

By midnight they are all at the consolidation point in the Drenica Valley. At 0315 Prek makes contact with KLA scouts from the 3rd Brigade, and at 0421 they arrive at Shala's headquarters, Skanderbeg.

Prek opens the front door of a large house and leads Travis and John into a dark front room. The rest of Prek's men enter a nearby barn.

Travis and John stand silently in the dark room, wondering if this is possibly a Serb trap. Maybe the VJ took the headquarters and are waiting for them. Trooper is ready to pounce on Travis's command while both men instinctively rely on each other's courage. With their weapons at the ready, Prek pulls aside a thick curtain that exposes a large, brightly lit, smoke-filled room. Five surprised KLA soldiers dressed in BDUs jump up from their chairs and scramble for their AKs. Prek makes some sort of joke in Albanian, and the men relax and roar back humorous remarks. One of the men points to the NATO officers.

"*Notto?*"

Prek grins. "Yes, American and British NATO officers!"

Travis and John feel like celebrities. All five of the KLA soldiers vigorously shake their hands, saying over and over, "Thank you, thank you!"

Trooper shakes water all over John, and everyone laughs again. John turns red, but remains speechless. One man, after petting Trooper, excitedly raises his index finger to the NATO officers in the international symbol to wait.

He calls out, "Julianna, Julianna!"

As the officers take off their heavy wet packs, a door on the opposite side of the room opens. What appears next is the last thing the NATO officers expect: a strikingly beautiful young lady with large brown eyes, high cheekbones, and long, black, silky hair. She has a certain air about her, a quiet type of beauty. Prek says something to her in Albanian.

She looks at Travis and John, and says in perfect English, "My brother is Colonel Josif Shala. He will be here very soon. Please have a seat." She casts a quick smile at the NATO officers and darts out of the room.

John finds the nearest chair and immediately collapses into it, placing his AK across his lap. Noticing Travis is still standing and staring at Julianna as she leaves, John takes his wet cap off and slaps Travis on the back of his legs.

"Quit gawking and sit down, Yank!"

Embarrassed, Travis takes a seat and notices all the KLA men are smiling at him.

Tall and unassuming, Josif Shala enters from the same door Julianna left through. He gives John and Travis hearty handshakes and introduces the five KLA in broken English. One of them is Josif's second in command, a large hairy man with squinty eyes named Bekim Mali. Travis thinks it odd how much hair is growing on the man's nose and ears.

Julianna returns holding a pile of towels. She smiles at John while handing him one, and he graciously thanks her. Prek grabs one from her arms and also thanks her, but Travis is tongue tied when he gets his. Julianna and Travis make eye contact, and she smiles pleasantly as he takes another towel for Trooper. She takes a seat at the end of the table while the officers remove their blouses and towel off their faces and heads.

Much to Trooper's delight, Travis vigorously rubs him all over. Afterwards, Trooper casually walks up to John and shakes one more time. John gives Travis a death stare.

Julianna interprets in perfect English between the KLA and the NATO officers. The conversation begins by welcoming the NATO officers in traditional Albanian Kosovar traditions. Josif pours locally distilled plum rakija into shot glasses and toasts to NATO. The KLA soldiers repeat "*Notto*" and slam their empty glasses on the wooden table. Josif pours another round and holds his glass high.

"To a free Kosova!"

"Kosova!" shout the men.

Travis glances at Julianna sitting at the end of the table. She has also joined in the toasts. Again, their eyes meet.

A KLA soldier enters and serves hot bean soup and bread. Everyone drinks from the bowls and tears off chunks from the large round bread. Another soldier brings in a case of Kosovar beer brewed in Peje. He puts a beer in front of each person and opens one for himself. The next few minutes are filled with the sounds of slurping, crunching, and guzzling. Afterwards most light cigarettes and grab more beers.

The NATO officers drink beer and look around the smoke-laden and clammy room. On the plaster wall is a large, red, silk KLA flag. A bronze-type profile picture of the old warrior Skanderbeg hangs next to the flag. Skanderbeg, an Albanian nobleman and military commander who fought for Kosovo's freedom over 500 years ago, still reigns in the hearts of the KLA, who see themselves fighting for the same cause.

Travis, still eyeing Skanderbeg's hard look, says to John, "I wouldn't want to mess with that guy."

John replies, "I wouldn't want to mess with the KLA."

Travis turns his attention from Skanderbeg, glances at John, then at the men in the room.

"You got that damn right," Travis says under his breath. "These guys are hard. All of them."

Josif smashes his cigarette in a full ashtray, puts both of his hands on the table and gently addresses his NATO guests.

"Please go and change your wet uniforms, and then I will give you an update of my zone."

John and Travis dig dry uniforms out of waterproof bags in their packs. Julianna leaves the room, and the KLA keep drinking beer as the NATO officers change. Julianna returns, gathers their wet uniforms, and wanders outside to hang them up.

Julianna is back in a few minutes and follows her brother, the NATO officers, Bekim Mali, and Prek Luga into an adjoining room.

The room is slightly smaller, cleaner, and not as musty as the first room. On the walls are various maps and VJ unit diagrams.

A long wooden table with metal chairs is positioned opposite the wall of maps. Josif points toward the chairs for the NATO officers. Prek and Bekim remain standing off to the side while Josif lights a cigarette and picks up a wooden pointer. Julianna sits two seats down from Travis to help translate.

Josif leans against the wall, takes a deep drag from his cigarette and exhales.

"Gentlemen, what you see is VJ and paramilitary activities in the 3rd Brigade's area of operations. This includes destroyed Kosovar villages, atrocities against Kosovars, and anticipated future VJ operations. The most dangerous VJ unit for us is consolidated in Klina, a Serb city. Klina is a logistical base from which the VJ run operations, and it also protects the Serb population from our reprisals."

"What do you mean from your reprisals?" asks John.

Josif hesitates, puts his right hand on his jaw, and thinks carefully how to respond.

"The KLA doesn't rape and kill women like the Serbs do to us. And we never harm children."

John pushes the point. "Then what exactly do you mean by reprisals?"

"We select our targets carefully. These targets are always men who are supporting the VJ or paramilitaries in some way. We have good snipers."

John doesn't give up. "Yes, we have reports that the KLA shoot the police and those that provide equipment and goods, but also intellectuals, like lawyers, doctors, and even scientists."

"Yes, certain ones. Those that deserve to be killed. Unlike NATO we have a good intelligence network on the ground. We know who they are."

Travis glances at Prek. "Say, Prek, are some of these good snipers your men?"

Prek answers, "Yes sir, the best ones are in my platoon."

"Good!" Travis fires back, then swallows a mouthful of beer. John gives Travis another one of his death stares.

Josif, glad to move on, points to a 1:50,000 scale map of central Kosovo, indicating the road networks.

"The VJ move by road in convoys of at least ten vehicles, and always with a gun jeep in the front, middle, and the rear. They have learned that anything less will be ambushed by our forces. That's bad news for us. The good news is that will give NATO airpower a better opportunity to acquire and target VJ columns moving on the roads."

John responds first. "True, but that will not happen until NATO gains air superiority and knocks out most of the VJ anti-aircraft weapons first. That can take time. So, where do you think the VJ in Klina will go next?"

Josif points to Kosovar villages in the west-central part of his AO. "There is no doubt that tank and mechanized VJ forces from Klina will hit the larger Kosovar villages of Skenderaj or Malisheve. The unknown is *when*. With the air war beginning, they may ramp up operations to control all of west-central Kosovo, then decentralize their forces within the occupied villages for protection against NATO air strikes."

Josif take a long drag on his cigarette and exhales as he continues. "Additionally, there are two Serb paramilitaries operating in our area, the Black Hand and Arkan's Tigers, named after their leader, Zeljko Raznatovic, whose nom de guerre is Arkan. They will attack the smaller villages. They do not have heavy weapons, but what they lack in weapons they make up with sheer brutality. They are the worst of the worst."

Travis, rubbing Trooper behind the ears, looks up and nonchalantly asks, "Tell us more about the paramilitaries. Who are they, and why aren't they in the VJ?"

Once translated by Julianna to everyone in the room, the question immediately causes an emotional response from Josif and Bekim, both speaking on top of each other.

Josif pauses and lets Bekim speak while Julianna translates for the NATO officers.

"These paramilitaries, terrorist groups, have been operating for years against not only the KLA, but against our people. They torture, pillage, rape and murder with great pleasure. The VJ coordinate directly with them because they know the area so well. The VJ also provides artillery support for these bastards."

John and Travis look at each other. The paramilitaries are listed on their priority target list from the NATO Special Operations Center.

Travis inquires, "How do we identify them?"

Josif answers, "They all wear black, and have a patch on their right shoulders indicating their unit."

Bekim throws two arm patches on the table. One is the black hand, obvious by a black hand on red background. The other is the Arkan Tigers, with a yellow tiger on a black shield background. Everyone remains quiet.

Josif breaks the silence. "There is another force you need to know about, the Serb Special Police. They wear blue uniforms and blue American Kevlar helmets. They are special police because they have a special mission . . . to hold the VJ to their duty."

Josif can tell the NATO officers are perplexed, so he continues. "Just like all communist-based governments, the special police enforce the political will of the army. They follow behind the VJ to verify they are attacking, and especially ensure Kosovar cleansing takes place. Most VJ soldiers are conscripts who live in Serbia and could care less about Kosovo, so they need to be carefully watched, and the special police do that."

John asks, "Well, what exactly do they do?"

Bekim replies in Albanian and Julianna translates. "The Serb Special Police shoot any VJ that does not do their duty."

Josif says in a low, serious voice, "You will see for yourselves."

Josif speaks in Albanian to Julianna and she leaves the room. Travis gets up and fetches a plastic bowl and some dry dog food from his pack. As he feeds Trooper, Julianna brings in sausages and bread, placing them on the table with a stack of plates. She fills two plates and gently puts them in front of John and Travis. Bekim brings in more beer, slamming it down on the table.

The group takes a break while eating and drinking once more. After consuming a fair amount of beer, Bekim leaves for the toilet, a porcelain hole in the bathroom floor. Travis and John speak together as Josif speaks with Prek off to the side. Julianna assumes the uniforms outside are still wet, but goes outside anyway to find something to do. As she inspects the uniforms she wonders why neither of the NATO officers wear underwear.

Everyone comes back together within twenty minutes. Travis has drawn a large question mark on a whiteboard by the map. Julianna has to translate what it is to Josif, Bekim and Prek. Travis stands up in front by Josif and speaks.

"So, what do we do now?" He points to the question mark.

That one thing is on everyone's mind. The NATO officers and Josif quickly agree it must be a NATO air strike on Klina. The VJ battalion there is the biggest threat in Josif's area, and the Drenica area is NATO's priority for John and Travis. The VJ must be targeted in a surprise attack before they strike the larger Kosovar villages.

Julianna does not say anything but feels hesitant about striking Klina. Miro's parents live there, and although they never approved of her dating Miro, they are, after all, still his parents. She keeps it to herself, but confronts Josif after the meeting. He tells her that the NATO air strikes will target specific VJ targets, and not civilians. Julianna is still uncomfortable about the plan, but accepts the necessity of hitting the VJ.

Bekim unrolls a map and places it on the table. Others put their beers on each corner as paperweights. Bekim points to

Klina on the map, then pulls out another piece of paper.

Julianna translates, "Here is a hand-drawn sketch of Klina. It is based upon the results of KLA reconnaissance from the last week. Basically it is a mechanized VJ battalion of approximately six hundred and fifty men, about thirty-three wheeled vehicles, five T-72 tanks, thirty-one BMP armored troop carriers, three pieces of towed artillery, at least one ZSU 23-4 anti-aircraft tank, and two SA-3 and one SA-6 air defense vehicles. I am sure they have mortars also."

John asks, "Do you have the coordinates of anything, especially the SA-3 and SA-6 sites?"

Bekim is confused by John's question, but Josif knows the meaning and answers. "No. We do not use coordinates because we have no aircraft or artillery."

Travis adds, "Well, that means another recon to determine the coordinates, but at least we have this sketch to guide us. To knock out the SA-3s and 6s, NATO aircraft need exact coordinates. There is another problem, especially with SA-6s; they are the best low-to-medium air defense system in Kosovo, and they are mobile, either on an armored chassis or in the back of a truck. We will need tomorrow as a planning and rehearsal day. Daylight is just a couple hours away, so we will plan and rehearse starting tomorrow afternoon and into the night. We will sleep the next day and conduct the recon that night."

Josif agrees to the plan and offers the NATO officers a place to sleep in the house, but they choose to lay out their sleeping bags in the barn with Prek and his special forces platoon. Prek speaks decent English, but not enough to discuss the Klina plans in detail. Travis hustles back inside the house and asks Joseph if Julianna can translate.

A few minutes later Julianna enters the barn. For the first time Travis sees Julianna smile, and a welcome sight it is in the dimly lit barn. Most importantly to Travis, the smile indicates she might be willing to translate on a regular basis—something the NATO officers badly need. Just as inside the house, Julianna translates perfectly, and within just a few minutes the timeline for the Klina operation is well understood amongst the KLA special forces. Travis thanks her, and she smiles once again as she leaves. Travis can't help but think of her as he sleeps with a smelly, damp Trooper.

By noon the next day, Travis, John, Josif, and Bekim have thrashed out a detailed plan to conduct a strike on Klina. Josif and Bekim will bring their own KLA troops who have previously reconnoitered Klina, about fifteen total.

For group one, Josif will go with the NATO officers and Prek's platoon to look for the SAMs while Bekim will go with group two to find tanks and ZSU 23-4 anti-aircraft vehicles. Group three is Josif's own special forces platoon, and they will lay low as a reaction force. All three groups will depart in separate vehicles at 2100 and link up at a designated point no later than 2145. From there the force will move in their three groups. Everyone will have an AK-47 and five grenades. Josif carries a radio to communicate with the other groups, and Travis and John will each carry a SATCOM radio to contact a designated NATO AWACs plane circling high above Kosovo or Albania.

Julianna will accompany the NATO officers, group one, to interpret. Upon the end of the mission, Josif will announce the code word *Hollywood* over the radio, meaning each group is to run to their awaiting vehicles and return to Skanderbeg on their own.

That afternoon and night everyone rehearses the plan over and over, including the *what-ifs*. Radio procedures are rehearsed, as are casualty evacuation procedures. Group three practices all the contingencies to reinforce another group or counterattack a VJ force. Travis makes contact with Pine Wood, the NATO Special Operations Center, to relay the plan and coordinate procedures for calling in the strikes on the VJ.

John radios General Gashi on Mount Pastrik to advise him of the operation. John is pleased to hear that Josif has already informed General Gashi. It will be the first NATO–KLA coordinated action in Kosovo, and the NATO officers know from their experiences in Bosnia that many things can go wrong. Travis just hopes more things will go wrong for the VJ. After all, the VJ battalion is consolidated in one point, an easy target for NATO air. Thus far, all NATO bombing in Kosovo has been directed at knocking out SA-6s and other SAMs sites. This would be the first blow to VJ ground forces, and the NATO officers are anxious to use airpower to deal a devastating blow to the VJ in Klina.

At 2100 the three groups depart Skanderbeg en route to the linkup point. At 2135 they link up and begin their six-kilometer infiltration to Klina. Josif, Travis and John have night vision goggles. Trooper constantly sprints ahead, back and forth between the groups, and even on the flanks looking for Serb ambushes.

All three groups move slow, trying to be as quiet and vigilant as possible. By 0100 all groups are in place near Klina. Group three, the reaction force, goes into hiding in the brush while groups one and two make their way toward their objectives. Both groups are well aware VJ guards will be roving inside and outside the city. It is also standard procedure for the VJ to have static guard positions at all entrances into Klina. Travis sends Trooper to find any guards along their line of advance. It does not take long for Trooper to return and sit in front of Travis. Travis gets the attention of a KLA soldier, then points toward the general direction of the VJ guard. The KLA soldier moves toward the guard with a large K-bar knife. Six minutes later the KLA soldier returns, and not a word is exchanged before the group's movement continues.

Group one slowly creeps toward where an SA-6 is positioned on the hand-drawn map. Fifty meters from the position, Travis and Josif crawl on their bellies. Seventeen minutes later they are crawling in mud tracks to find the SA-6. The problem is that SA-6s are highly mobile and displaced often to hide from NATO air reconnaissance.

The only option is to follow the tracks and low-crawl through the mud until they see something. It doesn't take long before they spot the vehicle, hidden in a grove of trees still outside the city. Travis removes his laser gun, a digital handheld device that records exact coordinates. He "paints" the SA-6 and receives a digital twelve-digit grid coordinate that is automatically sent to an overhead AWACS and a forward United States Air Force air controller.

The two, with Trooper following, crawl quickly back, where John is quite amused to see Travis transformed into a mud clod. Travis is all too happy to tell John the next one is his.

John soon learns SA-3s are difficult to locate even with night vision. He and Josif crawl for over an hour looking for it; just like the SA-6, the SA-3 has displaced to evade NATO surveillance. They finally find it when they see a crewman from the SA-3 outside the vehicle smoking a cigarette. The man shouts something to a crewman inside the vehicle. A voice responds back from inside, but the VJ soldier smoking the cigarette says nothing. John and Josif hug the ground.

Unfortunately, the VJ soldier starts walking down the muddy tracks, right toward them. John rolls off the tracks to the left while Josif rolls to the right. Josif understands Serbian, so he knows the VJ soldier is a grumpy guard who has not been replaced on time. He is going back into Klina to find his replacement.

Without the ability to communicate with each other, John and Josif cannot plan what actions to undertake. As the VJ soldier comes closer, John and Josif look at each other. Both pull their knifes. When the soldier is thirty meters away both men are ready to jump up and attack. Two knives against one AK-47. Josif and John are thinking the same thing, concentrating on jumping up at the same time, and moving fast enough to plunge their knives into the approaching man before he can yell, much less fire his AK-47.

The man slops through the mud, smoking his cigarette with his weapon slung over his left shoulder. Twenty meters away, fifteen meters, ten . . . Both men lie in the mud with pounding hearts. Just as they are about to jump up, a large dog appears from nowhere and attacks the man from his left side, bringing him swiftly down into the mud. The man jumps up screaming and running as fast as he can back toward the vehicle while the dog nips at his trousers. By the time the man makes it back to the vehicle and turns to shoot the menacing mutt, the dog has disappeared.

Meanwhile, John gives Trooper a big hug and whispers sarcastically to him, "Don't you ever tell Travis I hugged you!"

The USS *Vella Gulf*, a newly commissioned Ticonderoga-class cruiser, is positioned in the Adriatic Sea as part of a larger US Naval task force. Her mission is to engage Serb forces, specifically anti-aircraft positions and key infrastructure targets within Kosovo and Serbia. As their first action in combat, the captain and crew prepare to launch at least two missiles into Kosovo, and possibly more if necessary, to destroy anti-aircraft targets vicinity Klina.

The operations officer aboard the *Vella Gulf* receives two grid coordinates for confirmed SA-3 and SA-6 vehicles, and time is of the essence to launch before the vehicles move to new positions. Although the cruiser is new, the crew has trained long and hard for what they are about to execute, launching nine-foot-long Tomahawk cruise missiles at subsonic speeds over hundreds of miles to precisely hit key targets.

At 0458 hours the *Vella Gulf* launches two Tomahawks at

550 miles an hour toward Klina. The crew is confident in the ship's technologies and in their own abilities. They can navigate the missiles, even change their course if necessary. This would require information on the movement of the targets or locking onto the targets before they move. Flight time is twenty-three minutes.

Fifty-five miles to the north of the *Vella Gulf*, two tank-busting A-10 Warthog aircraft are alerted and scramble from Aviano Air Force Base in Northern Italy. Flying at 355 miles an hour, US Air Force captain Chad Russell, known as Tracker, is flying the lead aircraft. A veteran of Operation Desert Storm, Tracker is considered an experienced and proven combat pilot capable of acquiring and destroying enemy tanks, just as he had in the wide-open deserts in 1990.

This time engaging enemy tanks will be significantly different, and much more difficult. Nestled inside the city of Klina, the Serb tanks are surrounded by buildings on narrow streets. Additionally, tanks are very mobile in urban terrain, and once threatened by aircraft, they can move amongst the streets and buildings. Because of this mobility, it is difficult for the pilots to target the tanks without damaging the city's infrastructure.

Flying alongside and just slightly behind Tracker is First Lieutenant Scott Gainey, a skilled pilot but untested in combat. Known as Apollo, this will be his crucible ride into combat, but even so, he realizes many factors play into a successful mission.

First, the anti-aircraft systems must be destroyed by the cruise missiles launched from the USS *Vella Gulf*. If the SA-3s and 6s are knocked out, then the A-10s must arrive on station immediately, catching the BMPs and tanks in the streets. If the armored vehicles scramble into garages or barns, then the NATO rules of engagement forbid the pilots from indiscriminately destroying buildings.

For the American pilots, surprise is also key to survival. Somewhere in town is at least one ZSU 23-4, a lethal killer that can shoot four 23mm autocannons at low-flying aircraft. With its four autocannons mounted on a tank chassis, it can send up a wall of steel that would chew up even the titanium bottom of an A-10. Additionally, VJ in the town have a man-portable air defense system, or SA-7.

For the pilots, this means coming in fast and low to keep the SA-7s from acquiring them. Tracker and Apollo have extensively trained as a team at the gunnery ranges and in aerial maneuvers. Urban combat at Klina would add another dimension of complexity, in not only timing after the destruction of the SA-3 and 6, but also flying as a team over the city engaging targets.

On the ground one kilometer outside of Klina, the NATO officers, along with Josif and Bekim, are all assembled. The air controller sends Travis the weapon systems and timings for the Klina engagements. There is only one thing left to do before departing: confirm that the SA-3 and 6 are hit by the Tomahawks. In an open field, everyone lies on the ground in a large circle, weapons pointed out for security. Hugging the ground is a damn good idea considering what is about to happen.

Travis and John expect the explosions to be earth-shattering. Besides the munitions in the Tomahawks, the three large missiles on each SA missile system will explode. Standing up is not a good idea, even half a mile away.

The silence is almost unbearable. The sun rises, and the birds begin their morning chatter. Time clicks by slowly, and nerves are more than a little frayed waiting on the air strikes. In the back of everyone's mind is *What if the missiles never arrive?*

They don't have to wait much longer. About twenty meters over their heads, a missile swooshes by, followed by a second one. *Swooosh . . . swooosh!* They fly by so fast it is difficult to actually put eyes on them, and within seconds one tremendous explosion, followed by a second, sends vibrations through the ground, airwaves, and their bodies. Hundreds of parts blow high into the air and over 500 meters distant. Travis grabs his radio mic and holds it up to his right ear, screaming as loud as he can that the two targets "have been serviced." Josif announces "Hollywood" over the radio.

Tracker and Apollo are coming in fast and low just five kilometers from Klina when they received word from the AWACS that the systems are destroyed. The mission will be *a go*, and the pilots' stomachs churn from butterflies. Apollo, the inexperienced pilot, is concerned he will vomit in his mask. Tracker sees the explosions and gives directions of attack to Apollo, which forces him to refocus on the mission instead of his stomach.

They are two minutes out from Klina when they see the NATO officers and KLA running away from the city. Tracker reminds Apollo to disregard them. At the same time, the NATO officers and their accompanying KLA watch the A-10s fly right over them, sending chills down their spines with a sense of great expectations. Most stop and watch the Warthogs make their initial gun run into Klina.

Tracker and Apollo spot numerous VJ soldiers running onto the streets of Klina, apparently running to their battle stations. Slowing down to 150 miles per hour, the Warthogs attack their prey: tanks. As per the reports, all three tanks are still in their positions inside the city. Their gun tubes are oriented to the fields outside the city in case of a KLA ground attack. Tracker designates to Apollo the tank each will engage.

The pilots then swing around in a half-circle movement while elevating their aircraft to dive-attack at the best angle on the tanks. The planes' supersonic turbo fans whine loudly in their fight with gravity. They hear the ping of small arms fire on the bellies of their aircraft as they start their descent, but nothing below 23mm can penetrate the titanium bottom. Diving at 125 miles an hour, Tracker is first to engage his target. With tremendous concentration he flies between the tall buildings and fires his depleted-uranium 30mm shells in three-second bursts from a seven-barrel rotary cannon. Smoke pours out the end of the cannon, and the large bullets break the sound barrier with a thunderous *brrrrt, brrrrt, brrrrt*, hitting first the street, then the top of a tank. Once he feels the concussion of the tank explosion, Tracker pulls back on his stick to quickly elevate, then veers the Warthog away from Apollo's attack lane.

Like Tracker, Apollo uses the same tactic to dive toward the tank between buildings, this time high-rise apartments. Unlike Tracker, Apollo is too tense and fires his initial burst from the gun off target and into the apartment buildings. The 30mm rounds explode upon impact, and the apartments burst into flames. Because of his bad gun run, Apollo strains his turbo fans by pulling up and away to re-circle and make another run. This time he pulls himself together and relies on his training.

In the meantime, Tracker begins a run on the last tank two blocks away from Apollo. Situational awareness is the trademark of any skilled pilot, and now Tracker and Apollo have to adjust in unison to precisely align their guns on their targets.

Apollo storms in for the kill on his second run. Although the apartment building is on fire from his first attempt, Apollo is determined to make up for lost ground. While he maneuvers to get into a good diving position, the tank has moved to another street. In its place is a ZSU 23-4 waiting to chew Apollo's Warthog to shreds. Apollo spots the ZSU 23-4 but assumes it is the tank. After all, they look very similar, the only difference being the turret—the top of the tank.

The ZSU 23-4 aims its four large guns straight upward and sends a steady stream of lead into the sky. When Apollo realizes his situation, he panics. In a split second he takes evasive action and veers as hard as he can to the left. His left wing clips antennas on top of an apartment building, and he loses his situational awareness. He struggles to control his plane, flying at rooftop level without any sense of where Tracker is on his run.

Tracker dives on his tank, destroys it, then elevates and veers his aircraft. At 150 miles an hour, Apollo is still trying to gain control when he narrowly misses Tracker's plane on his ascent. Tracker is alarmed but immediately orders Apollo to fly away from the city to regain his composure.

Tracker is hell-bent on killing the third tank. Through his sights he tracks the tank moving down a narrow street. He goes for the kill. Suddenly the ZSU 23-4 pops back out into the open on the edge of town, turning its turret in Tracker's direction. Tracker does not see it, but high above, Apollo spots the ZSU 23-4, locks on it, and fires a Maverick missile. The missile slams into the side of the ZSU 23-4. A fireball erupts, sending red-hot shrapnel over 300 feet. Trucks, trees and lampposts disintegrate.

Undeterred, Tracker continues his run on the tank. He sends a stream of 30mm right through the top of the turret, then at the last second dramatically elevates through the smoke and flames, missing a building by inches.

As Tracker flies a half circle above the city to head back home, he sees BMPs and VJ jeeps at what appears to be a bus station. Tracker instantly recognizes it as the VJ headquarters because of all the antennas, and makes a dramatic run, unloading his 30mm gun on the entire complex. Seconds later Apollo follows suit and makes a run on the complex from the opposite direction. Both pilots release flares from their aircraft to throw off any VJ soldiers firing SA-7s. Tracker and Apollo look one more time down at Klina for any targets, but smoke covers the entire city.

*Boom!* Apollo's left engine takes a hit from an SA-7. The engine has serious damage, and the entire aircraft shudders. Apollo stays focused on remaining airborne and is able to keep it flying, albeit at less than half speed. Tracker calls the emergency to the air controller and is instructed to land at Petrovec airport in Skopje.

# 06: NORTHERN MITROVICE

**EVEN THOUGH THEY ARE** battered and sore, Miro and Niko slumber during the entire five-hour bus trip. They wake up once the bus comes to a halt, and the driver swings a lever to open the door. Miro looks out the window and notices a VJ sergeant holding a clipboard.

"Not this again," Miro mumbles to Niko. "I can't take another reception like the welcoming committee at indoc."

The sergeant boards the bus and gazes silently at the recruits. Once he determines that everyone is awake he announces, "Welcome to 1st Company. We will now go inside and I will in-process each of you. That way we can get you on the rolls and start being paid. After you are done, go and get some chow before it closes. The chow hall is one block to the left. After you eat come back here and I will issue your equipment and weapons. By the way, I am SGT Luka Kovac, the supply sergeant. I have already eaten, so I will be in my office all evening."

Niko sits up in his seat and asks SGT Kovac where they are. He smiles and states loudly so everyone can hear, "Kosovo, northern Mitrovice."

Miro is relieved. Not only has he survived the indoctrination battalion, but now he is apparently with a regular VJ infantry unit, and hopefully without the brand of *coward* hanging over his head. He imagines being in the VJ might be tolerable, especially stationed in Kosovo with Niko.

The busload of new recruits stretch as they exit the bus and enter the supply sergeant's office to sign paperwork—just routine administrative forms to sign in to the company, says the clerk. One form pertains to pay, including 5,000 Dinar paid in cash up front. Right off the bat, happy soldiers. Another form asks questions concerning ethnicity, address, name of parents, father's occupation, relatives in the VJ who are officers, and education type and level. Miro fills in all the answers quickly and truthfully.

At this point he isn't about to try and get away with anything and get himself in trouble. Not after what he has just been through. Niko lies on almost every answer except for ethnicity. He doesn't want the VJ to know what village he is from or how to contact his family. He makes up answers, including that he is a high school graduate and a medical technician.

The clerk looks over the forms and asks Niko if he has his medical technician certificate, or at least can state where he attended school. Niko's plan to avoid the infantry falls flat when he can't remember the school's name. He even tries bribing the clerk with a pack of American cigarettes, but the guy doesn't smoke.

Miro, on the other hand, states where he obtained his electrician's license in Belgrade, and the clerk gives him credit for it.

"So, why is it important to know all of this information?" Miro asks.

The clerk looks up from his paperwork. "In case you are missing, get wounded, or get killed, we know who to notify. As far as your education and skills, the VJ needs to fill certain positions with qualified people."

"What am I qualified for?"

"Let's see, electrician. Hmmm, most likely a signalman."

"What's that?"

"A fancy term for a radio operator. Now move on so I can get these other guys taken care of."

Miro and Niko walk at their own pace to the chow hall. It feels strange, but in a good way, that no one is yelling or harassing them. Once there, they stand in a short line, eventually signing their names to the food roster. They pick up metal trays and make their way down the chow line. Miro holds out his tray, and soldiers mechanically slap food onto it. Niko does the same but keeps holding his tray out until the servers add more food.

"You guys look like you need to eat. Well, it's not the best food in town, but you are welcome to more if you want it," laughs one of the servers.

After getting Jelen-brand beers out of a cooler at the end of the line, Miro and Niko sit down and inhale their best meal in weeks. Not a word is exchanged between them, only grunts and groans of wolfing down fried veal and pickled beets. After eating, they gulp down the ice-cold beer. Niko looks back at the beer cooler, then back at Miro.

"Hell, why not," Miro grunts while choking down his last bite.

Niko grabs two beers and slams them hard on the table. They both let out a short laugh and pop the cans open.

"Here's to our liberation," barks Niko.

They toast and again take large gulps. Miro finishes first and lets out a loud burp. Other soldiers in the mess hall laugh, some even clapping. Both men flush and give a courteous wave back to their impromptu audience.

Upon their return to the supply sergeant's office, Sergeant Luka Kovac has Miro and Niko sign for their equipment and AK-47s. Luka states that he has some "extra" equipment if they lose anything. As both are receiving and organizing their issued items, Luka looks at a piece of paper.

"Miro, looks like you are to stay at a house about five blocks from here."

"A house?" Miro responds with utter surprise.

"Yep, that way we all won't be killed if NATO bombs our barracks! Nice, huh?" Luka says with a short laugh. "You will have to find your way. The family has volunteered to sponsor you and expects you tonight. Tomorrow be back here by 0730. *Sober.*"

"Yes, Sergeant!" Miro happily answers while pocketing his money.

"Niko, looks like you are staying in an apartment within walking distance also. You will be sharing it with a couple of other soldiers."

Niko holds his money up to the light, inspecting the authenticity. He nods approval to the sergeant and takes the address and map. Both men store most of their equipment in a locker and pack some items in their rucks to take with them. They check in their AKs at the arms room, and begin their journey on foot to their temporary homes. After a few blocks Miro slaps Niko on his shoulder and wishes him a good rest.

Niko lights a cigarette and casts a glance at Miro. "Maybe a few drinks first?"

"Naw, it's getting dark and I need to go meet these folks while I am sober." Miro laughs.

So they go their own ways, both with address and map in hand. Northern Mitrovice is Serb, so it is fairly safe to walk alone at night. Miro gazes at the city's lights as he makes his way through the beautiful old part of the city.

The city is divided by the Ibar River, which has served as the dividing line for a long history of conflict. The north side of the river is Serb, and on the south side are Albanian Kosovars. Miro takes his ruck off and rests on a bench while looking across the river. On the other side is the KLA, waiting for the VJ to cross into their territory. But it seems so peaceful with a light breeze and points of light glimmering off the slow-moving current. Miro stays for most of an hour, thinking about all that he has been through. He stretches his back as he stands up, glancing once more across the river, wondering where Julianna is.

After enjoying his evening stroll, Miro locates the house in an affluent neighborhood. Walking up to the front door, he feels hesitant to knock because he has never met them. He double-checks the address and knocks lightly. He hears movement and voices inside the house. Moments later the door slowly opens, and standing in front of him is a young blond girl, perhaps eight years old.

She immediately becomes excited, turns around and yells, "Papa, Papa, Papa!"

A small plump man with a short mustache appears with a wide grin.

"Come in, come in, please. Let me help you with your things."

Miro enters into a simple but meticulously clean front room. As the man helps with Miro's pack, a blond woman wearing a white silk nightgown strolls into the room.

She looks at Miro warmly and holds out her hand. "Welcome to our home. We are the Marins: Filip, my husband, Ana, my daughter, and I am Suzana."

Miro gently shakes Suzana's hand, but hesitates shaking the man's hand while he is handling the ruck.

"I am Private Miro Cadikovski. Thank you for such a warm welcome."

The man drops Miro's ruck, shakes his hand and excitedly states, "Cadikovski, Cadikovski, yes, I picked you because your brother is a good friend of mine. Colonel Cadikovski is the commander here and well known for his leadership of the Guards Brigade!"

Miro is speechless; apparently his brother, Dragan, is the brigade commander.

"Uh, yes, yes, that's right, he is my older brother. I have not seen him for some time, though, as I have been going through difficult training."

The Cadikovski link seems to greatly please the Marins. The man, Filip, frantically tries to help Miro in any way he can.

"Are you hungry? Let's have a drink! Upstairs is your room. We hope you are pleased and comfortable!"

Overcome with the Marins' hospitality, Miro shyly asks if he can first bathe, at which time Suzana scurries up the stairs to start his bathwater. Filip and Miro walk up the stairs while little Ana follows dragging his ruck. Miro is led to a small but cozy room. After thanking Filip and his daughter, Miro takes a clean uniform from his ruck and heads down the hall to take a much-needed hot bath. The tub is almost full when he enters the bathroom. He closes the door and starts undressing. Miro can't remember the last time he had a bath. He dips his right foot in first to test the temperature, then lowers his sore body into the hot water.

Suzana opens the door and walks in carrying a towel and washcloth. She stands next to Miro, looking eagerly at his body.

"Filip is on the phone, so I brought these for you. Anything else you need? Maybe your back washed?" Suzanne asks half-jokingly.

"No, ma'am, I am fine. Thank you all the same."

Suzana turns and slowly walks back out, turning and casting a big smile at Miro as she slowly closes the door.

Miro figures she is just teasing him, and the last thing he needs is to dive headlong into trouble, especially with a married woman. Then there is Julianna, who he wishes had entered the bathroom instead of Suzana. Miro soaks his stiff body until the water is cold, then towels off and dons his fresh VJ uniform. He looks at himself in the mirror. He despises wearing the VJ uniform, but at least he feels human again.

As Miro reappears downstairs, Filip and Suzana are patiently waiting to present toasts. Suzana hands a small glass of vodka to Miro. Miro grins, glad he did not go out with Niko drinking. At least this vodka is free.

"To Serbia's province of Kosovo," toasts Filip, raising his glass.

Miro notes both Filip and Suzana down the entire glass, so he follows suit.

Filip recharges the glasses.

"To the VJ soldiers," Suzana softly toasts while gazing at Miro.

Again, they take a shot and Filip recharges the glasses once more.

"To peace and prosperity," Miro proudly toasts.

By 0730 the next morning Miro arrives clean shaven outside Luka's office with the other newcomers. Niko is already present, but looking slightly pale. Miro, recognizing a hangover when he sees one, offers him some biscuits that Suzana gave him on his way out the door. Niko grins and graciously accepts. As Niko stuffs his mouth, he hears other soldiers discussing their previous night's experiences on the town. Niko realizes he isn't alone with an aching head.

Luka opens the door and greets the men. "Good morning, Privates. Your platoon commander, Lieutenant Buha, will be here shortly to meet you. Miro Cadikovski, you are to report to the brigade headquarters at 0800."

On hearing the order, a bolt of lightning shoots up Miro's spine. He anticipated that his brother would want to see him, just not this soon.

Luka points up the street. "Just go two blocks, take a right, and it is the large building with the flag. We can introduce you to Lieutenant Buha later. You better get going now."

Miro departs in a fast walk, thinking about what his brother will say to him, and how he will respond. Dragan knows about his capture in Montenegro, his time at the indoctrination battalion, and possibly about his marriage to Julianna.

Upon entering the brigade headquarters, Miro wanders up to a VJ private sitting at a desk. Miro takes his hat off and states he is reporting to Colonel Cadikovski.

"Yes, the commander is expecting you."

The private leads him up a flight of steps. He tells Miro to go through the closed double doors at the end of the hall and have a seat by the secretary. Miro notices VJ officers walking about the building, but luckily paying no attention to him. He walks down the hall and spots a sign on the double doors: *Commanding Officer*. Hesitantly, Miro opens the right door and peeks in. A lady is busy typing. She looks up, annoyed.

"Yes?"

"I am Private Cadikovski," Miro says in a low voice. The lady, wearing a dress a size too small, immediately gets up and waddles into an adjoining office.

Miro hears her say, "Private Cadikovski is here, sir."

He also hears a snap in his brother's reply. "Tell him to report."

The lady struts back to Miro, her high-heeled shoes clicking on the hard floor. Without looking at Miro she says, "Report to the colonel; he is waiting on you. *Hurry up.*"

Instead of hurrying up, Miro slowly walks past the annoyed secretary toward his brother's office. The door is open, and he sees Dragan's back while he looks out a window.

"Private Cadikovski reporting as ordered, sir."

Dragan slowly turns around, and with a scowl he stares at his younger brother. Miro is taken aback. The two have not seen each other in years. His older brother is just that—looking older, much older. He is a hard-looking man, seeming unemotional and distant. Standing just a few inches higher than Miro, he is straight as an arrow, fit and trim with closely cropped gray hair. His eyebrows slant down over glaring gray eyes that would rip the soul out of you. Both stand silent as they look each other over.

Miro breaks a faint smile, but Dragan remains stone faced.

"I had you assigned to my brigade, Miro. That way I can keep an eye on you so you don't cause our family any more shame. When I received a report from the VJ border police you crossed into Montenegro, I sent the special police to find you at the airport. Even I could figure that one out, especially since we don't know anyone in Montenegro, much less related to anyone."

Colonel Dragan Cadikovski takes several steps and picks up an envelope from his desk.

As he clutches the envelope in both hands, he steps closer to Miro. "I know all about you, Miro, and what you have done. Including running off with an Albanian woman. Did you know that her brother, Josif, is a brigade commander in the KLA?"

Miro gulps loudly but remains silent as he nervously gazes away from Dragan's wrathful eyes.

The colonel's upper lip is now raised, his teeth clenched. "Well, did you or did you not know Josif is in the KLA when you ran off with his sister?"

"I did know, but I never interacted with him. He is older and was your friend long ago, before the troubles began. It is his sister, Julianna, that I love. Our marriage has nothing to do with Josif, nor the KLA."

"Marriage, huh! You married her on the way to the airport?"

"Yes, and I am glad I did. I want to return to her and leave the war."

"And that's precisely why I sent you to indoctrination training, and why you are here today—to hold you to your duty. Any more trouble from you and off to the penal battalion you go!"

"I may not be as committed as you want, but I will be compliant as long as your orders are not against the Geneva Convention."

"Why should I believe you? You lied to Mother and Father about joining the VJ, and instead you married the sister of a KLA commander and tried to sneak away."

Miro tries his best to keep from looking intimidated, but it isn't working. Standing at attention, he is petrified. In a trembling voice he manages a weak, "Yes."

Colonel Cadikovski somberly marches up to Miro, staring coldly into his eyes. He hands Miro the envelope. It is the letter Miro sent to his parents in Klina, but it has never been opened. The envelope is stamped *DECEASED*. Horrified, Miro is stunned. He stares at the envelope but can't speak.

Colonel Cadikovski snaps, "I hope you are proud of yourself, running out on Mother, Father and your country like a fucking coward."

He spins around and struts back toward his desk, then suddenly turns back, facing Miro with a red face of rage. *"They were burned alive in their apartment during a NATO air strike. The same apartment you were raised in."*

# 07: GOODBYE

**JUST SEVERAL HOURS AFTER** returning from Klina's mission Travis wakes to the sounds of Prek's men moving about inside the barn. Travis unzips his sleeping bag while Trooper gives him the usual good morning love lick under his chin. John gets up and stretches in the barn's damp clamminess. Prek comes in with hot coffee and sets it down on a small folding table. After Prek's soldiers fill their canteen cups, John lights a cigarette and enjoys a sip of the hot joe.

"Ahhh, that's the dog's bollocks."

Prek stares at John with bewilderment. Travis figures John is talking about Trooper but really doesn't get his point. As usual, he feeds Trooper first before pouring a cup of the precious black Balkan coffee.

With the Klina operation behind them, John and Travis realize this is the beginning of a long and difficult air–ground campaign. Nothing is going to be that easy in the future. The reserve force Josif brought along wasn't even needed, but the Klina strikes were a surprise to the VJ. In the future they will be more vigilant. Most concerning is what the VJ will do next. That's why the NATO officers and the KLA at Skanderbeg are getting up after just three hours of rest.

As John put it when they got back from last night's mission, "The Serbs will do *something* to retaliate. Soon."

The NATO officers hurriedly down their coffee and enter the house where they will plan more operations. An urgent meeting is called by Josif for the NATO officers and KLA leaders. The central topic to discuss is what move the VJ will most likely make and how to counter their operations, especially if it is a punitive retaliation against Kosovar civilians. Josif and Bekim know all the villages in their area, and are trying to anticipate which one, or ones, will feel the wrath of a vengeful VJ.

The discussion focuses around evacuating the remaining Kosovars from nearby villages, specifically Skenderaj. Josif has the forces within his 3rd Brigade to undertake such an operation. The coordination of buses and civilian trucks will be his biggest challenge. John and Travis, through interpretation from Julianna, listen silently. They certainly endorse evacuating innocents, and preventing Serb atrocities, but they also have a mission. A mission that cannot lapse, even during humanitarian operations by the KLA.

John radios Pine Tree to give the daily situation report. A point of contention arises when John asks Pine Tree if NATO warplanes can escort, or at least protect, 3rd Brigade's civilian evacuation operation from the Skenderaj area. Specifically, he requests that NATO overfly departing buses and trucks as they travel to the Macedonian border.

It takes several hours to get an answer back, not because of communications problems, but because NATO senior military leaders had to discuss the matter. In the end the request is denied, specifically because NATO has already finalized a target list and allocated aircraft for today's bombings further north and in Serbia proper.

Josif doesn't like the answer and strongly protests. Both John and Travis counter that typically the VJ leave evacuation buses alone, happy to see the Kosovars leaving. Josif still complains that these people will be women with their children, and older Kosovars. They will be completely defenseless against rape, robbery, or worse.

John radios back his NATO superiors. Eventually, a compromise is hammered out, one that seems to make sense. On-call CAS will be limited to two A-10s on station, and NATO will allocate a few aircraft to overwatch major routes heading toward Macedonia, but only to target VJ convoys, especially armored vehicles. In theory, the VJ will then be forced off these routes, and thus enable a safer and quicker passage for the evacuees. Josif agrees to the compromise, and then returns to work out the more detailed logistical planning.

John, Travis and Prek go to another room to discuss their next combat mission and Skenderaj.

John repeats the requirements just given to him on the radio. "Pine Tree needs to know what VJ forces occupy Skenderaj. Intelligence gleaned from satellite surveillance and signal intelligence indicates an enemy presence. However, the picture is still unclear. They need to know the size and type of enemy units, and if atrocities have occurred."

Prek says there is a small KLA presence there. John asks what they have reported.

Prek opens the door to the communications room and asks in Albanian if anyone has heard from the KLA in Skenderaj lately. No one answers. Josif overhears Prek's question. He enters the communications room and runs his fingers nervously through his hair while ordering his radioman to try and make contact with them. The radio operator tries several times but receives nothing back from Skenderaj.

John and Travis enter the radio room with Josif. Bekim follows.

Josif, miffed, guesses that perhaps the KLA in Skenderaj might be busy trying to evacuate the civilians. Everyone in the room, including Josif, knows that is wishful thinking.

Bekim in his native Albanian states to Josif, "The KLA in Skenderaj should still be monitoring the radio."

John feels sending Prek and his platoon to recon the city is all that is needed. "Besides, NATO just wants to know what forces, if any, occupy the city and if the civilians are okay."

Travis disagrees. "John, they want to know the size and type of enemy, and I think it would be unfair for Prek to be the eyes and ears for NATO's bombing campaign. *That's our job.*"

Upon hearing a higher pitch in Travis's voice, Trooper wakes from his nap. He nudges Travis's hand to get a response. Travis rubs the top and back of Trooper's head to soothe the dog and himself. John squirms in his chair trying to get comfortable, but can't because of the tense conversation.

"Trav, this is a recon mission, not a bombing run. Prek knows these villages and cities better than we ever will. Once he brings back the information, we can plan a mission if necessary."

Travis shoots back, "Why execute two missions if we can do it all in one? Besides, by the time Prek makes it back with the information, the A-10s may be off station and the enemy will probably have moved anyway."

John relents. "Okay, but we still need Prek. We also need to remind Pine Tree to have air on call the entire time we are there in case something happens."

"Something happens? You mean an opportunity to target the enemy?"

"Of course, but also if we get in a pinch," responds John in a low, serious tone.

Josif sits patiently, listening to the NATO officer's logic. "I agree this should be a combined operation between NATO and 3rd Brigade. We cannot pull off a large-scale evacuation operation if the VJ occupy the city. I think we will need close air support on call, like in Klina. I will be taking most of my force for evacuation operations, but if a large VJ force is there, our first priority will be to reinforce you guys."

John reluctantly agrees. "Okay, but we better start getting ready. Anything can bust loose today after what we did last night."

Josif, proud of himself for wrangling the deal, states, "My leaders are already planning the evacuation. Let's get back together in two hours."

Travis leaves the room to find Julianna. She will be needed to translate in two hours for the planning phase of the upcoming operation into Skenderaj. He walks quietly down the hall with Trooper in tow and taps on her bedroom door.

Julianna opens the door slightly, sees Travis and Trooper's heads poking through the crack. She lets out a short laugh and opens the door. Travis notices a lady reading a book to a young boy on the bed. As Julianna introduces Travis to her, Deidra quickly rises and shakes his hand. She lays her left hand over their joined hands and looks him in the eye.

With the few English words she knows she repeats, "NATO, thank you." She then gives Travis a warm hug and a faint smile.

Travis knew another woman and her child were in the house but has not seen them until now. Deidra is little more than skin and bones, and her child appears to be malnourished.

Travis looks at Julianna as Deidra lets go. "What is she thanking NATO about?"

"NATO is bombing the people who did these terrible things, and that's why she is thanking you."

Julianna tells Travis Deidra's story while Shabin holds on to Travis's right leg like a little monkey. After hearing Deidra's horrifying experiences, Travis sits on the bed and places the little boy in his lap. He tickles Shabin while bouncing him on his knee. Shabin reaches up to touch Travis's face. He finds the stubby beard fascinating, and giggles with delight. Travis holds the little hand and looks at it with sympathy, then softly hugs the little boy.

Travis stands and carefully hands Shabin to Deidra. He doesn't know what to tell Deidra. He is at a complete loss for words. Travis puts his hand on the side of her face and smiles, then starts to leave the room.

Julianna asks, "Was there something you needed?"

Travis, embarrassed he forgot why he came to her room, requests she interpret a discussion with Josif and his men in two hours.

"Before the meeting, John and I need to brief you up on the mission."

As usual, Julianna is anxious to help. She follows Travis out of the room, but not before kissing Deidra on her cheek and soothing her in Albanian.

Julianna accompanies Travis and Trooper to the plans room. John, who is studying a map of Skenderaj, looks up. "Oh perfect, do you have time now for a quick briefing on our mission?"

"That's why I am here," she replies while glancing at Travis.

After the NATO officers' brief Julianna on Skenderaj, she requests to go with Travis and John on the operation.

"Of course, that would be wonderful," Travis enthusiastically responds. John quietly takes note of Travis's eagerness.

Travis tells John about Deidra and Shabin. He recommends to John and Julianna that Deidra and her child be part of the evacuation being planned by Josif. John, being married with a son, empathizes with her situation. In the back of his mind he is always worried what will become of his family if he does not make it home.

Julianna hesitates, then says, "That was the plan when we got here, but we have become such close friends. I used to feel sorry for myself until I met her. She is not very strong, and without us to help her—"

"But what about the boy?" Travis quickly asks, then continues, "Sooner or later Josif may have to displace from here as the VJ gets closer. The child's life will be endangered. They simply can't be part of this headquarters."

Julianna's face is gloomy. She puts her head down, then quietly responds, "Yes, little Shabin must be cared for. I have grown so very fond of him also, like family. But I suppose you are right. For their safety they must be evacuated to Macedonia."

"Right, now that's the attitude," says John. "So, you will talk to your brother about getting her on a bus?"

Julianna nods approval.

Travis asks Julianna something that brings her out of her despondency. "Are you going with her and Shabin?"

Surprised by the question, Julianna stares hard at Travis, then John. "No. I am staying to fight for my country."

"With John and I, as an interpreter?"

Julianna ponders the question. "I will need to talk to Josif. Yes, I want to. *Very badly.*" She looks at Travis.

When Julianna finds Josif, he has no issues with Julianna interpreting for the NATO officers. Like the NATO officers, he wants Deidra and Shabin to be evacuated with the others from Skenderaj as soon as possible. "This could be their last chance."

✯✯✯

Julianna spots Deidra outside on a blanket with Shabin, enjoying the spring weather. She unconcernedly wanders outside and lies on the blanket with them. They make small talk for a few minutes, mainly discussing the birds singing and flowers blooming. Deidra has Shabin pick some flowers to put in Julianna's hair, which Shabin gladly accomplishes. Julianna mentions how the beautiful spring is such a wonderful time in Kosovo. Deidra merely bows her head and says nothing. Her son continues to pick flowers and bring them back to the ladies.

Julianna says, "You must get away with Shabin as soon as you can. Things are getting worse. Despite the air campaign and the KLA's efforts, the VJ are still advancing. You and Shabin are in great danger. You must leave for Macedonia the soonest. I am sorry; you know what you mean to me."

Deidra looks up and stares at Julianna with dread. "I knew this time would come. I was just hoping that somehow the VJ would be defeated, or at least halted because of the NATO bombing. You know I do not want to leave, and wouldn't if not for Shabin."

She rolls over and places her left arm on Julianna. "Come with me, Julianna. I am afraid to go alone. We could live in safety in Macedonia until after the war, then come back . . . that is, if the VJ is beaten."

Julianna sits up. "And that is precisely why I am staying to fight. To help in any way to stop the atrocities and win independence. Besides, I think Josif will let me stay with the NATO officers, to interpret for them. I think that will be a very important job."

Deidra also sits up, placing her hand on Julianna's cheek. "Promise me you will be careful, and that after hostilities you will find me. Promise?"

Julianna holds Deidra in her arms, then kisses her once again on her cheek. "Yes, of course, I promise with all of my heart. Where do you think you will go in Macedonia?"

Deidra ponders silently for a few moments, then states, "Probably to where your parents are, or at least in the large Kosovar community. Maybe I can stay with your parents and it would make it easier for us to connect afterwards."

Julianna reveals one of her wonderfully spontaneous smiles. "That sounds perfect. What a wonderful idea, and I know my parents would love to have you. I will write a note you can take with you."

As Julianna leaves, butterflies dance in her stomach. Deidra has not only provided emotional support at this critical time, but she is also now Julianna's closest friend. They have connected in a way that even surpasses Julianna's link to Miro. Maybe it is because they understand each other as women. Either way, she has just made a promise to one day find Deidra, and it is one she plans on keeping.

The thunderous echoes of NATO bombings are heard and felt in the far distance. Every so often a NATO aircraft is spotted high above. John and Travis watch, listening in to the pilots' frequency. Based upon the pilots' conversations, NATO targeting is not as effective as they had hoped. As anticipated, the VJ quit massing their forces and are operating in a much more decentralized manner, hiding vehicles in barns or garages. All the warplanes can do is find targets of opportunity: a single vehicle, or a small convoy if lucky.

As the NATO officers watch and listen to the air operations, a car arrives to pick up Deidra and Shabin. They will be driven ten miles to the east where buses are waiting for the first load of Kosovars. Josif and Julianna follow Deidra and Shabin as they come out of the front door and walk toward the car. Both Deidra and Julianna are solemn. As they embrace goodbye, their eyes moisten, and Shabin's face is pouty. Julianna picks Shabin up and gives him a tight hug, whispering something to him that others cannot hear.

Travis brings over Trooper to cheer Shabin up. While saying goodbye Travis squeezes the boy as firmly as he can, feeling his little heartbeat. He wishes Shabin were his. John looks on from the door thinking about his son.

As they drive off, Julianna stoically watches until the car is out of sight, then runs into the house. Josif, standing silently, walks up to John and Travis. All three look upward, watching the NATO warplanes.

# 08: PLATOON

**MIRO LEAVES HIS BROTHER'S** office with tremendous guilt. He feels responsible for his parents' death, and for the first time questions his own actions in running away to Montenegro. Having failed his parents, brother, Julianna, and now even himself, devastating feelings of self-loathing flood him. He convinces himself he is a complete failure and has nothing to hope for in his future. Having to serve in a VJ unit that will soon cleanse Kosovars is against everything he stands for. Miro contemplates suicide.

The contemplation soon transforms into a deep plea somewhere inside his psyche to end his life. He carries his AK-47 everywhere he goes while on base, so it will be easy to follow through on his suicidal thoughts. Miro walks behind his brother's headquarters.

Too many people are around.

He walks amongst various buildings until he finds a vacant warehouse. Walking behind the building through weedy grass he finds the perfect spot between two small trees. Kneeling down on his knees he awkwardly chambers the first round in his AK-47 and places the cold and hard barrel under his chin. He thinks of his parents and how they cared for him while growing up. How his mother kissed him every morning before going to school. Then he pictures the horrible death they suffered, and he begins to squeeze the trigger, expecting bullets to rip his skull apart at any time.

Tears rain down his face, mixing with thick mucus flowing from his nose. He is ready to accept an end to what he now considers himself—a miserable failure. With his eyes closed he puts more pressure on the trigger. He starts to hyperventilate and pulls the trigger harder. Nothing happens. He pulls it as hard as he can; still nothing. He isn't familiar with the weapon, and tries to look at the AK through his watery eyes. The safety is still on. He clicks the switch to *Fire* and repeats the process—barrel to the underside of his chin, eyes closed.

Julianna appears. She is looking at him with her big, brown, dreamy eyes. She needs him, probably now more than ever. She tells him if he goes through with this, she will forever be a broken woman because of his cowardice. She doesn't want to be left behind as a widow. It will ruin her life, also.

Miro throws his weapon down and places his hands over his face, crying hysterically. After perhaps an hour, maybe two, Miro heads toward his platoon area. Once there, he enters, having no idea what to expect. The room is crowded with soldiers packing their gear. No one even looks up at Miro until a sergeant approaches him.

"Are you Private Cadikovski?"

"Yes, Sergeant," Miro quietly responds, still trying to pull himself together.

"I am Platoon Sergeant Bogdana Komazec, but most call me *Bog*. I need to bring you on board fast because we move out for training tomorrow. Be in full combat gear by 0730 tomorrow morning."

"Yes, Sergeant."

"You're going to be driving one of those trucks, so you need driver's training today. Vuk, your squad leader, will get with you on that. By the way, it must be nice having a brother that is our brigade commander! I guess we must treat you special nice," he says with a grin.

"*Listen up, everybody,*" Bog yells. Everyone stops their packing and looks up. "This is Private Cadikovski, straight out of training. He will be assigned to 2nd Squad as a driver and radio operator. He is from Klina, so he knows his way around Kosovo. That is all; now get back to packing. Oh yes, briefing at 1100 by our platoon leader, Lieutenant Buha. *Be here!*"

Bog turns back to Miro. "Better start sorting through your gear. You can take your ruck tomorrow if you like. Training will be on the range tomorrow to learn about the AK-47, firing it single shot and fully auto. Anyway, welcome, Miro; it is good to have you!" Bog shakes his hand and moves on.

Miro appreciates the platoon sergeant's kind words, but he still feels like a loser. He begins to sort through his equipment, wondering what to take. He is looking for Niko to assist when a corporal appears and shakes his hand.

"I am Corporal Vuk Kovac, your squad leader. Glad we got you. We are full strength on personnel now. Here, let me help you." Corporal Kovac starts sorting equipment for Miro. "You need this, you don't need that; rain gear is a must, keep it on top of your ruck. This is a helmet cover, and it attaches like this . . ."

Miro is stunned at the hospitality of his platoon leadership. After what he has experienced, Miro expected to serve with a platoon of ruthless bloodthirsty criminals. His anxiety eases a bit.

"Oh, and meet me in the motor pool after Lieutenant Buha speaks to us in a few minutes. I will train you on how to drive a truck. You do know how to drive, I hope?"

"Yes, Corporal."

"Call me Vuk."

At 1100 Lieutenant Buha enters the room and everyone jumps to attention.

"Please take a seat, men. I just want to go over the details on our training tomorrow. Many of you haven't even fired a gun, much less an AK-47. The first thing you need to know is that they are *loud*. We will have hearing protection on the range, so be sure to put them in your ears good and tight. Second, safety is always a priority. Bring the ammo you are issued, but don't insert the magazine until you get on the firing line. We will have more ammo available on the range. Keep your weapon downrange when you are on the firing line. When you are not on the firing line, no goofing off. I want you to be watching the soldier in front of you on the line. Each soldier firing will have their squad leader coaching them on how to shoot the weapon correctly. The KLA already know how to shoot, and many of them are experts, so take this training seriously. It could save your life. Any questions? Okay, see you in the morning. Oh, and *sober*."

Several soldiers laugh as the platoon leader leaves the room.

Miro gazes at his AK and realizes his first attempt at firing one was to blow his own brains out. He feels fortunate now that he didn't know what a safety was.

"What are you so preoccupied with?" Niko asks.

"I saw my brother this morning. It didn't go well."

"I didn't think your visit with him would go well considering our recent past in the VJ."

"He told me our parents were killed in an air strike. I didn't think NATO would target civilians, so I guess I am pretty naïve. NATO may be just as ruthless as Milosevic's regime, I suppose."

"This happen in Klina? I heard that a couple of A-10s busted up the place, but didn't want to mention it because I knew you are from there. It just would have made you worry to the point of . . . giving up."

"You're right. I came close to offing myself after my brother told me. I'm still shook up. Damn, Niko, I don't know what to do."

"Stick with me. I think we have fallen in with a good platoon.

All the guys seem normal, not nationalist zealots aiming to kill a bunch of folks. That includes the lieutenant on down. I have a feeling the tough part is over. Don't give up now. She needs you."

Miro perks up when Niko mentions her. He didn't think Niko had seen her in the car with him at the border.

Niko says, "She is out there somewhere, waiting for you to find her."

Miro still feels a little despondent. "Out there *somewhere* is right. Wherever *somewhere* is."

"Keep your chin up, kid. Now head to the motor pool. You don't want Vuk waiting on you. Besides, it will be cool to learn how to drive one of those monster trucks."

Miro jogs to the motor pool and arrives just as Vuk is walking up. They pace down the line of trucks until Vuk points out bumper number *13*, the 2nd Squad truck Miro will drive.

Vuk places his hands on his hips as he looks at the truck. "It's a TAM-150 6x6." Vuk opens the driver's door, and Miro puts his foot on a metal step to look inside. "It just seats two in the cab, including the driver. It can reach about eighty kilometers an hour; although that doesn't seem very fast, if you are sitting in the back, you wouldn't want to go any faster. I will be your sidekick while you drive, and I will have a radio so I can communicate with Bog and the guys in the bed."

Walking around the back of the truck, Vuk points to the bed. "As you can see, the cargo area can easily carry our squad and quite a bit of gear. A drop-side folding wooden bench seat is on each side, and a tarp goes on top. The sides stay open for security. Now, let's give her a try."

Vuk climbs into the passenger's seat while Miro ascends into the driver's seat. He is surprised at how high up he is. It is a little imposing after driving his small Crvena Zastava.

"There's the button to start it. Just pull the throttle out, then push the button once. After it starts, slowly push the throttle back in. There is no key. You wouldn't want to be looking for your keys while under fire, would you?" Vuk snickers.

Miro follows Vuk's instructions, and the truck roars to life. A large puff of black diesel smoke billows out of the exhaust.

"Okay, push in the clutch and put the gear shift into reverse."

Miro finds the clutch to be stiff, and it takes him a few seconds to push it all the way to the floor. He grips the stick shift with his right hand and grinds it into reverse.

"Easy now. You will have to get used to exactly where the gears are without grinding to find them."

Miro backs the truck up slowly, then mashes the clutch in again and finds first gear without a problem. He drives the large truck around the motor pool, learning how hard it is to turn the steering wheel and work the clutch simultaneously. *It turns like a battleship,* he thinks, but it is enjoyable and somewhat exhilarating.

After Miro gets the hang of it, Vuk has him drive out the gate and onto the road. They drive around the outskirts of Belgrade, bouncing in their seats while going over potholes and climbing curbs. The wooden seats in the bed rattle loudly, especially when Vuk tells Miro to put it into 6x6 and drive off-road.

"This is what the truck is built for, off-road," shouts Vuk.

Miro realizes Vuk is right. For the size of the truck, it creeps over hills and valleys without any problems. He practices for about another hour driving on slanted terrain and through creeks. Considering how horrible the morning has been, he is having fun, and he feels guilty.

Once back in the motor pool, Vuk instructs Miro how to maintain the engine. Vuk unlatches a large metal clip outside each door and tips over the entire cab, exposing the 9.57-liter V6 engine. After going through the maintenance checks, they carefully lower the cab and securely latch it back in place.

Vuk takes a few steps back and gazes proudly at the truck.

"This is your baby, Miro. Take good care of her and she will take care of you. You're an important asset for us. You know Kosovo, can operate a radio, and drive this brute. Sometime in the near future you will drive this truck over the Ibar Bridge and deep into Kosovo. The lives of your comrades will be in your hands, literally. I recommend every chance you get to take her out and practice, but always be sober and take another soldier with you."

"Thanks, Vuk. This has been a real learning experience for me. Who knows, maybe I will want to be a truck driver someday instead of an electrician."

"You may not think so after driving in combat," Vuk plainly states.

Miro doesn't waste any time. He finds Niko still messing with his equipment. They go on a ride along the same route he and Vuk took earlier. Niko says he has been in dump trucks but not a truck like the TAM-150.

Miro drives to the top of a hill that has a large miners' memorial overlooking Mitrovica. He cuts the engine and they take in the landscape.

"You know we could leave right now," Niko states.

"You mean *leave* leave? Like going AWOL?"

"Yep, that's exactly what I mean. You could look for your girl, and I would make my way to Macedonia."

The thought sends chills down Miro's spine. "How far do you really think you would make it wearing a VJ uniform? Where in the hell would I go to find her? Walk to the nearest KLA headquarters dressed like this?"

"Just dreaming, I guess. I don't know where we could go. That is, without getting caught."

"And getting caught would mean bad news. Like dying in the penal battalion. As bad as I want Julianna—uh, that's her name—I say we stick it out where we are. You have to admit we have it pretty good in this platoon."

"So far. But one of these days we will deploy in this truck to war, and that won't be as fun as driving across country. People on the ground and from the air will be shooting at us."

"It's just bad timing right now, Niko. Once we get further into Kosovo, we might have a much better chance of escaping, especially if we can get some civilian clothes."

Niko pulls a cigarette from a celluloid pack, strikes a match, and lights it. He inhales a deep drag and blows the smoke out with a sense of discouragement. "I've got a feeling a lot of folks are going to get killed, soon."

Returning back to base, Niko and Miro finish getting their gear ready for the next day.

The platoon leader, Lieutenant Buha, is across the room and approaches Miro once he spots him. "Private Cadikovski, I have not met you yet. Please come see me in a few minutes once you are done here."

Miro sounds off, "*Yes sir!*"

He hurriedly finishes his packing. Before leaving to report to the lieutenant, Miro asks Niko, "Have you met the platoon leader yet?"

"Nope."

On his way, Miro has a hunch why the lieutenant wants to see him, and it has to do with his last name.

He raps three times on the lieutenant's door.

"Report!"

Miro enters, stands at attention, and salutes Lieutenant Buha. After returning the salute, the lieutenant tells Miro to have a seat and relax.

"Private Cadikovski, I am Lieutenant Aleksandra Buha, the only one in this platoon that knows that you are coming from the indoctrination battalion. It will stay that way unless you or one of your comrades you came with tells someone. I don't care why you had to go there, but I do care about our mission, to clear Kosovo of the KLA."

Miro sits upright, silent in his chair, grasping the armrests tightly.

Lieutenant Buha stands and starts pacing the room. "The sooner we can save Kosovo for Serbia, the sooner this war will be over. If we can evacuate the Kosovars, these ethnic Albanians who want to secede from Serbia, without harming them, then maybe NATO will back off on their bombing. The problem we have right now is that our leaders, like your brother, advocate ethnic cleansing by means of targeted violence. These leaders think that killing all young men will keep them out of the KLA, and killing many of the civilians will give the rest a sense of urgency to leave faster."

Lieutenant Buha stops to look at Miro's expression. He fully realizes what he just said about Miro's brother is treasonous. Miro sits expressionless.

Lieutenant Buha continues, "The way I see it, violence is counterproductive. We can push the people to leave without killing them as long as we show resolve in hunting down and destroying the KLA. We vastly outnumber and outgun them. Basically, we can just sweep them aside."

Miro is astonished; he has never heard this soft approach before from a VJ officer.

Miro asks, "Why do you feel this way, sir? I mean, I have never heard this language from an officer."

Lieutenant Buha pulls up a chair and sits down. "I am an American."

Miro's mouth opens.

"That's right, I am an American from Chicago, where I go by Alex, and educated at the University of Chicago. My parents left Pristina in 1981 after Tito died, and made their way to Chicago where there is a large Serb population. About a year ago I came back because I strongly feel Kosovo belongs to what most people around the world still call the former Yugoslav Republic, which includes Montenegro and Kosovo. Because I had a college education, they sent me through officer's school and made me a lieutenant, so here I am."

"Do they—that is, the senior leadership in the VJ—trust you?" Miro asks as he squirms in his seat.

Lieutenant Buha laughs. "Well, after all I am just a lieutenant." In a more serious tone he continues on. "Look, let me explain my rationale for leaving the States and serving in the VJ. Let's say that a certain ethnic population immigrated into Texas over the years and decided they wanted independence from the United States, to claim Texas as their own and secede from the Union. Let's say in doing so, they started to target police and the military, sniping at them and blowing up their buildings.

"Would the US government stand idly by? Of course not. They would enter Texas with massive force to rid the insurgent secessionists and migrants from taking the state away. That is only logical. The US Army would wage war, even killing the secessionists. So what is so different than our situation? If we had not committed atrocities against helpless civilians per Milosevic's guidance, then NATO wouldn't be bombing us. I am telling you this because we will keep a high ethical standard in this platoon, even if it costs me my job."

Miro states, "I have lived here and seen how the Serbs treated the Albanian Kosovars—no equality in anything, just more suppression. That is one of the main reasons the KLA formed." Miro pauses. "Why are you telling me all of this, sir?"

Lieutenant Buha interlocks his hands behind his head and leans back in his chair. "Quite frankly, though you are just a private, Colonel Cadikovski is your brother. Maybe you have some sway with him. He and I do not see eye to eye on how we conduct operations. I feel the Geneva Convention is important, and guides NATO's purpose for the war. Unfortunately, our company commander, and especially your brother, do not view it this way. But if the whole brigade would conduct operations in accordance with the Geneva Convention, then maybe the Serbian generals would see that is the best way to complete liberating Kosovo from the insurgents."

Miro stands. "Sir, there is something I need to tell you, I think. First of all, I applaud your approach. I disagree with the aims of our government, especially Milosevic's murderous rhetoric. But I have no pull with my brother. He detests me and always has. I think I am in his brigade just so he can ensure I serve and do my duty. Having said that, just to save one innocent Kosovar life, I will do what you ask. I will approach him any time you wish; I just don't think he will listen . . . he cares more about his own career than doing the right thing for Kosovo."

Lieutenant Buha's interest piques. "So *what do you* think is the right thing for Kosovo?"

Miro shoots back, "Simply for everyone to live in peace, just like we all did during Tito's time."

Lieutenant Buha studies Miro's face. "Well, Tito is not around anymore, is he? And for one, I don't want another era of communism. We have to be realistic as to the situation we are in right now, and deal with it the best way we can; there will be difficult times ahead, so we must be strong."

After Miro's suicidal thoughts earlier that day, the platoon leader's last words strike home. Maybe everything will work out as long as he stays in the lieutenant's platoon.

Miro has dinner with the Marins that night. When he arrives Suzana answers the door with her usual sensual smile and desirous eyes. Filip is not home yet, so Miro shyly smiles at her and hurries to take another hot bath, this time locking the bathroom door. While soaking in the hot water he thinks about what Niko said. He and Niko could be on the run right now after ditching the truck.

Miro hears Filip come in and tell Suzana he is going to change his clothes. As Filip walks by the bathroom, Miro wonders what Filip does for a living. He decides it is none of his business and he won't be rude and ask. They are very generous people, and Miro appreciates the homemade hot food and bath, not to mention a real bed.

During dinner Filip is full of questions for Miro. The question that really catches Miro's attention is when Filip asks about his American platoon leader.

"He seems level-headed, I guess. Sir, how did you know I had an American platoon leader?"

"Your brother told me. We ran into each other today and he told me about him, and I thought it was interesting because he is the only American in the VJ—that I know of."

"He sincerely believes that Kosovo should remain part of Serbia. That's why he came back to Serbia. That's what he told me."

Filip remains quiet for a few minutes, playing with his food.

"What do the men think of him? Do they trust him?"

"He is highly respected. My comrades all admire his leadership by example. He always leads from the front and trains us well. I think he is a good man. He doesn't believe in the hard approach, but instead feels that we can overpower the KLA while treating the civilians with dignity and respect."

"Is that what he *tells* his men?"

"I don't know; that's what he told me."

"Why would he tell you that?"

Miro grows agitated. He tries to hide his feelings by making light of the question. "Only because I am the brigade commander's brother," Miro laughs. "He thinks I will make him look good if I brag to my brother about him."

"Oh, I see," Filip chuckles. "He probably thinks he has to make a good impression with his bosses because he is an American in the VJ."

"Yeah, I'm sure that's it," Miro lies.

The next morning Miro drives his squad to the range. It is the first time he has worn his battle gear: helmet, web gear, cartridge pouches with ammunition and canteen. As the platoon sergeant, Bog is in charge of the training at the range, while Lieutenant Buha observes the quality of the training.

With his platoon seated in bleachers, Bog stands perfectly erect in front and holds up an AK-47. "This is an *Avtomat Kalashnikova*. It is a gas-operated rifle firing the 7.62 cartridge and has an effective range of 330 to 440 meters. You will see on full automatic the volume of fire will amaze you, and so will your inaccuracy. It will take practice to fire this weapon effectively, and your chance is today. You will not leave the range today until fully qualified. Squad leaders, take over."

Vuk spends the remainder of the day training 2nd Squad on the AK-47, from disassembly, reassembly, performing a functions check, and firing in both single and fully automatic modes. It is a hot day, and although firing the heavy weapon is somewhat fun, by midafternoon the sun is taking its toll on the soldiers still struggling to qualify.

Miro is impressed with Niko's knowledge of the AK-47 and how fast he qualifies. It is evident Niko has used the weapon somewhere before. Miro thinks the weapon is heavy and clumsy. It takes a while for him to even come close to the targets on full auto, and he spends a couple of hours qualifying. Even so, he does better than many others.

With their helmets off, Miro and Niko sit in the shade watching the last men qualify. Niko sucks on a cigarette while Miro tries to drink water from his canteen. His hands are still shaking from firing the AK on full auto for a couple of hours. He swallows a couple of gulps, then pours the rest on his head.

"Strange thing happened last night at my sponsors'," Miro gasps.

"What's that?" Niko responds with little interest.

"The man, Mr. Filip Marin, asked me about Lieutenant Buha."

Suddenly interested, Niko quickly turns his head toward Miro. "What about? Why is it his business to know?"

"That's what struck me; why would he care? I don't think he trusts Lieutenant Buha because he is an American."

"What does this Marin guy do, and how did he even know about the lieutenant?"

"He said my brother told him. Maybe he wants me to keep an eye on him, I don't know. I have no idea what the guy does. He doesn't wear a uniform of any kind that I have seen."

"Maybe you should tell the lieutenant."

"I think I need to be a quiet private and not stick my neck out."

"So, who is your loyalty to?"

Niko's question catches Miro off guard. He quietly ponders. Deep inside he knows someday he will have to decide who his loyalty is with, and it will be an ethical dilemma for him wrestle.

Three T-72 tanks roll up behind the range and stop. The drivers cut the engines and the crews dismount. Bog yells for everyone to gather around once more.

"Okay, we have all qualified on the AK-47. We are not done, gentlemen. Next we are going to learn how to mount, ride on, and dismount a T-72 tank. You're probably wondering why we need to learn to ride on a tank. Well, we only ride on trucks for so far. During direct action with the enemy, we as infantry support the tanks and the tanks support us. Tanks need us to provide security from enemy snipers and RPGs, while we need tanks to provide high-caliber firepower with the 125 mm smoothbore main gun. Each tank also has machine guns that can stop an enemy infantry attack in seconds."

Each squad leader leads their men to a tank. The crew

demonstrates how to mount the tank from the left rear, then crouch forward to grab the handles on the turret.

Vuk looks at his men. "I will demonstrate what the crewman just said."

Vuk slings his AK on his back, climbs up the tank and moves quickly to grasp the handles on the outside of the turret.

"You have to hang on tight, really fucking tight. There will be three men on each side of the turret, so six to each tank. If you fall off, there isn't anybody going back to save your ass. When you get the command to dismount, then just jump off the side. There is not time to dick around by taking turns to climb down the way you came up. Once you are on the ground, unsling your AK and find me. Any questions?"

Niko, as usual, has a question.

"Once we find you on the ground, how do we move with the tanks?"

"We will move on their flanks looking for enemy infantry. Any other questions? Okay, everyone needs to practice, each time going faster. I will tell you when you have mastered the drill. Until then, keep going."

Vuk jumps off the side of the tank while Niko climbs up first, followed by Miro and the remaining squad members. The tank crewmen smoke and enjoy watching the soldiers.

★★★

Miro shows up late at the Marins' that night. Tired and sore, he quietly taps on the door. Suzana cracks it open.

"I was beginning to wonder if you were going to come over tonight, at least for some drinks."

She opens the door, and Miro quietly walks into a dark and silent house.

Wearing a pink evening gown, Suzana comments, "Filip and

Ana are already fast asleep. I waited up for you. Come on in the kitchen."

Miro follows Suzana through the living room, dining room and into the kitchen. He awkwardly sits in a chair at the kitchen table, groaning after a long day of shooting at the range and jumping off a tank ten times.

"I think I could use a drink about now," Miro whispers.

Suzana pours stiff drinks as Miro discusses the day's training. They have several more, and Miro starts feeling better, especially when he takes off his shirt so Suzana can give him a neck massage. She digs deep in his shoulder muscles, causing him to close his eyes and lower his head in ecstasy. She starts using one hand, then the other. Opening his eyes, he sees her evening gown on the floor.

★★★

At 0730 roll call the next morning Bog seems a bit nervous. He double-checks to make sure everyone is present and announces that Lieutenant Buha will be addressing them shortly.

"At ease for now, but everyone stay in place; this is big," explains Bog as he excitedly scurries back inside the platoon building.

Rumors swirl. Most have heard the same thing: a deployment in the next day or two. Obviously it will be further into Kosovo, but no one knows where.

Bog comes back out and calls the platoon to attention. Lieutenant Buha appears out of the building and puts the men at ease.

"Smoke 'em if ya got them," Bog calmly announces. As several soldiers light up, Lieutenant Buha clasps his hands behind his back and struts back and forth in front of the platoon.

"The brigade starts rolling at 0500 tomorrow in echelons. Our battalion is scheduled to start at 0520 and our company at 0530. We are the lead platoon in our company, so at 0530 we must leave on time to not impede with the movement tables. Like usual, three trucks for us, one truck per squad."

Lieutenant Buha holds up a piece of paper. "Here is the complete movement timetable and routes on paper. I will give it to Bog, who can distribute it down to each truck. We are moving in echelons and along different routes so that NATO warbirds are less likely to target the entire convoy. If you see them flying overhead, radio me and wait for my order to pull over to the nearest building. Try to remain out of sight until the birds have left station. Our brigade mission is to secure Skenderaj, a Kosovar village."

Buha swallows hard, then continues. "Colonel Cadikovski is assuming NATO won't bomb us there, fearing killing Kosovar civilians. Our platoon mission in Skenderaj is to be given an area to disarm the civilians, then send them on their way with their personal items toward Macedonia. Do not shoot anyone unless they are a threat to you. When I say anyone, that includes men. If you suspect them of being in the KLA, bring them to me and I will interrogate them, not you. *No harm to anyone.* Am I clear?"

Most soldiers sound off, "Yes sir!"

"Good! That is all. I will be in my office if anyone needs me. Bog, release the platoon no later than 1500 to give everyone personal time before the mission tomorrow."

Bog salutes, and Lieutenant Buha walks calmly back inside.

"We will train on one very important task today: how to clear a building. Squad leaders, break your men into pairs and use the old abandoned house just outside the gate."

All three squads practice for a couple of hours, eat lunch, then prepare for deployment. In the early afternoon, squad leaders inspect their men's packs, then supervise the loading of necessary items onto the trucks. Vuk seems to be everywhere at once, from inspecting his men's equipment, to ensuring the proper loading and securing of ammunition, combat gear, and supplies of all types. He inspects Miro's truck for a full tank of gas and extra tie-down straps. The men work with a sense of urgency, and Vuk is pleased with their preparations. He releases them in early afternoon. He knows the big show is about to come to their little world.

Miro and Niko walk into town and drink some beers at a small pub on Koloshini Avenue overlooking the Ibar River. Niko smokes one cigarette after another, while Miro is more concerned with drinking beer.

"Tomorrow we cross," Niko spouts out, anxiously.

"Tomorrow I start looking for Julianna."

"How are you going to do that?"

"I will have to look for opportunities, like asking captured KLA if they know her, or taking the truck to Drenica."

"Well, I guess you have sorted out who you are loyal to."

Miro still isn't comfortable with *that question*. He fidgets in his chair and gulps beer. Slapping money on the table, Miro gets up and tells Niko he has to go. Niko, sensing Miro is not thinking clearly, offers to go with him.

"I'm fine, I just need some time—to think by myself."

"Hey, one other thing. When you go to the Marins' tonight, try to find out what that guy does."

Miro half-turns around and gives a thumbs-up, then goes on his way. Stumbling out of the pub, Miro is well oiled. He immediately heads toward the Marins'. He tries to enjoy the beautiful walk, but a strong sense of dread hijacks his thoughts. It seems to him that every time his situation begins to get better, it only gets worse. He desperately wants to experience something that takes his mind off of the mission. Seeing Suzana, and a good home-cooked dinner with the Marins, might just be what he needs.

Upon arriving at the Marins', Suzana meets him at the door wearing a colorful summer dress. She says she is surprised to see Miro so early. Miro explains his departure the next morning and the time off granted by his platoon leader. Suzana grabs Miro's hand and tells him she is happy to see him again. Miro, slightly startled, but more embarrassed, strides with her hand in hand to the sofa. Sitting close together, and with Suzana still grasping his hand, it is an awkward situation for Miro.

Suzana's lips almost touch Miro's left cheek.

"So, you are leaving tomorrow for deployment further into Kosovo. Oh, that is so dangerous. I am so proud of you, but I will also be worried!"

At a loss for words, Miro turns his head toward her, shyly smiling back.

"Well, we have time. Filip will not be home for a couple of hours. He picks up Ana from school at 1630."

Miro's anxiety level peaks. "Excuse me, Suzana, is there something you need done before Filip gets home?"

Suzanna replies joyfully, "Oh no, I just have a going-away present for you!"

She lets go of his hand and hurries barefoot into her bedroom. Miro hopes it will not be a bottle of champagne or vodka. He doesn't want to have a hangover during the next day's deployment.

In a few minutes Miro recognizes the sound of high heels clicking into the living room. From behind him she walks around the couch and into his view. Besides her black high heels, she has only her bra on. Her light-brown curly pubic hair is in full bloom. Miro's face flushes while she aggressively straddles Miro's lap, then sucks his tongue into her mouth. While she runs her fingers through his hair, Miro reaches around and unclasps her bra. He throws it behind the couch and onto the floor as her hard, pointy nipples stand erect, inviting him to indulge.

Two hours later, after taking a bath, Miro and Suzana sit on the sofa watching the Serbian news on TV. The VJ are portrayed as the saviors of Serbia as they aggressively carry out Milosevic's ethnic-cleansing policies. Piles of dead civilians are graphically portrayed, but blamed on the KLA by the newscaster. There is also footage of VJ proudly posing with dead KLA.

Suzana once again grasps Miro's hand, but this time she squeals with delight as she adds, "The ridding of all Kosovar criminals."

Miro feels sick. He thinks of Julianna and wonders what kind of person he is becoming. Not only has he cheated on her, but he might even be watching her death on TV. Additionally, he is wearing a VJ uniform, about to deploy.

The front door springs open, and Ana comes tumbling in, happy to see her mother. Filip is close behind wearing a dark-blue uniform. Miro stands up to shake Filip's hand, then realizes he is an officer in the Serbian Special Police. Filip, totally oblivious of Miro's expression, shakes Miro's hand heartily, then with a pep in his step walks to a table near the TV.

He lifts a vodka bottle and methodically pours three drinks. He slowly turns, looks at Suzana and Miro, and stands straight as an arrow with a smirk on his face. Ana wanders around carrying a size 39D bra she has found on the floor.

Abruptly, Filip announces in a boisterous voice, "I have something important to say to you two. Something happened today that will change my life forever."

Miro, his stomach in knots, knows Filip has quickly figured out what occurred between Suzana and him. After a few moments of uneasy silence, Filip gazes oddly at them both, then continues.

"It is a special day! I was promoted to colonel. Now I command my own special police brigade, and we will be deploying with your brother's brigade starting tomorrow to Kosovo!"

Filip hands a glass to Suzana, then Miro. He then takes a glass for himself and proposes a toast.

"To Milosevic."

# 09: SKENDERAJ

**SKENDERAJ IS A SMALL** city that lies halfway between Skanderbeg and Mitrovice. It is composed exclusively of Albanian Kosovars, and is right in the path of the VJ's current movements into Kosovo from the north.

With little information to go on, John and Travis will conduct a reconnaissance. If VJ forces are already intermingled with local Kosovars, the mission will become much more complex, if not impossible. The only possibility would be to somehow separate the VJ from the Kosovars, a daunting and dangerous task.

This time John and Travis are intent on reducing, if not totally eliminating, any civilian casualties. After all, the aim of the entire war for NATO is to stop civilian casualties, not increase them. In the mission review after Klina, the NATO officers discussed the unintended civilian deaths during the A-10 attack that accidently strafed apartment buildings and houses. It was a public-relations disaster for NATO, as the Serb media exploited what was really an accident into an example of American airpower targeting Serbian civilians.

The KLA didn't like the deaths of innocent Serbs either, as any erosion of international political support for the NATO war effort could result in tighter rules of engagement, and thus a reduced amount of air support.

Julianna was very upset by the civilian deaths, even a bit shaken. Josif knows why, as the safety of Miro's parents is on her mind. Although they do not like her because she is Kosovar, they are still Miro's parents.

For the Skenderaj mission, the NATO officers and Julianna as an interpreter will operate with Prek Luga's KLA special forces platoon of fifteen men. Josif and his 3rd Brigade forces can be called on if necessary, but in the meantime will be conducting large-scale evacuation operations in an area east of Skenderaj.

The operation will begin similarly to the previous ones, with echeloned car movement to a rally point, then dismounted movement to the objective. However, on this operation, two cars will leave at a time. John and Travis learned this technique from the KLA. If the first car runs into trouble, then the KLA in the following car can respond.

At midnight the first two cars depart, with Travis, Trooper and Julianna in the first car, and John and the KLA in the second. Fifteen minutes later the next two leave with Prek in the second vehicle. The last two cars are all KLA special forces. Thirty-five minutes later they assemble at the rally point.

Again, like the Klina operation, the force will be broken into three groups. Group 1, with both NATO officers and Julianna, approaches the city from the south. Group 2, led by the Prek, will set up a security force along the route from the north. Group 3 to the west is the reserve force with three *be prepared* missions: to reinforce one of the first two groups, counterattack an attacking VJ force, or set up an ambush.

For security reasons, the rally point is east of the city near Josif's brigade. After reviewing communication procedures at the rally point, the three groups split to execute their missions. From there, Group 1—the NATO officers, Julianna and two KLA soldiers—positions on the south route out of the city, observing traffic for VJ or paramilitary movements. Group 2, Prek's northern force, moves to the main route from Mitrovice in order to look for any VJ units or approaching VJ vehicles. Group 3, the reserve force, moves to a concealed location west of the city.

Prek reports by radio to the NATO officers that there is no activity on the road from Mitrovice into Skenderaj. No refugees are heading north either, as they eventually would run into the VJ.

The NATO officers, observing the route out of the city to the southeast, spot no movement except for refugees fleeing the city. They are stopped by the KLA and told to move east toward Josif's evacuation points. All three groups keep a vigilant watch all night while Josif uses trucks to evacuate civilians from the east. Julianna tries multiple times on the radio to communicate with the local KLA, but with no luck.

With a heavy mist covering the ground, John, Travis, Julianna, and two KLA special forces soldiers stealthily enter the city from the south. The scene is surreal as they cautiously move like ghosts throughout the city, AK-47s at the ready. John and Travis agree something is amiss. John taps on the shoulders of the KLA, signaling for a quick huddle behind a closed commercial building. With Julianna translating, the consensus is that something is not right; it just seems eerie.

They stay in place while Travis sends Trooper ahead to smell for explosives or cadavers. It doesn't take long for Trooper to return, whining to Travis that he has found something.

Trooper, followed by Travis and a KLA soldier who speaks some English, goes forward while the others stay behind the building. They covertly dash in between houses, at times stopping and listening. The city remains eerily quiet. Trooper eventually leads them deep into the city. The dog trots to a ditch behind a house. Peering into the ditch, Travis can see something, but the low-hanging mist covers the contents. The KLA soldier provides security as Travis enters the ditch with a somewhat controlled slide in the mud. He loses his balance and falls, landing on top of a warm human body. Travis jumps backwards onto the ditch's muddy bank. Quickly gaining his composure, he carefully treads in the watery ditch and counts seventeen warm corpses, all in KLA uniforms.

Travis motions his KLA soldier into the ditch, shining a flashlight onto the dead men's faces. The special forces soldier is not from the Skenderaj area, and does not recognize any of them.

Along with Trooper, the two make their way back to the others. Arriving behind the building, Travis whispers to Group 1 the gloomy news. Because the bodies were still warm, everyone in the group expects the killers to still be in the city. The identity of the murderers remains a mystery.

Julianna radios Prek in Group 2, advising him about the KLA bodies. Prek responds he sent a small reconnaissance force into the city from the north, but they returned empty handed.

As Travis and John discuss the situation, the KLA soldiers speak to Julianna. Julianna then interrupts the NATO officers.

"The soldiers just told me they think they know who killed our comrades."

Travis and John are all ears.

"Paramilitary. These groups stealthily sneak into a town prior to the VJ's arrival. Their job is to assassinate the KLA so the VJ can enter without being ambushed."

John asks, "Do you think they are still here?"

Julianna questions the KLA soldiers, and they quickly respond. John and Travis can tell what the answer is by their anxious tone.

"Yes, they always wait until the VJ arrive to make sure the KLA do not reenter."

"How many?" asks John.

Julianna, after getting an answer, states, "Twenty, maybe up to thirty."

Travis has Julianna radio Prek and update him.

While she is radioing, John and Travis again discuss the situation. With up to thirty Serb paramilitary in the city, they are outnumbered, even with Group 3's reinforcement. They don't want to divert any of Josif's forces either, as evacuation is paramount for the safety of the city's civilians.

To make things more complicated, Travis and John fully realize they must destroy paramilitary groups. They are on their priority target list from Pine Tree.

Travis asks Julianna what group would most likely be in this area. Julianna, after questioning the KLA soldiers, states, "Arkan."

Travis and John look at each, knowing what the other is thinking. Arkan's Tigers are the highest-rated target on the paramilitary list.

John whispers, "Julianna, if you would, radio Group 3 and have them come to our location."

At twilight the NATO officers lead Groups 2 and 3, a total of ten KLA special forces soldiers, on a direct-action mission into town. Direct-action missions, to find and destroy the enemy, are rare for John and Travis.

Because the NATO officers' primary task in Kosovo is to call air strikes, direct action is only permissible for specific enemy forces, such as Arkan's Tigers. Arkan is the leader of the most notorious paramilitary group from Serbia. In reality Arkan and his Tigers are a criminal gang wanted by Interpol for murders across Europe since the 1970s. Arkan was also indicted by the UN for crimes against humanity, and is considered the most powerful crime boss in the Balkans.

Time is of the essence. With the Tigers' presence, a VJ force is on its way to Skenderaj. Prek, to the north, should spot and report any VJ movement. Considering all the factors, the risk is high, but the NATO officers and their accompanying KLA special forces soldiers have the element of surprise, and a deep desire to eliminate the ruthless Arkan and his men.

The wet mist has turned to a low fog as the sun begins to rise, making visibility about twenty meters. After Prek is notified of their mission, Trooper leads the way for the assault team. The special forces soldiers, followed closely by the NATO officers and Julianna, disperse and run in quick rushes from one building to another. Stopping and listening, they continue methodically down each street. It is a tense and exhausting process. Everyone expects contact—eventually.

After about an hour of searching, Trooper returns, again whining. He has found something, either explosives or cadavers. The assault group follows Trooper, still spread out for security reasons. Approximately five blocks into a housing area everyone hears it: a woman's blood-curdling scream.

The sound echoes amongst the buildings, and the assault force stops to assess the situation. One of the KLA soldiers spots two armed men wearing black sitting on a hill behind a two-story house, the house from which the screams seem to be resonating.

Travis and John confer quickly, call the reaction force to stand by, then send three special forces soldiers to eliminate the two guards on the hill. Within ten minutes both guards are silently killed. The three KLA, one a sniper, stay on the hill behind the house to overwatch the assault force.

Travis sends two more soldiers to guard the back of the house while the remaining five assault the house. Staying behind with Trooper, two radios and Julianna, the NATO officers observe the action.

The five KLA soldiers spring across the street and place their backs against the house. The lead soldier tries the front door—locked. One KLA soldier kicks the door in while another throws a stun grenade into the front room. The lead KLA soldier rushes inside with the others close behind. Inside, eight men dressed in black are clumsily reaching for their AK-47s.

Within seconds the first three KLA soldiers entering the front room release an earsplitting cacophony of automatic weapons fire, killing all eight. The other two enter, and all five KLA soldiers quickly search the main floor, weapons ready. No more enemy are found, but an elderly couple lie in a pool of blood on the kitchen floor. One soldier quickly places his fingers on the couple's throats, checking for a pulse, but he doesn't need to. Both have been shot in the back of the head.

All five soldiers stand still, listening. The screams have stopped; complete silence. Quietly, and without a word, the KLA soldiers regroup into their assault line-up at the bottom of the stairs. The lead soldier begins to climb the creaky wooden steps, taking one step at a time, then pausing and listening. In a tight formation, one just behind the other, the five point their weapons in a 360-degree orientation.

More people are going to die, and very soon.

Outside across the street, Julianna receives a call from Prek. She looks at John and Travis, who anxiously wonder what is happening inside the house.

Julianna, with a shaky voice, states, "Someone has alerted the VJ. Two BMP armored personnel carriers are heading toward town at top speed."

"Tell Prek to ambush them; they must be stopped!" John shoots back.

Travis, on his radio, requests emergency close air support to knock out the BMPs.

Prek anticipated the ambush order. Two of his four men have RPGs, and he sets them up along the same side of the road while hiding in the tall grass. He and his other two men have AK-47s, and they will rise from the grass once the BMPs are hit by the RPGs, looking for any soldiers escaping from the vehicles.

The BMPs are still over 100 meters away, one directly behind the other. The KLA soldiers get into place, nervously rehearsing in their mind when to rise, take aim, and fire. The lead BMP will be hit first; then, once the second BMP hits the brakes, a second RPG will slam into its side.

The BMPs are moving fast for tracked vehicles, maybe fifty kilometers an hour. The KLA soldier responsible for knocking out the lead BMP must time his actions precisely, or the entire ambush could be disastrous.

Fifty meters and closing, forty, thirty, twenty—the KLA soldier quickly rises to one knee, aims calmly at the approaching BMP. The track commander on the lead BMP spots the KLA soldier aiming the RPG at him and turns his mounted machine gun toward him. The RPG and machine gun fire simultaneously. The RPG warhead hits the left front quarter panel of the BMP, penetrating the vehicle's armor, instantly killing the driver and igniting the vehicle in flames. The machine gun burst from the BMP rips through the KLA soldier's chest, instantly killing him.

The second BMP, instead of coming to a screeching halt as anticipated, diverts off the road away from the ambush, driving at full speed into a farmer's field.

Meanwhile, VJ soldiers jump out of the back of the lead BMP on fire. Prek and his two soldiers with AK-47s gun them down without mercy. The last two VJ dismounting the burning BMP are on fire. Prek orders his two men to hold their fire; no point wasting precious ammunition.

The BMP in the farmer's field makes a large half-circle turn, stops, then faces the KLA soldiers from a distance of about 100 meters. Besides a machine gun, the BMP also has a 73mm cannon, and it can easily range the KLA.

Prek and his remaining three soldiers are facedown, trying to present as small a target as possible. The BMP fires a round, hitting the paved road just a few meters in front of Prek. With an ear-splitting sound, the round explodes, showering Prek with asphalt and gravel.

The BMP inches slowly ahead, raking the ground with machine-gun fire close to Prek and his men.

Prek yells to his soldier with the remaining RPG, "Once in range you must hit the BMP or we will all be killed."

The soldier with the last RPG realizes it will be suicide to try and shoot the vehicle once it is within range. Because the BMP is approaching head-on, Prek yells at him to low-crawl to get a better flanking shot. The KLA soldier low-crawls slowly, trying to not be detected. Closer the BMP comes; soon it will be able to detect Prek and his men lying in the grass. The machine gun on the BMP will then make quick work of them.

Prek again yells at his soldier with the RPG, "When I start firing at the BMP to get their attention, you fire!"

Back at the house, at the top of the stairs, a hallway goes in both directions. What the KLA soldiers see on the left stuns them. About three meters away is a large bald man dressed in black, sweating profusely. He squats behind a young nude woman, her round eyes glowing with terror. The man is undoubtedly an Arkan Tiger, as indicated by his arm patches. Holding her tight with his left hand over her mouth, in his right hand he holds a large revolver to her right temple. Speaking in Serbian, the man screams at the KLA soldiers to leave or he will kill the woman. In a split second the first two KLA quickly raise their AK-47s, pointing directly at the man's head.

The tenseness grows unbearable for the man in black. Sweat stings his eyes, and he starts to pant. The KLA soldiers don't break a sweat or flinch.

"A VJ reaction force will be here any second. I radioed them myself. Leave now or be killed."

The nearest KLA soldier, still aiming his AK-47 at the man's head, states in Serbian, "Okay then, you have thirty seconds to let the girl go."

The man holding the pistol becomes extremely agitated.

"Give up, hell! Why would I give up to be killed by Albanian terrorists?" Then in a thunderous voice he screams, "*Now!*"

The KLA soldiers know something violent is about to happen. The door at the other end of the hall bursts open. An Arkan Tiger stands in the doorway with an AK-47 pointed at the KLA soldiers on the stairs. Before he can get a shot off, he is gunned down by the two soldiers on the steps, whose job it was to watch the door. Simultaneously, the two KLA soldiers aiming at the man's head kill him, his blood and pieces of his head splattering on the wall and young woman. Unhurt, she faints.

Suddenly, the crack of a rifle is heard outside. It comes not from one of the two KLA soldiers guarding the back of the house, but from the KLA sniper on the hill behind them. He has shot an Arkan Tiger about to jump out of a second-story window. The Tiger falls on the ground, never to get up again.

In the farmer's field, Prek jumps up and fires his AK-47 wildly at the approaching BMP. The VJ soldier manning the machine gun on top of the vehicle is hit and falls inside the hatch. The BMP comes to a halt, and VJ soldiers dash out of the back. The KLA soldier with the RPG rises from the grass and takes careful aim, only to be shot by a VJ soldier before he can get the round off.

Travis receives a call: "TOT 30 seconds, over."

"Roger, out," Travis responds. He stares at his watch: 30, 29, 28, 27, 26, 25, 24, 23—*oh Lord, why are the seconds counting down so slow*—22, 21, 20, 19, 18, 17, 16, 15—*come on*—14, 13, 12, 11, 10, 9, 8, 7, 6, 5, 4, 3—*let's go*—2, 1.

Everyone in Skenderaj except Travis is alarmed by a huge explosion. Travis is smiling.

Prek can't believe his eyes. A missile hits the top of the BMP, and it explodes into a huge fireball, sending pieces of the vehicle flying hundreds of meters. Every VJ soldier is instantly vaporized. Prek looks into the sky. High above he sees a jet circling; then it leaves station. Prek smiles.

As the KLA search the house and surrounding area, thirteen dead Arkan Tigers are found covered with a tarp in the back of a truck. Obviously, the KLA in Skenderaj put up a fight before being overwhelmed by the Tigers. Arkan, the malevolent leader of his Tigers, is not among the dead.

Although hopeful he might be present, this is no surprise to the KLA, as Arkan has many enemies, both amongst the Kosovars and Serbs. He rarely goes anywhere except to make speeches, and then never without a large bodyguard contingent. He relies on his subordinates to carry out the assassinations.

John and Travis expect the VJ, and possibly more Tigers, will soon be in town. Retributions against the local population is a given, and the less people in town, the better. Josif's troops are now hustling civilians out of their homes for evacuation. The hidden cars are dispatched by Josif to expedite evacuation orders to the locals. John and Travis agree one hour can be spared before departure.

They are not sure what to do with the traumatized Kosovar girl, who is now conscious. Julianna cleans her with a wet cloth in the upstairs bathroom. A few minutes later Julianna and the Kosovar girl, now clothed but still badly shaken, come outside to speak with some local people emerging from their houses. Julianna is approached by a man and woman who say they are her relatives. She immediately notices they are not Kosovar, but Romani. They say that the girl is fifteen years old.

They enter the house and verify the dead couple in the kitchen are her grandparents. They state her mother died several years before from cholera, and her father is a member of the KLA in town. They don't know what has happened to him.

Travis and John glance at each other; the girl's father is most likely among the KLA in the ditch.

# 10: DEPLOYMENT

**MIRO HASTILY LEAVES THE** Marins' house in the middle of the night, placing a thank-you note and some chocolates filled with brandy on the living room table. He has not slept at all, as his head is still swimming with thoughts of the previous day's events: Suzana's sexual aggressiveness, his submission to her, and Filip's possible knowledge of their affair and promotion in the notorious Serbian Special Police. Miro is glad to be deploying. If he stays, it will be just a matter of time before Suzana gets drunk and lets the affair out to someone, and he doesn't want to think about the consequences once Filip figures it all out.

Miro is so preoccupied with these thoughts he doesn't notice how fast he is walking. As always, in the back of his mind Miro also thinks of Julianna. He considers his actions with Suzana as just sexual, with no emotions involved, just like his animal behavior during his time at the indoctrination battalion. And just like at indoc, he does not want to feel guilty for his actions.

For the time being he convinces himself his actions were out of his control, and others are to blame for putting him in these predicaments.

At 0330 Miro enters the military base and immediately goes to the motor pool where the vehicles are lined up for the morning's deployment to Skenderaj. Walking down the line he finds his truck with 13 stenciled on the front and back bumper. Miro climbs into the cab, cranks up the loud diesel engine, and checks all the gauges. He jumps out of the cab and inspects other critical components of the truck: fluid levels, tire condition and pressure, lights and the steering linkages. He climbs into the truck's bed and lowers the side wooden seats. Everything looks good, and he wants to ensure his truck is as ready as possible. He knows Kosovo well, and he is anxious to leave his recent past behind him—and start looking for Julianna. He jumps back into the driver's seat, presses his head on top the steering wheel, and prays for forgiveness and strength.

By 0400, VJ troops are wandering about the motor pool, loading gear, weapons and ammunition. Vuk and the other squad leaders supervise the entire process; first they take personnel accountability, then scrutinize everything.

"Weapon and bayonet?"

"Check!"

"Basic load of ammunition?

"Check!"

"Equipment loaded?

"Check!"

"Food and water?"

"Check!"

"Identification tags?"

"Check!"

Bog inspects the man-pack radios, making the soldiers turn them on and make checks with other radios. At 0430, the VJ troops start to load into the back of the trucks, with one squad designated per truck. Second Squad loads into Miro's truck, including Niko, who is first—probably a habit from his indoc training. Because he is first, Vuk makes Niko the designated radio men in the back of the truck. The other radio will be in the cab, with Vuk in the passenger's seat. Miro admires Vuk Kovac because he is a smart and experienced soldier who has always been supportive of his men in 2nd Squad. He is leveled headed, always serious, and never loses his composure. Miro wants to get on Vuk's good side, and stay there.

The first truck, occupied with 1st Squad and the platoon leader, Lieutenant Buha in the cab, departs the garrison at exactly 0500, followed by Miro's truck and the 3rd Squad truck with Bog.

The sun is rising over one of the most beautiful cities in Kosovo: Mitrovice. The trucks roll down the tree-lined streets and past magnificent buildings with traditional Balkans architecture as they head south toward the Ibar River. Few people or cars are on the streets at this time, and the large trucks rumble down the cobblestones while the soldiers in the back bounce up and down, pointing their AK-47s skyward.

Once the Ibar is in sight, Vuk radios Niko in the back of the truck for every soldier to face about with their AKs and watch for ambushes. The Ibar is a somewhat small river but a tremendous symbol of the Serb and Kosovar divide.

Mosque spirals, narrower streets, and the increase in the density of homes make crossing over the bridge and into southern Mitrovice feel like entering another country. Gutted buildings and debris lie everywhere. The fighting has forced the residents to flee, and the KLA take advantage of the hollow buildings and rubble for sniping and ambushes. The VJ units that patrol south of the Ibar play cat and mouse with the KLA snipers. It is a never-ending and bloody game.

Behind the wheel, Miro keeps his distance from the lead truck. Stand-off between trucks is critical for security. If something does happen, he is to follow Vuk's orders, although Miro has no idea what those orders might be. He will soon find out.

A single shot rings out. The truck just behind Miro's, with Bog, swerves and hits a light pole. The truck in front of Miro pulls onto a sidewalk and stops close to a building. Vuk orders Miro to do the same.

Troops in all three trucks dismount and stand next to the nearest buildings. Miro and Vuk jump out and run behind the truck and a dilapidated building. VJ soldiers from the last truck, the one that crashed, are ordered by Bog to hunt for the sniper. They dash off in two groups.

Miro and Vuk move slightly to huddle in a doorway.

"This is typical. One sniper holds up a whole damn column. I would like to see what happens if we catch him," Vuk mutters.

"I wonder why the truck crashed?"

Vuk grabs Miro by the arm. "I will show you why."

Both men crouch and scuttle a few dozen meters toward the wrecked truck to get a better view. Miro notices blood splattered on the outside of the driver's door.

"That's who they always aim at: the driver," Vuk solemnly mumbles while Miro stares at the blood.

Miro whispers, "Maybe we should check on him. He might still be alive."

Vuk lets out an ominous laugh. "If you want to survive, follow me and you might live."

He grabs Miro's arm again, leading him back to their previous safe position between the building and truck.

A loud firefight erupts with automatic weapons, echoing through the vacant buildings and alleyways. After half an hour the 3rd Squad returns empty handed, but claims they have wounded one. Who really knows. No blood is spotted. At the same time, a BMP arrives escorting a replacement truck for 3rd Squad.

Within twenty minutes the column is rolling once again, but behind schedule and traveling deeper into an area often inhabited by the seemingly invisible KLA. The trucks intermix with civilian traffic to avoid NATO air strikes. The men in the back of the trucks continuously scan for any sign of aircraft. Miro knows the drill. If an aircraft is spotted, everyone dismounts as fast as possible and runs fifty meters before dropping to the ground.

The rest of the morning is uneventful. The column passes through numerous small Kosovar villages. Void of people and severely damaged, many homes and cars are burned out, and starving dogs wander aimlessly. Worst of all is the smell, the combined noxious odor of decaying bodies and busted sewer lines. Most of the VJ soldiers put rags over their faces in a vain attempt to minimize the terrible smell. While driving, Miro gags and his stomach turns over. It is the worst smell he has ever experienced, and it clings inside his nostrils even after leaving the villages.

In an odd way Miro looks forward to arriving at Skenderaj, a Kosovar city that he has visited many times with Julianna. The people are friendly and, according to Lieutenant Buha, have not been touched by the war. It lies just fifteen kilometers ahead, and the signs of the war are starting to disappear. For the first time all day, Miro can sit back and try to relax. A warm spring breeze blows through the cab, and he sees farmers out in the fields. *Crazy*, Miro thinks, *how someone would stick around and farm with a war raging all around them.*

Abruptly someone in the back of the truck spots an aircraft high in the sky. Miro pulls over, as do the other trucks. Men jump out of the back and scatter as fast as they can into farmers' fields, lying facedown.

Everything remains quiet. Many gaze above, wondering if the aircraft is still around. Some even sit up and smoke, enjoying the pleasant surroundings. As fast as it disappeared, the aircraft appears again. Those who are looking witness the aircraft fire a missile at supersonic speed across the sky. The missile vanishes over the horizon, but soon thereafter an explosion shakes the ground.

Lieutenant Buha radios his company commander, who is twenty-three kilometers away in another village. After reporting the bombing, his company commander orders him to stay in place while he radios his superiors. Within eight minutes the company commander radios back telling him that two BMPs have recently been sent into Skenderaj as a reaction force, and they were most likely the aircraft's target. He states some of Arkan's Tigers are in town and have been in a fight with the KLA. They still need rescuing, and Colonel Cadikovski is sending in tanks and BMPs from all around the area toward Skenderaj. The order to remain in place stands for Buha's platoon, and to not mount back on the trucks until ordered.

For the next forty-five minutes they camouflage their trucks with vegetation. At one point Miro spots three T-72 tanks crossing the fields, moving toward Skenderaj. Shortly afterward, Buha receives orders to move into Skenderaj and engage the KLA.

Buha picks up the mic and radios his trucks, "Mount up. We are going in to kill the KLA."

Vuk yells at his squad to mount up, and Miro runs clumsily across the plowed field. By the time he arrives at his truck, all the squad's soldiers are in the back. Vuk curses at him to hurry. Miro jumps in, starts the truck and slams it into gear. He nervously pops the clutch, and the truck lurches forward onto the road. Even over the roaring truck's engine Miro can hear angry voices coming from the back. He looks in his side mirror and sees that Niko, who is wearing the squad radio, has fallen down in the bed.

Miro grins from ear to ear as he watches Niko struggle to get back up, then thinks it odd how soldiers can laugh at each other during times like these—maybe because it helps to reduce anxiety. Besides, Miro is paying Niko back for the soup he tossed in his face while in prison.

The three trucks blast at full speed toward Skenderaj. If any NATO aircraft come back, they will surely go after armored vehicles, Miro hopes. Within a few minutes the two burning BMPs come into sight, as do the burned VJ bodies. It is the first time Miro has experienced the reality of combat, and he has a sinking feeling in his stomach. He looks at Vuk, who sits quietly with a stone face.

Miro gathers his wits and drives on, hoping what he just saw is not the beginning of more horror to come. Upon reaching Skenderaj, a VJ soldier motions the trucks to park on the other side of some large buildings.

Miro parks the truck inside the city next to the designated building. He grabs his AK and dismounts with Vuk and the rest of the soldiers. Lieutenant Buha quickly arrives and assigns each squad a sector of the city to search for any surviving Tigers—and the KLA.

As each squad enters the city, it becomes apparent the search is going to be difficult as hundreds of Kosovars panic and flee in the opposite direction, toward the east. Between the cars, carts, and people on foot, it will be too easy to become separated, so most VJ soldiers stay behind the masses for the time being.

"The tanks and BMPs must have circled around the city to cut off the KLA," Vuk yells. "There is no way they could have come this way with all the people in the road."

Vuk takes a mic from the radio Niko is carrying on his back. It doesn't take long to receive instructions from Buha. Vuk bellows orders as loud as he can so his men hear.

"We are to wait here and not let anyone escape north. Colonel Cadikovski wants to cordon the town to trap the KLA. Our entire platoon's zone is the north."

Miro and Niko are relieved to hear this. All they have to do is stay in place and wait.

Niko kneels close to Miro. "You keep popping that damn clutch, I'm going to give your ass to the KLA."

# 11: BAD NEWS

**JULIANNA ACCOMPANIES THE NATO** officers and Prek's KLA special forces platoon as they speed away from Skenderaj. Simultaneously, Josif's brigade halts evacuation operations. The destruction of two BMPs north of town means a VJ hell-storm will soon descend upon the city.

Colonel Cadikovski's VJ Guards Brigade are indeed closing the noose around Skenderaj with BMPs and T-72s, just as the last of Josif's vehicles, packed full of civilians, flees town.

The trip back to Skanderbeg isn't one of rejoicing. There are still many civilians in Skenderaj. John and Travis discuss their required report to Pine Tree as they watch in despair the numerous disheartened refugees plodding along the roadside. The killing of Arkan's Tigers will be good news to their NATO bosses, but the NATO officers know VJ retributions on Skenderaj's remaining Kosovars will be forthcoming.

Skenderaj was a pyrrhic victory.

Arriving at Skanderbeg, all are drained physically and psychologically. Prek's KLA soldiers brought back their two dead hurriedly stuffed in car trunks. Prek pulls each one out and carries them to the back of Josif's headquarters where they lie for a short memorial service, then burial. The other dead KLA soldiers are still in the ditch at Skenderaj. There they will remain, rotting in the stagnant water. There is no time to retrieve them. All they can hope for is that locals will bury their defenders. Such is the cost of war.

As Prek leads the short memorial service, Julianna stands with her head down and hands interlocked in front of her. Tears stream down her solemn face, not only for the two dead KLA soldiers she has known for many years, but for the unknown fate of Miro.

It all hits her at once.

Although it was just a little over two months previous, their rendezvous to Montenegro and subsequent marriage seem like another lifetime ago. She can't help but think Miro is in a Serbian prison, or worse.

While others leave after the service, Julianna is frozen, staring at the gravediggers, mesmerized in deep thought. Her anxiety skyrockets, and she catastrophizes about the future. Deep inside she knows the deaths of Prek's two soldiers are just the beginning of horrors yet to come. What will become of them all? Will she ever know what happened to Miro? Will her parents ever know what happens to Josif and her? A terrible, sickening pain in her stomach paralyzes her.

She is jolted back into reality when Josif takes ahold of her hand. Anxiety still has a strong grip on her, and she gasps for air as he slowly escorts her back into the house.

Although they couldn't understand a word Prek said, John and Travis also attended the service. They are impressed with the courage of Prek's men, and consider themselves blessed to have Prek and his KLA warriors with them. Standing stoically, both try to come to terms with the usefulness of their operations in Skenderaj.

The NATO officers' concern now is how to stop the VJ from pursuing violent retributions on Skenderaj's populace. Many were evacuated by Josif, and more probably escaped after the VJ arrived, but many more are still trapped inside the city. They would be the VJ's fodder: the old, young, sick, and disabled.

Tramping slowly back inside Josif's headquarters, the officers sit by their radio gear in one of the rooms. Trooper guarded the room during the service, and he lies by Travis's chair, stretching his long muscular body and groaning with pleasure. Travis slowly strokes Trooper's stomach and gazes at his cherished dog and close companion.

John sits across the radio table, leaning his chair back against the wall with his arms folded, lost in thought. The men from two different English-speaking countries discuss their dire situation.

John says, "The time has come to huddle with the KLA leadership in some desperate attempt to turn things around in Kosovo."

Like a rocket, Travis jumps from his chair. Trooper turns over, cocks his head, and stares at his master walking out of the room. Travis finds Josif consoling Julianna at the kitchen table.

Josif glances at Travis. "Yes, my friend?"

"Sorry, but John and I were wondering if we could discuss some matters with you and your deputy? When you find the time, of course."

Josif cups his hand on the back of Julianna's head and kisses her forehead. She makes her best attempt to smile back at her brother, but her eyes still pool with tears.

"Go ahead. I will get Bekim," Julianna whispers.

A few minutes later the five of them are in the room with the big map on the wall. Everyone is seated except Travis, who is too energized to sit still. He reads Josif's, Bekim's, and Julianna's body language; they are all downcast. Trooper lies behind John without a care in the world.

Travis addresses the small group. "I know it has been a tough twenty-four hours, and we are all tired. We did the best we could, and we are now confronted with two issues. One is the retributions the Serbs will take out on the civilians still in Skenderaj, and the other is much larger: How to stop the VJ onslaught."

Josif crosses his arms and sits silently. He is here to listen to foreigners tell him how to win an unwinnable war. He thinks of Vietnam and how the Americans developed a losing strategy, then abandoned the South Vietnamese to slaughter.

John stands and breaks the silence. "The VJ will not kill or force out all the Kosovars every time they capture a village. They will keep as many women and children close to them as possible, so neither the KLA nor NATO can attack them. I bet that's the situation we have in Skenderaj right now."

Julianna interprets for Bekim, who adds, "There isn't much we can do about Skenderaj if they are holding the people hostages. We can't touch them. At least they are not killing everyone this time."

Josif somberly states that the VJ will keep the children, mothers, old and sick as human shields, but the special police will still execute the men—all of them.

"They will even execute any VJ they think is not doing their duty. That's what they do. Evil."

John adds, "NATO won't even try precision bombs on the tanks and BMP inside Skenderaj with the hostages close by. Even if we sneak in Prek's snipers, and they kill a high-value target, let's say the VJ brigade commander, the Serbs will execute many of the hostages."

Travis, stroking his short whiskers, thinks out loud. "We have got to figure out how to get more bombs on the tanks and BMPs. If we can neutralize their armored formations, then the KLA will have a fighting chance to stop their light infantry."

John retorts, "Even when they do move their armor, the VJ have adapted their offensive tactics to a more decentralized approach to avoid our airpower. They spread out their forces while on the move and won't linger in Serb cities like Klina, where they would become prime targets. I think they learned their lesson on what happened there. Except for fast-moving reaction forces like those that surrounded Skenderaj, most VJ military vehicles are moving in small groups dispersed within civilian traffic, making it almost impossible for our aircraft to attack them without causing civilian casualties. Every time the VJ capture a Kosovar village, the more hostages they have around them."

Travis scans the room. "Any ideas?"

Silence occupies the room as everyone thinks.

Travis lays his hands flat on the table and stares at them in deep thought. "Well, we can hit the field and start calling in pinpoint air strikes with our laser designators, or we can have General Gashi set up ambushes throughout Kosovo, but neither will win the war, only delay the inevitable."

Josif suddenly stands up. "We the KLA *must* go on the offense with a surprise attack. One that will send the VJ reeling back, and give us good press internationally. We just have to pick the right time and place, with a large ground and air attack. If we use the element of surprise, the VJ will never see it coming. They are convinced at this point they have figured out how to win, and you know what, they are right unless we do something they will never expect."

Travis and John sit in silence. John rises slowly. Trooper snores.

"You may be onto something. You had better get with General Gashi on that one. It will take much more infantry than your brigade. We would also need to talk with our superiors."

Josif walks across the room and studies the map on the wall. Bekim joins him, and they discuss something in Albanian.

The two decide that one of the NATO officers should radio Pine Tree to voice concern over the unchecked VJ forces advancing into central Kosovo. So far the air strikes have not slowed their advancement, and something has to be done before they take all of Kosovo.

The first KLA recommendation is to immediately insert more NATO special forces in Kosovo. Without more special forces and air force air controllers on the ground to spot VJ targets, NATO aircraft would continue to struggle identifying lucrative targets from the air.

The second recommendation is to seriously consider a NATO ground invasion force attacking from Albania into Kosovo. The NATO air war is not working because of the VJ's ability to adapt their tactics, and unless a larger force can stop them, it might mean the Serb occupation of all of Kosovo by midsummer. This would complete Milosevic's policy of genocide, the worst since WWII. A third recommendation is what Josif explained, a large offensive against the VJ, with the KLA as a ground force and NATO providing air strikes.

John put Josif's points on paper, washes his face, and uses his SATCOM to radio Pine Tree. Within minutes he is speaking with Brigadier Basil Lewis, his SAS commander in Albania. Much to John's delight, the brigadier says there is an American task force arriving in Albania. Its mission is to be prepared for operations into Kosovo against the VJ.

The brigadier continues, "It is a political decision whether to launch the task force. If it was a military decision, we would have deployed them already. The problem is that the politicians in NATO are promising no boots on the ground to their citizens back home, and that airpower alone will win the war."

"Then why is the task force even in Albania?" John asks.

"Well, NATO has developed an attack plan into Kosovo with thousands of forces, but we are only allowed to posture the American task force in Albania, hoping the Serbs will view the US force as too big a risk to continue their attack. We are lucky we could do that much. As a last-ditch effort we are hoping the politicians will let us deploy them to prevent catastrophe. Look, John, the plan is that the KLA will provide the ground force while NATO provides the airpower. The airpower seems to be picking up—heck, today we pounded a Serb column just south of Pristina. We have got to keep the air campaign going, and you and Travis Savage are the link between the two forces. The British and American people don't even know you are in Kosovo, and to send more special forces would risk the politicians losing their credibility about no boots on the ground. Besides, four US Army scouts were just captured by the VJ as they were scouting on the Macedonian/Kosovo border."

John asks how he and Travis should proceed, considering the VJ are attacking almost unhindered.

"Stay in contact with General Arsim Gashi. He is the only one that can unite and maneuver the KLA to best attack the VJ."

John replies, "Affirmative, over."

"By the way, John, good work in Skenderaj. Serb media is reporting the deaths of the Tigers by the KLA. Lots of hand-clapping back here."

John realizes the brigadier is just trying to perk him up about Skenderaj. He put the hand mic down slowly, knowing working with the KLA on their offensive planning will be difficult at best.

Travis, petting Trooper between his ears, says, "Looks like it's about to get exciting."

Josif, Julianna and Bekim Mali return shortly after John's radio call with Brigadier Lewis. Josif sits on the edge of the table facing the NATO officers.

"The VJ are getting closer by the day. Abandoning Skanderbeg will be a necessity within a week or two, unless something is done." Travis and John are all ears. "I spoke with General Gashi. He understands the situation even better than we do, as he is monitoring operations throughout all of Kosovo. He agrees that we need to go on the offensive to destroy as much of the VJ as we possibly can. Otherwise, well, the VJ will continue to capture one village after another."

Travis, excited to hear the KLA are taking the initiative to attack, asks, "So, any ideas, especially where and when to attack, and with what forces? We will need to coordinate the air."

"Not yet, but it must be soon as possible. General Gashi knows that also. I will confer with him shortly. His staff is working the plan right now."

John adds, "We are going to talk with General Gashi also. The air planning cycle will take a couple of days to flesh out. While you and General Gashi plan the attack, keep us informed."

A KLA soldier enters the room and whispers something to Bekim. Bekim, a huge bearded man, walks over to Josif and speaks quietly in his ear.

"Excuse us, something urgent has come up. We must go outside and wait on a message."

Josif and Bekim hurry outside into immediate discussion with some of their soldiers. Josif lights a cigarette without thinking about it. The NATO officers move to another room and peer out a window with their AKs in hand.

A fast-moving car is heard coming up the road into the compound. Everyone outside grabs their AKs just in case the guard at the entrance has made a mistake, or has been killed. The speeding car suddenly appears and comes to a squealing halt in front of Josif and Bekim. In a cloud of dust, a KLA soldier jumps out of the passenger side and quickly runs to Josif, saluting him. "Commander, I have urgent news—bad news."

"Well, go ahead. Let us have it," Josif says.

"A bus full of sixty-four Kosovar refugees has been destroyed by a NATO strike. We fear all are dead."

Josif, alarmed, asks, "Are you sure? Why would NATO bomb our bus? Where and when did this happen?"

Still standing at attention, the KLA messenger responds, "Outside of Pristina this morning. The bus was amongst a column of VJ vehicles. The American A-10 pilot must have mistaken it for a VJ bus when he raked the entire column with his Gatling gun."

Josif swears and throws his cigarette down. The giant Bekim remains silent and pale. The messenger stays still, facing Josif.

"Is there something else?" Josif demands.

"Yes, Commander." The messenger swallows hard. "The woman and her son that stayed with you, Deidra and Shabin, were on that bus."

# 12: SEARCH AND CLEAR

**MIRO KNEELS AGAINST A** wall, surveilling the route out of the city. With his AK-47 at the ready, he wonders how he will discern KLA soldiers from civilians trying to escape the chaos. What Miro witnesses are no KLA, or even Kosovar civilians, but truckloads of VJ soldiers roaring past the destroyed BMPs and into the city. It is a noisy and dirty position. The trucks' huge, loud tires bounce by with their high-pitched diesel engines spewing plumes of black exhaust.

As each truck passes, a cloud of dust and dirt envelops Miro. He covers his nose and mouth with a green handkerchief and squints to keep as much dirt out of his eyes as possible. After a long line of trucks, Miro spots his brother's green staff car being escorted by the special police in their dark-blue bulletproof jeeps.

More trucks come. One of the huge troop-carrying trucks pulls off the road beside him. The tailgate bangs down, and out jump VJ soldiers. Their squad leader yells instructions as other trucks and armored vehicles drive into the city. A tank rumbles by, and the ground vibrates as the monster slows down, neutral steers, and points its gun tube toward the open fields.

From behind, Vuk taps Miro on the shoulder, nearly causing him to jump out of his skin. Vuk points to the truck that stopped and unloaded troops. He tells Miro that another VJ platoon are relieving them as Skenderaj's perimeter guards. Miro doesn't have to be told twice. He follows Vuk closely as he scampers around the squad's perimeter and gathers the rest of the men. Once together, they double-time to link up with the rest of their platoon huddled by the three squad trucks.

Lieutenant Buha stands in the middle studying his men as they sit or kneel quietly on the ground. What he sees are scared and nervous young men, some even trembling. He can see it in their faces: no talking, no smiles, just big eyes gazing at him or the ground. Buha knows what his men are anxious about: searching and clearing buildings—a dangerous task, considering the KLA could be hiding anywhere, waiting to take revenge on any VJ soldier they can. Buha issues orders to kill or apprehend any KLA soldiers, plus guidance from higher headquarters:

"All males between eighteen and sixty are to be arrested and escorted to the center of town for questioning, as some might be KLA. Other civilians are to be issued instructions to walk down a single road through a final VJ checkpoint, then begin moving to Macedonia."

Next, Bog gives specific search instructions to each of his three squads. Vuk's squad is given a residential street to clear, and Vuk teams up Niko and Miro to start on the right side of Tito Street. At 1800 everyone will rally at a pre-designated point near the center of town for chow. Once Buha and Bog finish giving orders and fielding questions, the platoon's soldiers salute and begin their precarious task.

Niko and Miro walk a short distance to Tito Street, then crouch down and study the first house. It is a modest two-story brick structure. The front door and shutters are closed. With what little training they have had on how to search and clear a building, they decide to enter through the rear.

As Niko and Miro walk cautiously around the right side of the home, tension mounts; they are aware the unexpected is always close at hand. Behind any door, window, or piece of furniture, death can be waiting. In truth, they are both scared to death of the KLA.

Niko puts his hand on the handle of the back door. He is surprised to find it unlocked. Easing the door open as quietly as he can, Niko, then Miro, quietly make their way inside a kitchen, straining to hear even the slightest of noises. They soon find out hearing anything is difficult with the loud vehicles rolling by. Staying together, their AKs at the ready, they cautiously amble from one room to another. They nervously twist and turn around the furniture and try not to step on the clutter covering most of the floor.

The house is in disarray, with items thrown about as if someone hurriedly left the home with whatever they could take. The downstairs bedroom is such a mess that Miro and Niko begin to think it is the work of looters—clothes thrown about the room, drawers left open, the bed turned over. Family pictures are still on the dresser. Miro picks one up and looks at it. People of all ages standing, the younger ones up front with a pup. Smiling, holding each other. It appears to be three generations. He carefully places the frame back, feeling guilty for sticking his nose into someone else's house and personal belongings.

Niko and Miro clear the bottom floor without incident. Upstairs is next. This time Miro leads, slowly climbing each step, trying to be as quiet as possible. Even so, the stairs squeak and moan as he places each foot down. Miro stops several times to listen, really more out of fear than anything else. At the top are three bedrooms, one in the middle and one on each side. All with their doors closed.

Miro cautiously walks to the left room. He stands on the left side of the door while Niko is on the right. Miro puts his left hand on the handle and pushes the door open. Both men flatten themselves against the hallway wall, but nothing happens. No shots, no screams, no pleading, nothing. Miro enters with Niko close behind. It is a child's room, also in disarray. Miro picks a doll off the floor, looks at it sadly, then tosses it on the bed. The room stinks like mold and shit. The closet door is closed.

Niko motions with his hand toward the closed door. This time Miro places himself on the right side of the door with Niko on the left. Again, Miro puts his hand on the handle and flings the door open. Stuffed animals and other toys from the top shelf fall out of the closet onto the floor. Both men jump back. They stand in silence for a few long moments before regaining their composure. They look at each other in nervous contempt for what they are doing, then start for the middle room.

The door isn't fully closed, just ajar. Niko pushes it slowly open but with a loud squeak. Another child's room, this one with a crib. It stinks worse. The closet door is already open and stuffed full of clothes. Filthy clothes. Bad enough to make Miro retch.

Finally, the last room in the house. As he has twice before, Miro opens the door. Both peer into the room and see an ordinary bedroom with an unmade bed and clothes on the floor. The closet door is closed.

Niko grabs Miro's right arm and whispers, "I have a bad feeling about this."

A jet flies over and rattles the windows. Hearts are pounding. Niko and Miro pause, listening for exploding bombs. No explosions. Who knows whether it was a NATO or Serb fast-mover. Unnerved, both walk back into the hall. Niko wants to leave the closet be. Just leave. Miro objects, worried that innocent people in desperate need of help may be hiding inside. He tells Niko to just wait in the hall and cover him as he opens the closet door.

Miro silently walks back into the bedroom. He stands before the closet door and hears a noise inside. He lifts his AK and freezes. His stomach has butterflies. He feels like shitting. His breathing comes too fast, and his own heartbeat throbs in his ears.

Miro gathers enough courage to throw open the closet door. Niko aims his AK from the hall.

Miro sees someone on the floor. He puts pressure on his trigger just as he did before to off himself. This time he knows the safety is off.

Three people are on the floor: a woman, a young girl, and a teenage boy huddled in each other's arms. They have wide-open, terrified eyes on pasty faces of gloom.

Miro exhales, as does Niko. The woman pleads in Albanian to spare their lives. Miro looks into her eyes and sees fear, a type of fear he has never seen before. No one has ever looked at him like this, and it makes him feel like a fucking monster. He lays his AK-47 on the floor and holds the lady's shaking hands. Speaking in Albanian, Miro tells them not to worry, that it is time to go to Macedonia where it will be safe. His words seem to have little effect on her. After all the terrible atrocities committed on the Kosovars, why trust a VJ soldier?

Niko, now standing behind Miro, approaches the woman and asks how old the boy is. The woman looks down and doesn't speak. Niko repeats the question and states they will not harm him. The woman blurts out he is an innocent boy of thirteen, and would never hurt anyone. Miro asks where her husband is. The woman states that they have not seen him in a long time, perhaps a year. She suspects that he was murdered by Serbs, as he was a good husband and father, and would never abandon his family.

Miro tells her to take what she can, as time is short and they must leave for their safety. She lets go of the boy and grabs a bag of food. The two children look confused as Miro gently grabs the woman's arm and leads them down the steps and onto the dirt road.

Outside is chaos; shouts and screams are only drowned out by tanks, BMPs or trucks. Bewildered Kosovars shuffle along the roadsides with all they can manage to carry. Niko instructs the woman to follow the other Kosovars out of town, and not to return until after the war. He and Miro keep a sharp eye on the three as they scuffle away, joining the stream of Kosovars all heading in the same direction. Toward Macedonia, and safety.

Miro and Niko hear fast-movers overhead. They gaze to the sky, covering their eyes with their hands to blot out the unforgiving sun. A distant jet explodes into an orange fireball while others make steep banking moves. More fireballs. In a matter of minutes, only NATO aircraft circle high above the city. Miro wonders if they will be bombed or strafed. Niko just watches in fascination.

Before searching the next house, the two look around and witness many other Kosovars being escorted out of their homes. One VJ soldier kicks and screams at an older woman he thinks is moving too slow. He points his AK at her and screams he will shoot her if she does not move faster.

Without hesitation, Niko sprints across the street and takes his anger out on the soldier. Miro tries to stop the bigger and stronger Niko, but to no avail. With his AK Niko butt-strokes the soldier in the face. The soldier goes down hard on the cobblestones. On impact his helmet pops off and his AK clatters to the ground. Bleeding from his lower lip, his expression is one of disbelief.

Some of his comrades attack Niko until several others soldiers, including Miro, force them apart. Niko and Miro don't recognize any of them. They must be from a different platoon, or company. They become rather agitated at Niko, cursing and threatening him. Niko aims his AK at the soldiers, waving it back and forth.

"Go ahead, fuck with me. I'll kill every motherfucker that kicks a woman."

Miro is freaking out. The other soldiers stand silent, suspicious of Niko's motivation. One eventually speaks. "Okay, okay, cool down, man. We are all on the same side. Put the gun down and go on. No harm done."

Miro tugs Niko gently by his shirt, carefully moving him back until they are behind the second house. Miro grabs on tighter to Niko's shirt and throws the much larger man on the ground.

"Have you gone crazy? What in the hell is the matter with you?"

Niko, picking himself up along with his AK-47, responds angrily, "Many of the VJ are savages. Beasts who prey on innocent people. I don't put up with that bullshit."

Miro looks coldly at Niko. "So, you prefer to join the penal battalion or be shot by the special police? You go right ahead, but I tell you this is just the beginning, and we have no choice. I am not going to sacrifice myself out of principle. Now, let's finish our job before we get into more trouble."

Niko and Miro clear four more houses on their side of the street, only finding one elderly dead man who shot himself in the head. Without hesitation, Niko takes the dead man's revolver, wipes off the blood, and tucks it into his waistband.

Miro stares at the corpse, thinking how the man would rather kill himself than endure a long, painful walk that he most likely would not even survive.

Niko slaps Miro on his arm. "We're done. Let's get the hell out of here."

Miro throws a shirt from the floor over the dead man's face.

A few minutes later they meet up with the rest of their squad on the street, then walk a few blocks to join the rest of the company for dinner. It is beef goulash, but Niko can't eat, nor even sit still, especially after seeing the soldier he butt-stroked sitting just meters away. The man is trying to eat out of the side of his mouth that is not swollen.

Niko gives Miro his portion and walks back to the platoon

area. Miro takes his tin plate and continues to eat while he follows his friend.

Niko climbs up the back of the squad truck, sits on the wooden bench and pulls out a cigarette. He strikes a wooden match on the seat, lights his cigarette and takes a long drag. Miro sits beside him, finishing his food.

Exhaling cigarette smoke Niko says, "What a fucked-up day. Are we going to do this shitty work all the time?

"It can always get worse."

"What's worse than kicking people out of their house, then making them fucking walk with their kids to another country?"

Miro puts his plate down, feeling like a glutton. He remembers what Lieutenant Buha told him about using influence with his brother. *It's worth a try*, he thinks.

Without looking at Niko, he throws his plate away and says, "I am going to see my brother."

Miro hustles toward the center of town looking for his brother's headquarters. He hopes to persuade Dragan to issue orders for soldiers to treat the local Kosovars as humanely as possible. As Miro walks along the cobblestoned streets he passes two Kosovar men lying facedown, both shot in the back. He checks their pulses. Both dead.

Upon arriving in the town's circle, Miro sees a large group of wire-encircled men sitting under the watchful eyes of VJ guards. He walks up as close as he can to the wire before a guard threatens him to move back. Miro is close enough to notice they are all either young or old. Hardly any of them are fighting age.

Miro recognizes the young boy from earlier in the day at the first house they searched. The boy sits cross-legged and shaking. He notices Miro looking at him and begins to sob. Miro, flushed with anger, turns to find his brother.

The command post is not far away and easy to spot. Numerous command vehicles with multiple antennas and blue special police jeeps are parked outside a restaurant. Since he is only a private, Miro knows he will have to bluff his way past the guard by the door.

He looks inside his brother's command car and spots a dispatch folder. Acting like a driver, he casually opens the door and takes it. He walks up to the guard and confidently tells him Colonel Cadikovski needs his dispatch folder. It works; the guard lets him through without so much as a word.

Upon entering Miro feels uncomfortably out of place. He has never been inside a command post. Everywhere radios are buzzing and officers converse in various groups. No one is idle but him, so before someone notices a private with nothing to do, Miro walks with a sense of purpose through the main room and into the restaurant's back office.

There sits his brother standing behind a large desk speaking loudly to three officers standing at attention: ". . . keep pushing, keep pushing. We must control the city by dark. I don't want any terrorists attacking us tonight. Report to me once your sectors of the city are cleared and your defenses complete."

Without a word, all three salute and strut quickly out of the office, sweeping Miro aside as if he were not even there. Miro regains his balance, then stands in the doorway at the position of attention.

Colonel Cadikovski immediately spots Miro and asks, "What do you want, Miro? Food not good enough for you?"

Miro nervously states, "I saw your dispatch folder was still in your car, so I thought I would bring it to you."

Colonel Cadikovski reaches for the folder and smirks. "Okay— take a seat. Looks like the soldier's life has finally appealed to you. It has been a huge success today; be sure and tell your comrades. It is all about being efficient and effective. We have efficiently cleansed the city, and now we will effectively make sure they don't fight back or return."

Miro uneasily sits straight in his chair, and responds in a weak voice, "What of the prisoners outside, Dragan? What are you going to do with these young boys and old men?"

The colonel seems surprised by his brother's question. "Why would you ask this? They would cut your throat if let loose. What do you think we should do to them? The only thing logical. Look inside the bed of the truck out back and you will see dead Tigers. Kosovar men killed them. Maybe the KLA or just men from this city, but either way we must eliminate all the terrorists or they will continue to kill us. It is that simple. This is war, Miro. The quicker it is over, the better."

"But they are mostly young boys and old men. Why not just let them go, or hold them if you really think they are a threat?"

"That's up to Marin and his secret police. I have nothing to do with that situation except to provide guards." Colonel Cadikovski sits down, then leans back in his chair, lost in thought while staring at Miro. "Actually, we are establishing a makeshift detention facility, just across the street in the gymnasium. We are not harming them. Having some of the Kosovar civilians here will keep NATO off our back. Don't concern yourself with these criminals. Now go back to your unit before you get in trouble. For once in your life, do your duty and make me proud. At the rate we and the rest of the VJ are going, this war will be over in a few weeks."

"Can I speak with Colonel Marin about the prisoners? I know him; I stayed with him and his family in Mitrovice."

Dragan hesitates, then says, "I will talk with him."

Miro pops up, stands at attention and salutes. He feels odd saluting his brother, but again, he does it more out of habit from his recent baptism of military indoctrination. His brother quickly returns his salute without emotion.

Miro exits the door and runs directly into Filip Marin. Dressed in the dark-blue uniform of the special police, Marin doesn't even glance at Miro, and pushes him aside. Miro is relieved Marin didn't recognize him. Thoughts of what he and Suzana did in their living room are still fresh on his mind.

Quickly leaving the headquarters, Miro has little hope for the captured Kosovar men. The friendly Filip Marin who was so hospitable in Mitrovice is now Colonel Marin, a detachment commander of the dreaded Serbian Special Police. By Serbian law, the special police outrank the VJ. This means Colonel Marin outranks Colonel Cadikovski. Miro is well aware of what the mission of the special police is—to exterminate Kosovars and shoot any VJ soldiers suspected of noncompliance in the war effort. In effect, the special police are Milosevic's guarantee that the VJ will carry out his atrocious objective of a Serbian-pure Kosovo.

As Miro passes the detained men he notices a food kitchen is being set up against a wall inside the wire, a good indicator they will not be executed, at least not anytime soon.

"Get in line. Let's move," bellows a VJ sergeant to the prisoners.

At first none of the prisoners move, but upon prodding by the guards, they slowly rise and stand in line. Miro continues his walk back to his platoon, stepping up his pace before someone of importance notices him gone. As he returns, Vuk is first to eye him.

"Enjoy your outing, *Private*? Since you were not here, you get the 0200 to 0300 guard shift. Chow is gone too, so hope you found something to eat."

"Yes, Corporal," Miro says, then sheepishly pulls his sleeping bag out of his pack. He finds a spot on the ground by Niko, who smiles at him while leaning against a wall smoking.

"Where in the hell have you been? Keep this up and you will find yourself in the penal battalion. As tainted draftees we are on a short leash, you know."

Miro doesn't say a word as he spreads out his bag and settles in. He sits and is taking his boots off when shots ring out.

# 13: THE WARRIOR BEAST

**JOHN SIPS ON A** cup of coffee and watches Travis tinker with the secure tactical satellite radio. As Travis sets the dials, Trooper tries to help, but his big nose gets in the way. Trooper gets a pet on the head, then a gentle rejection push.

"Pastrik, this is Razorback, over. Pastrik, this is Razorback, over."

"This is Pastrik, over."

"I need to speak to the commander, over."

"Hold one, over."

In a few minutes General Gashi's recognizable voice comes over the net.

"General, Lieutenant Colonel Phillips and I are still at Skanderbeg. We understand you have discussed with Colonel Josif Shala, the 3rd Brigade commander, about a major offensive?"

"Yes, and we are working out the details now. I also spoke with Pine Tree just a few minutes ago, and they seem to be supportive—that is, if they agree with the plan."

"When can we get a draft of the plan, General? That way we can start planning the air."

"We will be sending the FRAGO in a few hours by secure fax

to Colonel Shala at your location. He will be able to brief you on the general scheme of maneuver."

"General, one other thing. It is imperative that we have enough KLA as a ground force, meaning it will require more than what Shala has here."

"I understand; I will wait until Colonel Shala briefs you for any more questions."

"Roger, over."

The radio goes silent. Travis packs up the radio while John hunts for Josif. John finds him in the plans room, reading the order from General Gashi. He returns to get Travis.

"Come on, mate. Josif is reading the order."

John and Travis enter the large plans room. Josif walks up to the paper map on the wall, attaches acetate over it, and draws with a black marker.

Travis glances at the map, then stares at Josif in disbelief.

"Malisheve? That's foolish, Josif. There is an entire VJ mechanized brigade there, and they are in a Kosovar-inhabited city. Who told you this? Gashi?"

Josif glances at Travis, then back to the map.

"Yes, by order of General Gashi. Gashi's plan is to mass two KLA brigades near the city. The KLA 2nd Brigade from Pristina attacks the VJ at Malisheve, then withdraws to cause the VJ to pursue them. Once the VJ pursues the Pristina brigade out of the city, my brigade ambushes them—with the help of NATO air support."

Travis plops down in a chair, looking very concerned. "I have a bad feeling about this. Too many things can go wrong. What if the VJ brigade in Skenderaj attacks us while we are ambushing the VJ coming out of Malisheve?"

John speaks up before Josif can respond. "Too many things have already gone wrong, Trav. Lady Luck has never been a friend of ours, but we have to wrestle back the initiative from the VJ somehow. And best of all, this is Gashi's plan, not NATO's. It will give the KLA ownership and legitimacy for their part in the war."

"So the air support has already been coordinated with NATO?" Travis curiously asks.

The expression on John's face is telling. Travis quietly says, "Guess that's our role in all of this."

John nods, then asserts, "We are here to support you, Josif. You command your forces and we will call in the air support."

The next evening Josif meets with his key leaders and the commander and staff from the KLA 2nd Brigade from Pristina.

Josif addresses the assembled leadership, with Julianna translating for the NATO officers. "This is going to be a different type of battle, more of a conventional fight as we mass our two brigades to fight toe to toe with Serb ground forces. Previously, we have only used guerilla tactics, a hit-and-run type of warfare that has had minimal effect on the VJ's offensive into Kosovo. General Arsim Gashi has given me an order to win a *big battle* to turn the tide of the VJ offensive. Malisheve was at one time the headquarters and pride of the KLA, a city of Kosovars who remain loyal to Gashi and the KLA forces. The VJ forced most of the KLA out of Malisheve a month ago and occupied the city with an entire armored brigade.

"Symbolically, the VJ occupation of Malisheve is a significant Serb victory. Gashi reasons taking it back from the Serbs will not only be a moral victory, but possibly turn the tide of the war in our favor. This victory will prove that we can mass forces and beat the VJ on the field of battle. Gashi knows he must change our tactics to have any chance of winning the war against a force much more powerful than our own. He needs to do something with his forces that is bold and audacious; a battle that would be so decisive it would throw the VJ back on their heels in retreat. *Malisheve is going to be that battle."*

The NATO officers brief next, with John taking the lead. "NATO planners have never planned air-combat operations off of a KLA plan. Pilots' lives are at stake, not to mention the possibility of more civilian deaths in Malisheve. In the end, NATO has agreed to support the KLA mission but with specific limitations. Only VJ combat vehicles will be targeted, and only if they are outside the city, away from the civilian population. Even then, pilots might be reluctant to fire because of the close proximity of your fighters. But we, Lieutenant Colonel Savage and myself, are here to do precisely this: to plan NATO air attacks in support of freeing Kosovo from Serb aggression. If either one of us can get an accurate *eyes on* a Serb target, then they will execute the attack. We will do the very best that we can."

Once Julianna finishes interpreting John's message, the men all stand with thunderous applause. The warrior beast stirs in the hearts of the KLA.

While carrying their gear to their cars, Travis and John see Josif speaking to Julianna along the wood line. Travis's ego slightly deflates when Julianna doesn't even glance at him, instead listening intently to her brother. A few seconds later Julianna suddenly collapses into Josif's arms.

The officers run toward them, knowing Josif has told Julianna of the deaths of Deidra and Shabin. Julianna is hysterical as Josif says something to her in Albanian; she breaks from Josif's grasp and runs aimlessly into the woods. Josif starts to go after her, but lets her go, knowing she needs time to process the tragic news. He slowly walks back, glances at the NATO officers, and enters the house.

As Julianna walks through the woods, she tries to persuade herself it must be someone else rather than Deidra and Shabin.

She reasons of all the buses that were on the way to Macedonia, chances are that it was not the bus they were on, so it must be a mistake. "*It must*," she says aloud, collapsing on her knees with tears streaming down her face.

Julianna weeps steadily as the reality of Deidra's and Shabin's deaths sink in. She never wanted to let Deidra go, and only did so for Shabin's security. Julianna blames herself for sending them off. If she hadn't done so, they would still be safe inside the bedroom. She doesn't know how she can continue on. If she only knew whether Miro were still alive, there might be a reason to live. But she concludes he is most likely gone also.

Tears clouding her vision, Julianna looks up and sees a man in uniform. The man lifts Julianna to her feet, then embraces her. Julianna at first resists until she realizes it is Travis. They hug and kiss passionately. After a few minutes Julianna places her head on Travis's chest and feels his thundering heartbeat.

Julianna looks at the ground in despair. "Are you kissing me because you love me or because you feel sorry for me? Or is it because you are feeling guilty about the NATO air strike?"

Travis still holds Julianna tight. "All three reasons, I suppose."

He is overcome with guilt. For the first time he questions NATO's presence in Kosovo, and if they are doing more harm than good. Julianna gazes at him and wonders what he is thinking.

Travis stares back at her, deep into her watery eyes. They embrace each other once again, sharing a moment of sadness and desperation.

Walking back with Julianna to the house, Travis notices John outside talking on the satellite radio. Julianna enters the house as Travis approaches John. John covers the mic with his hand.

"NATO is still trying to confirm the civilian bus strike. They think it could just be Serbian propaganda."

Travis sits down on the front doorstep. "Once the strike camera footage is analyzed, NATO should be able to verify if it's true."

John finishes speaking on the radio, then tosses the mic down. "Price to pay for an air war, I suppose."

Travis angrily snaps back, "Price to pay? Every pilot by now knows that the VJ intentionally place Kosovar civilians in their columns as human shields. This is pure fucking incompetence. We had an agreement with the KLA that our planes would only strike VJ military vehicles, not buses."

John is stunned by Travis's outburst.

"Whoa there, cowboy. You have to keep the bigger picture in mind. We are here to save these folks. NATO follows the rules, but shit like this happens and you know it."

Travis's anger only increases. "Save these folks? Every time we do something, the Serbs counter with a vengeance and gain on us. We are losing this war, John, and the Serbs know that. The Serbs are outsmarting us and are making significant gains. The KLA just doesn't have the power to be an effective ground force, and retributions by the Serbs after our air strikes have only made the situation worse."

John remains silent for a few moments while Travis shudders with anger.

"What?" Travis blurts.

"We have a long way to go, Trav. You know that. Just follow the rules and don't cop an attitude."

Two nights later, John, Travis, Trooper, Julianna, and Lieutenant Prek Luga with his KLA special forces platoon are on the move toward Malisheve. Prek and his soldiers lead the way, and at 0230 Prek's men capture a VJ observation post in a small hut sitting atop a hill overlooking the western route into Malisheve—the route of Josif's attack. Three VJ soldiers are at the post, with two asleep in their cots and one sitting in a chair manning the radio. Prek's soldiers surprise them, capturing them alive and binding their hands with flex cuffs. The NATO officers and Julianna occupy the hut while Prek has a VJ soldier call in a routine radio check with the VJ headquarters in Malisheve. Prek speaks Serbian, but if he spoke on the radio, his Albanian accent would cause suspicion.

Once the NATO officers and Julianna arrive, Prek takes his radio and departs to help his men set up a defensive perimeter around the post. John and Travis set up their radios while Trooper lies down and listens.

From this vantage point they will be able to see most of the attack area and the KLA ambush position. Now the only thing to do is wait. Radio-listening silence is instituted among the KLA; the VJ have the ability to pick up their radio transmissions and, given enough time, determine the KLA's positions.

As John and Travis scan the area below with night-vision devices, within minutes a light sprinkle turns into a driving rainstorm, making it impossible to see more than a few feet in front of them.

Travis looks at the three VJ prisoners just feet away. Huddled together on the floor, young and scared, they are most likely conscripts away from home for the first time in their lives. Travis asks Julianna to tell them they will not be harmed. Julianna obliges, then questions whether the young men know Miroslav Cadikovski. All three are so frightened they seem to not even hear Julianna. They are in shock, and not one of them says a word.

John takes out a pack of American cigarettes and puts three in his mouth. He pulls out his lighter, lights all three, and puts one in each of the prisoners' mouths.

"Do any of you lads speak English?"

Two of them nod while the other spouts out the side of his mouth, "John Wayne!"

John looks at Travis and says, "Your American fags work every time!"

Travis quips, "Guess I will have to add cigs and pics of John Wayne to my packing list!"

John and Travis agree that the KLA attack might actually be more successful if carried out in the rain. Certainly there will be a greater chance of surprise. The VJ guards in Malisheve will most likely be more concerned with staying dry than watching for a major KLA attack.

The NATO officers also discuss the weather's possible impact on NATO's ability to conduct air strikes. John states the British Tornados are all-weather aircraft and have the capability to make bombing runs in the rain using thermal sights.

In a driving rain, the battle starts at 0415 with a tremendous explosion inside the city. Moments later the VJ radio in the observation post comes alive with chatter. Julianna, with her ear to the VJ radio, explains the radio transmissions are about reports of numerous KLA inside the city. The VJ brigade headquarters has been blown up with an RPG, and more KLA are pouring into the city through a gap in the western defensive perimeter. VJ reinforcements are ordered to fill the gap, and mortar fire is being called outside of the perimeter.

Breaking the radio-listening silence, John has Julianna call Josif on the NATO radio and warn him about the VJ reinforcements and incoming mortar fire.

VJ mortar rounds start to land on suspected KLA avenues of approach into the city, briefly lighting up the areas of impact. Inside Malisheve, pounding torrents of rain amid hand-to-hand fighting make for mass confusion on both sides. KLA RPGs hit VJ tanks, causing tremendous concussions followed by tank ammunition exploding into the sky like giant fireworks, illuminating most of the city. Lightning and thunder add to the surreal scene, as if man and nature have coordinated an orchestra from hell.

Even at the NATO observation post, the noise is a continuous series of deafening explosions. The concussions rock the hut so hard the roof and walls start to collapse. As the rain pours in, John's radio crackles something about NATO aircraft.

Just seconds later, fast-movers add exponentially to the cacophony of loud noises, flying low to acquire VJ tanks. At the same time, Prek's snipers, old Yugoslavian starlight scopes mounted on their Dragunovs, pick off VJ running about in the city.

John and Travis grab their radios while Julianna takes the VJ radio and they run out of the collapsing hut. Trooper drags the VJ prisoners out one at a time by their collars.

Huddling together in the driving rain, John is on the radio with the NATO aircraft flying over the battlefield. There are four British Tornado jets, and John knows one of the pilots from his time at Sandhurst. The pilot explains they spotted a ZSU 23-4 in the city, but people are around it in a circle, most likely civilians forced to act as human shields. The "Zoo," as the ZSU 23-4 is nicknamed by the pilots, starts to fire randomly into the air, hoping to catch a fast-mover flying in for a kill. The pilots are forced to focus on knocking out the Zoo instead of the tanks.

Julianna yells to Travis that she just heard the VJ on the radio state tanks from Skenderaj are on their way to counterattack the KLA from the rear. Travis grabs the mic from John and calls for close air support to target the approaching tanks.

# 14: THE SPECIAL
# POLICE

**MIRO HEARS MORE RAPID** gunfire. Electricity runs up his spinal cord and throughout his body. He knows it is either a full-blown KLA attack, or worse. He suspects the latter. It is full dark, and he hurriedly laces his boots back up.

Niko retorts, "Where in the hell are you going? Trying to get yourself killed?"

Miro grabs his AK-47. *"Come on, let's go!"*

Miro runs through the dark as quickly as he can, past other soldiers of his platoon who are grabbing their weapons and forming a defensive perimeter. Most assume it is a KLA attack, as they have no reason to think an execution could be underway.

With Niko in trail, Miro bolts as fast as he can move, but his stomach is tied in knots and his legs feel like rubber. His mind moves faster than his body. Coupled with his nervousness and anxiety, after a few hundred meters he suffers muscle fatigue and falls hard on the cobblestone road. His AK bounces loudly and skids along the cobblestones. He rolls on his back, trying to regain his breath. Niko catches up and drags Miro by his web gear to the side of a building. Miro is on the verge of a panic attack. Niko consoles him.

"Take it easy, buddy. Everything is going to be alright. Stay here until you can catch your breath."

Both see Lieutenant Buha sprinting past in the same direction, not even noticing Miro or Niko by the building.

A few more single shots ring out. Trying his best to follow his lieutenant, Miro struggles to his feet to retrieve his weapon but instead goes down on a knee, still trying to catch his breath. Niko helps Miro back up. Then they both chase after Lieutenant Buha.

Finally arriving at the source of the gunfire, the first thing Miro sees is Lieutenant Buha in a heated discussion with Colonel Marin. Miro can't hear it all, but he witnesses Lieutenant Buha in Marin's face, threatening him with a loud voice. Marin shoves Buha aside and called his cronies to subdue the lieutenant.

Miro forces himself to keep going, as he fears something so horrible is occurring that it will forever damage his soul. He is right. The male prisoners he saw earlier have been shot by a machine gun. Most lie motionless on the ground, while a few are still alive, clawing at the ground to escape death. The special police walk about inside the razor wire with their pistols, shooting the survivors at close range.

Miro desperately searches for *the boy*. He runs along the outside of the razor wire, straining his eyes in the dim light. Finally, he spots him. The boy is on his knees crying and begging for his life. A special policeman holds a pistol to his head.

Miro screams at the top of his lungs, "*NO!*"

The policeman looks briefly at Miro, smiles, then shoots the boy between his eyes, killing him instantly.

Miro, in a fiery rage, raises his AK-47, but his weapon is snatched out of his hands by someone behind him. Miro, startled, instantly turns and sees Niko.

"You're trying to get yourself killed, you idiot," Niko whispers as he keeps Miro from grabbing back his AK.

Miro collapses and starts once more to hyperventilate. It is so terribly surreal he prays he will wake up from a nightmare. Another shot rings out. At first Miro thinks he is being shot by the special police.

He looks up and hears Niko raving, "You *bastard! You will get yours!*"

On the other side of the compound Lieutenant Buha lies writhing in pain, holding his hands over his stomach. Standing above him, Colonel Marin points a pistol at Buha and shoots five more rounds into him, then calmly places his pistol back into his hip holster.

Niko helps Miro up, and they walk solemnly toward Lieutenant Buha's lifeless body. A stream of blood flows from his mouth. His eyes are wide open.

Marin is still standing above Buha, and in a cold and stern voice asks what they are doing.

Niko, thinking quickly, states, "We were just guards here, comrade Captain. We will take the body of this traitor for you."

Marin looks at Miro, wondering why he is having trouble breathing. Niko notices Marin's interest in Miro and quickly responds, "This soldier fought off a Kosovar that had jumped the wire. He is okay; he just needs to catch his breath."

Marin smiles. "Good job, soldier—wait. I know you!" Marin takes a few steps and looks closer at his face. "You are . . . *Miroslav Cadikovski*! Colonel Cadikovski's younger brother, and you stayed at my house before deploying! Well done, Miro. I will ask your brother to promote you for your brave actions here tonight."

Marin slaps Miro on the shoulder and walks away, barking orders at his special police. Miro is stunned, unable to process all that has happened so quickly.

Niko grasps Miro's arm tightly to get his attention. "Come on, let's get the lieutenant and get the hell out of here."

Niko picks up Buha's shoulders while Miro gradually picks up his legs.

Still putting on his clothes, Colonel Dragan Cadikovski runs up to Colonel Marin.

"I thought we had an agreement. You said that you would not execute the Kosovar men if I hold my soldiers to their duty in fighting the KLA."

Marin snaps back. "Your soldiers are not doing their duty. I shot three of them today for smoking pot. And I just shot one of your platoon leaders, the American one, for assaulting me."

Colonel Cadikovski has not seen Buha, Miro and Niko having just carried him away.

"You fucking killed who?"

Smiling slyly, Marin boasts, "Your American lieutenant, along with three of your conscripts."

"You murdering bastard. Not only was Buha a damn good officer but an American that we were using as a propaganda tool."

"I couldn't help it; the American was attacking me!"

"What for?"

"Shooting the criminals."

Colonel Cadikovski reaches for his pistol, but Marin puts his hand straight out.

"I wouldn't do anything stupid, Dragan. I can have you shot as well."

"Where is Buha?"

"Your brother and another comrade took his body away, I suppose to their platoon area."

It is a long trip back to the platoon area for Miro and Niko. Neither has ever carried a dead body, especially so far along dark streets. Lieutenant Buha's arms dangle to his sides. Several times Miro and Niko have to stop and rest.

The second time they stop is between buildings, offering them some concealment from KLA snipers. Miro sees Buha staring at him, eyes wide open. Niko closes Buha's eyes and rifles through his pockets. Finding a picture in his left top pocket, Niko shines a light on it. It is Buha with his family, all smiling with the ocean behind them. Miro and Niko weep silently. On the back of the photo is his wife's name and address. It is as if Lieutenant Buha foresaw his fate. Niko sticks the picture in his pocket, hoping someday to travel to the States to tell Buha's wife what happened—that he was a good man who died making a heroic stand against evil.

Once back at the platoon area, they lay Buha's body down amongst bewildered men. Sergeant Bog orders each squad to seek and destroy any KLA around the area. Niko approaches Bog and firmly tells him to stop the search. Bog looks inquisitively at Niko. Bog is a smart enough platoon sergeant to know Niko is serious.

Niko loudly announces, "Stop what you're doing and gather around me."

Bog stares at Niko, expecting him to share some type of exceptional information.

"The special police have just executed dozens of young and old men."

"All the firing didn't come from a KLA attack?" asks a soldier.

Miro sits against a wall, quivering with his hands on his face.

Niko continues, "No KLA attacked."

"Then who killed the lieutenant?" several men ask in unison.

"*Colonel Marin*," Niko bluntly reveals.

The platoon is in shock. Not everyone knows who Colonel Marin is, but immediately find out from those that do.

Most of the soldiers want to attack and kill all the special police, no matter the consequences. Bog has to calm his men down before they became a vigilante mob. Once cooler heads prevail, Bog looks at Niko and Miro. "What happened?"

Miro stumbles to his feet, finally getting a grip on himself.

He lurches forward and speaks.

"When the gunfire erupted I suspected it was an execution. I had seen the boys and old men corralled behind razor wire when I went to speak to my—Colonel Cadikovski. I saw the special police and I had a bad feeling."

"Why didn't you say something?" demands Bog.

"I suppose I was in denial at the time. I just couldn't bring myself to believe someone could do such a terrible thing. I was afraid."

"What did you tell your brother, Colonel Cadikovski, about then?"

Miro sees the faces of the other men in his platoon, even in the darkness.

"I went to convince him to treat the prisoners with dignity and respect, just like Lieutenant Buha has always preached to us."

Niko walks over to several soldiers he recognizes, the ones who abused the older lady earlier in the day. He scowls at them. "I still think some of us could be better at how the lieutenant wanted us to treat people."

The men lower their faces, silent.

"Go on," Bog demands of Miro.

"Niko followed me to the sounds of gunfire, but I fell on the cobblestones. We both saw Lieutenant Buha run fast past us after I fell. Niko waited with me because I had the air knocked out of me. When I was able to stand up and we arrived at the site, I saw the Lieutenant Buha yelling at Marin. That's when I saw the dead civilians, and I wanted to stop the special police from killing the wounded."

Niko intervenes. "I arrived just before Miro and saw the lieutenant in an argument with Marin. I froze. I didn't know what to do. The execution was pretty much over, so I looked for Miro. When I found him in the dark I stopped him from shooting the special police. Believe me, I hate them worse than the KLA, but we wouldn't have had a chance. We would have been gunned down like . . . well, like Buha."

Bog angrily spouts, "Come on, let's take care of the lieutenant."

The soldiers cover his body with a blanket, and every man prays by his side, many swearing revenge against the special police. Bog, having worked directly with Lieutenant Buha as his senior NCO, holds his officer's hand and whispers something no one can hear.

Miro lies down for two and a half hours before his 0200 guard duty shift. As tired and sore as he is, he cannot sleep. As he lies next to Niko, Miro's mind swirls on an emotional roller coaster; from despair at the violent deaths of the boy and Buha, to hatred of the special police. He wonders how much his brother supported the massacre. He has always known that Dragan is a power-hungry militarist, but not a cold-blooded murder, or someone that would condone such behavior. Marin must have threatened Dragan, or at least warned him not to intervene.

Miro's mind rambles, remembering fucking Marin's wife on the couch and on the dining room table. He laughs to himself, but feelings of guilt overcome him as Julianna comes to the forefront of his thoughts. He still feels guilty about cheating on her, even if it was with the devil's wife. He envisions Julianna's beauty, especially her smile. He can hear her voice, her laugh. He reminisces about their times together. How short their happiness had been after their marriage—before they were separated. If only the VJ had not attacked Kosovo that day, and they had made their flight—if he had not been arrested at the airport in Montenegro. They would be safe, and happy. Living a normal life of peace and love.

Miro's thoughts turn back to reality. He thinks about the possibility of her being raped and killed as so many Kosovar women have been. But maybe, just maybe, she is alive. There is always that chance. He again tries to figure out the most likely place she would be. She would have come back to Kosovo looking for him. Surely she would have gone home, but would have seen the empty destruction of Drenica. Maybe she linked up with her brother, Josif, or was able to make it to Macedonia. Maybe, maybe, maybe. He has the same reoccurring thoughts day after day. Miro lies on his back and looks at the stars, tears running down his face in silent agony.

Restless and unable to sleep, at 0200 Miro raises his sore body and relieves the soldier on guard. For the next hour and a half, he walks the perimeter with his AK-47 at the ready. He is a soldier in the VJ, a situation he is still very much against. But as a soldier he will protect his mates, and especially the lifeless body of Lieutenant Buha.

The next morning Lieutenant Buha's platoon buries him in a simple ceremony on the outskirts of the city. All in his platoon are present, but not anyone from his chain of command, not even his fellow platoon leaders or the company commander.

The company commander came by earlier that morning, but only to assign orders for the platoon sergeant, Bogdana "Bog" Komazec, to be placed in charge as the acting platoon leader. Miro saw the company commander pointing his finger in Bog's chest as he stood at attention. The entire platoon knows Bog is a strong leader, and he was close to Buha. The question in everyone's mind is how long Bog will last under such ruthless leadership.

Men jump to attention when a visitor shows up at Buha's gravesite. It is Colonel Cadikovski. Dragan puts the men at ease, takes his hat off, then kneels and prays. A few minutes later he stands, places his hat back on his head, and silently walks out of the platoon area.

Early that afternoon the platoon rotates to the gymnasium for showers and personal hygiene. On their way they pass the town square and witness a bulldozer next to the executed Kosovar bodies. The dozer takes one scoop at a time to a hole in a large field. For Miro it is a sickening sight, reminding him of the pictures he saw of the Nazi death camps in WWII. Ironically, Yugoslavia fought the Nazis, but now over fifty years later is carrying out the same Nazi policies of extermination.

Miro enters the gymnasium and sees hundreds of Kosovar women and small children sitting on the basketball courts.

Niko says, "The only reason the women and children are still alive is to serve as human shields against NATO air attacks."

Miro remembers his brother saying a civilian holding center was established to protect his headquarters. He stops and looks intently at the women and children sitting on blankets spread throughout the courts. He steps over the rope separating Kosovars from the showers. He walks amongst the women and children.

Niko is flabbergasted. "What the hell are you doing now, Miro . . . stop!"

Miro stops, turns about and hands Niko his AK-47. He continues to walk slowly among the civilians, looking closely at each one. He finds the mother of the executed boy. The mother he had promised as she sat shivering with her daughter and son that everything was going to be all right. There she sits, with her daughter on her lap, gently rocking back and forth, but with no son.

Her head is down and she doesn't see Miro as he approaches. Miro sits down next to her. Everyone in the gym is looking at him. There is a long silence as she either does not notice him or refuses to acknowledge his presence. The women in the courts remain absolutely quiet, all eyes on Miro. Only the occasional child's cry breaks the silence.

Finally, the mother slowly turns her head and stares through Miro. It is the saddest look Miro has ever seen, and at first he can't even speak. Pulling himself together, with his knees on the hard wooden floor he finally manages, "I am so sorry, so sorry."

The mother spits in his face. Miro, in shame, covers his face with his hands and hangs his head. The room erupts in chaos. Miro is assaulted from all directions by Kosovar women, hitting, biting and kicking him. Unable to get up, Miro coils into a fetal position, absorbing the countless blows on every part of his body.

Screams echo loudly throughout the gymnasium until a single gunshot stops everything. The next thing Miro remembers is Niko grabbing him by the collar and yanking him to his feet.

★★★

The following days are marked with the routine boredom of guard duty and preparing to attack further into Kosovo. Bog receives no information from the company commander as to when or exactly where they will be heading. The only instructions are *to be ready*.

Miro is fine with that, as he is so sore he can barely walk. He remains haunted by the deaths of Lieutenant Buha and especially the boy, whose name he doesn't even know. Normally a placid man, Miro is filled with not only guilt, but hate. Colonel Marin, who had graciously opened his house for Miro, is at the center of Miro's revulsion. Miro now realizes his brother had nothing to do with the massacre. That, at least, is some respite.

Miro and Niko take solace in each other. Though they have had their ups and downs, they depend on each other for emotional and physical safety. And although they still detest being in the VJ, Miro feels an obligation toward his comrades—an obligation only soldiers feel toward each other. To desert the VJ would be the moral thing to do, but to run out on one's comrades would be unacceptable.

The next evening, light rain falls, and both Miro and Niko don their wet weather gear. As they lie down they hear commotion throughout the city. Vehicles are starting and voices are yelling. Once again, everyone in the platoon knows something is up, and they stand, awaiting the unknown.

It comes quickly. The company commander runs into the platoon area, gives Bog orders, and leaves as fast as he came. Bog gathers the platoon together and explains that the KLA are attacking Malisheve, and their brigade is ordered to counterattack the enemy from the rear. They are to mount their trucks immediately and rendezvous at a predetermined point with the tanks for the final assault.

Miro and Niko quickly pack their rucks, then scramble to the truck with their AK-47s. Miro starts up the engine while the rest of the platoon climbs into the back. Bog hops into the passenger side, and within minutes they are moving out with the rest of the company's trucks.

As they depart Skenderaj, the rain is coming down in droves. For security reasons, all vehicles are in blackout drive, meaning their headlights are off, but small running lights to see the road are on. Both Miro and Bog squint through the rain to make out the truck in front. They drive for almost an hour until a VJ military policeman waves them into a field lined with trees. Miro drives through a muddy field as a ground guide with a red-lensed flashlight motions him to park.

Miro turns the engine off. In the distance is the sound of battle: thunderous explosions, all types of weapons fire, and jets screaming overhead.

Someone in the dark yells, *"Off the trucks."*

The one yelling is the company first sergeant. The company commander opens Bog's door as soon as the truck stops. Miro hears the commander tell Bog to mount six men to a tank, and only dismount to fight when ordered.

Lightning strikes nearby as Bog grabs the squad leaders to designate which tanks to mount. Vuk points Miro and Niko to their tank, a modern Yugoslavian-built T-72. They take off their wet weather gear and don small assault packs filled with ammunition and medical supplies.

They slog through the mud with AK-47s over their shoulders toward their metal beast. Niko is first to grab the muddy left sprocket and climb atop the tank's hull. The tank's huge diesel engine starts just as Miro climbs on the tank's back deck. Bog comes running up at the last moment, mounting the tank. They tightly hold the welded-on handles on the left side of the turret. Three others from their squad hold the turret on the right side.

Once the tank commander confirms all infantry are mounted, he gives orders to his driver for the tank to move out. Diesel smoke pours out the back of the T-72 as the tank rolls through the thick mud in the driving rainstorm. Other tanks are moving all around them, splattering mud and diesel smoke on soldiers desperately trying to hold on to the turrets' wet and slippery metal handles. As the tanks maneuver through the trees, rain pounds heavily on the men's faces while tree branches swat their bodies.

On top of the tank's turret are two hatches, one for the loader and one for the tank commander. The loader's is closed while the commander's is open. Bobbing up and down is the commander's head and shoulders. He wears a black tanker's helmet that covers his head and ears. A microphone is attached to his helmet, and Miro sees him speaking, but with all the noise he can't make out a single word. Miro and Niko grasp each other's hands. They know they are about to enter hell. Both wonder if death is close at hand. Miro thinks of Julianna, and wonders if she will ever know what happened to him if he dies. Little does he know that she will be in the same battle.

# 15: HELL

**SOAKING WET AND TRYING** to locate the VJ tanks attacking from Skenderaj, Travis again grabs his radio handset and contacts the A-10s circling the battlefield at 10,000 feet. While he waits for the pilots to answer, Julianna receives the VJ tank coordinates over her radio from Josif. His KLA brigade is just a mile north of the attacking tanks, but his scouts are forward enough to hear, then see, the T-72s rolling through the woods toward Malisheve.

Julianna passes the coordinates to Travis, and he repeats the locations twice to the A-10 pilots. The American A-10s fire Maverick missiles at the VJ tanks using a longer stand-off range so they will not have to fly over the Zoos' coverage. The biggest challenge for the A-10 pilots is hitting tanks zigzagging through the forest.

★★★

Miro, Niko, and Bog desperately clutch the turret railings. Miro spots Vuk and two other platoon members on the other side of the turret struggling to hold on as well. Miro's hands are wet and numb. He barely feels them. Even worse, his arms are becoming rubbery, the beginning symptoms of muscle failure.

Tanks are all around them, attacking at a blistering pace through the stormy woods. Most of the trees are small enough for the tanks to simply run over, but for the larger trees, the tanks must make dramatic and sudden turns, making it even more difficult for the riders to not lose their hold.

Miro witnesses a man lose his grip on another tank and fall backwards, disappearing into the dark, rainy gloom. The man has little chance of survival with the mass of tanks still to follow. Most of the tank drivers have their hatches closed and are just following tanks in front of them. They will not see a man in the mud.

As Miro tries to see what happened to the man, he loses his grip when the tank turret suddenly turns, looking for any enemy on their flank. Niko grabs Miro's assault pack and barely prevents his fall. Niko realizes Miro is about to get caught in the tank's track as it rolls along the support rollers' giant steel wheels. If that happens, he will be trapped in the track and crushed to death as his body passes over the tank's wheels and sprocket.

Flailing wildly, mud splatters Miro from head to feet. Bog sees the situation and grabs hold of Niko's other arm. As Niko pulls on Miro, who is weighed down with mud, with every ounce of strength he can muster Miro rises just enough to grab the top of the tank's hull, then climb back up to the turret railings.

A trees explodes. A tank about a hundred meters away explodes as well, vaporizing the infantry on top as the turret blows off the hull. The concussion from the explosion knocks VJ soldiers off five other tanks, including theirs. They fall helplessly into the quagmire five feet below. A missile rocks another tank approximately fifty meters away, again blowing the turret off the tank and setting off the tank's ammunition.

Hundreds of VJ soldiers jump from their tanks and land in the deep mud, where they desperately try to avoid the armored onslaught clanking toward them.

Sprawled where they fell, Miro, Niko, Vuk, Bog and the others are caked with mud and shaken, but otherwise okay. Picking themselves up out of the sucking quagmire, Bog and Vuk slog through the lightning strikes, rain and mud to consolidate the platoon together while tanks pass by, zigzagging through the woods to avoid missiles.

More missiles sail through the woods at supersonic speeds, shattering trees, destroying tanks, and killing soldiers trying to assault through knee-deep mud. Exploding tanks kill the crews instantly, while infantry on the ground are horribly maimed by large steel and wooden shrapnel and splinters that cut through flesh and bodies like sharp spears.

Bog and Vuk bravely endure explosions, concussions, shrapnel, splintered trees and upcoming tanks to move the platoon out of the kill zone. They lead as many as they can find up a steep, slippery ridge. Clawing on all fours, the men grab anything they can with their muddy, slippery hands: tree roots, rocks, and each other. Anything to keep them from slipping down the steep slope.

Niko is first to reach the top, and he assists Miro and others by holding onto a tree branch and grabbing their arms. Just below them the tracks on VJ tanks still squeak by, throwing mud and debris into the air while their diesel engines roar against the background of explosions and fire. Some of the men shake uncontrollably in the early stages of hypothermia.

Two fast-movers scream in low behind the VJ route of movement. The heat from their afterburners is intense as they ascend rapidly over Bog's platoon. The members of the platoon lie flat and cover their faces as the unbearable heat from the jet's afterburners scorches their clothes. They are the lucky ones. A tremendous explosion ignites behind them, incinerating the following tanks and troops.

Napalm.

The back third of Colonel Cadikovski's VJ brigade burns. VJ soldiers wriggle in pain as they whither in the inferno. The rain has no effect. Nothing will. Napalm even burns underwater. Out of mercy, VJ soldiers who survived the strike shoot their own flaming dancers. Swirling winds blow the sickening sweet smells of burning flesh and cordite around the battlefield.

At the front of Colonel Cadikovski's VJ brigade the attack continues unabated. Like mad hornets after their nest is disturbed, the lead VJ tanks spot the KLA Pristina brigade directly ahead and fire canister antipersonnel rounds from their main guns. Each tank round contains thousands of swarming steel flechettes, shredding anything within 500 meters.

★★★

From his position, Travis does not hear or see the fast-movers over the loud den of the battle. He does see the napalm and massive explosions in the woods as tanks and men are incinerated. The napalm smell reaches them as A-10s return to the battlefield firing Maverick missiles with a ferocity neither Travis nor John has ever witnessed before. John counts at least a dozen tanks destroyed.

Josif changes his brigade's mission. Instead of counterattacking any VJ force leaving Malisheve in pursuit of the Pristina brigade, he orders his troops to counterattack into the flank of Cadikovski's tank and infantry attack en route to Malisheve. If he can't stop Cadikovski's brigade, the KLA Pristina brigade will be trapped between two VJ forces: Cadikovski's brigade and the VJ forces from Malisheve.

Josif radios Julianna to relay a message to the NATO officers: *Stop all NATO air attacks. 3rd KLA Brigade attacking VJ tank force on their northern flank. Intent is to destroy VJ force, then link up with KLA Pristina brigade vicinity Malisheve.*

John relays Josif's cease-fire order to the air controller ten miles from the battlefield. He throws the hand mic down and takes a look around him. There they all sit in the driving rain, Travis and Julianna each with a knee on the ground and their AKs at the ready, Trooper guarding the prisoners, who are lying prone, and Prek a few yards away on the radio with his platoon.

Prek peers back at John with a concerned look. He low-crawls to John and speaks loudly in his ear. "My men just radioed that unknown forces were approaching them." Prek points toward the direction the forces are coming. "What do you want my platoon to do?"

"Ambush them, then break contact and have your men join us here. Once everyone is here we will displace quickly to the west."

★★★

The new VJ company commander spots Bog and his men on top of the slippery slope. He clumsily ascends the slope with assistance from Bog. The new commander bends over with his hands on his knees, retching up acidic smoke from the napalm strike. Still gasping for air he yells in Bog's ear to wait until all the tanks pass, then descend the slope and continue the attack.

The last few remaining tanks pass their position at the same time the air strikes stop. The company commander slides down first, followed by Bog and his men. Miro and Niko keep close together, sliding down the slope with their AKs at the ready. Once the entire platoon is off the hill, they link up with the rest of the company. The company commander leads the way behind the last tanks, ordering his three platoons to spread apart, but not too far that they lose each other in the rain and fog.

Other companies emerge from the battlefield, and a large infantry formation slogs forward. It is impossible to keep up with the tanks. Soon the tanks are out of sight from the following infantrymen. That's a big tactical mistake.

Niko trips and falls face-first in the mud. Miro rushes to help him up and notices he tripped over what is left of a KLA soldier, killed by tank fire. Soon they witness an uncountable number of bodies, mostly KLA, lying in muddy pools of blood and water. Up ahead they hear the tanks firing their machine guns instead of main guns, indicating the KLA are amongst the steel monsters. The tanks need their infantry, who are far behind.

Miro and Niko, with hundreds of other VJ infantry, cautiously advance by walking in the tank tracks. Explosions start again. RPGs rip through the tanks ahead.

Miro, his face white as a ghost, gives Niko a distant gaze. They are walking right into a maelstrom, and the company commander just keeps walking.

★★★

As John, Travis and Julianna monitor the battle, Prek's men suddenly open up with their AKs. A VJ infantry patrol has by chance made contact with their defensive perimeter. The VJ drop and try to see who fired at them. Because of the fog and rain, each side has yet to see the size of the other even though they are just meters away from each other. Prek's men quickly assault the VJ soldiers lying on the soggy ground. It instantly becomes a close-in fight, each man trying to gain an advantage over another in the hard rain and slippery mud. Prek's soldiers all carry brass-knuckle trench knives for situations just like this. The carnage is quick and bloody, with the KLA special forces making quick work of the unlucky VJ conscripts. Prek sprints back and gives the NATO officers the contact report.

"Be prepared to withdraw on a second's notice," John tells everyone. "There is a good chance more VJ forces will arrive."

Julianna receives another report over the radio. Josif asserts his brigade is counterattacking into the VJ flank, destroying the remaining tanks and VJ infantry. Afterwards, they will link up with the KLA Pristina brigade vicinity Malisheve.

***

Miro and Niko can only see a few feet in front of them as they drag forward in the thick mud through the rain and darkness. Their legs are weighed down with thick, gooey mud, making every step a herculean task.

Miro tightly grasps his AK with what is left of his strength. Niko, in much better physical shape than Miro, tries his best to see through the deluge and lead the way. Although the company commander issues instructions to keep each other in sight, most of the time they can't see any other members of the platoon. Niko grabs Miro's shoulder and motions him to take a knee. Listening intently, Niko points to their left. After a few moments Miro hears it also—men yelling in Albanian.

Miro mumbles, "What the—"

Niko yells as loud as he can to the company commander, "*It's a counterattack, probably by an entire KLA brigade!*"

Within seconds AK-47 fire from their flank is deafening, growing in intensity as the fight edges nearer.

The commander screams from the top of his lungs, "Stop and form a defensive perimeter!"

Miro and Niko fall in the prone with others lying next to them, waiting—to see who will show. Every trigger in the company has a shaky, cold, shriveled finger on it. What they soon make out is the outline of men firing AKs, but they cannot distinguish for sure who they are.

"It's VJ soldiers running toward us, don't fire!" screams the commander.

Some VJ soldiers fall while others stop for a split second to blindly fire behind them. What is left of the force joins the defensive perimeter.

Silence. Pouring rain, putrid smells, men crying out for their mothers.

Nothing happens.

KLA are yelling at each other. Some of the voices are in front, and other voices come from all around the circular perimeter.

Silence again. Miro pisses his pants and doesn't even realize it.

The company commander stands up. "Come and get us, you Albanian terrorists!"

Bullets rip through his chest, and the captain falls on his back with his boots still stuck in the mud. The KLA throw smoke grenades outside the VJ perimeter, producing flame and smoke, obscuring their attack.

VJ soldiers keep their heads down as bullets zip through the wet night air like swarming bees. The KLA circulate outside the entire VJ defensive perimeter. Every man in the perimeter anticipates a quick death. They pray it will be painless.

Julianna says Joseph reports his men are in heavy contact with the VJ infantry behind the tanks, routing them and causing widespread confusion.

Julianna stares at the NATO officers. "He thinks the conditions are set for the KLA Pristina brigade to break out of the Malisheve area and link up with his men."

Welcome news for Travis and John, but they now feel useless.

John announces, "Nothing we can do with air; both KLA brigades are too close to the VJ."

Travis, listening to the battle's moving cascade of explosions, takes Trooper for a recon of their exit route, making sure no one is setting an ambush for them.

Julianna loses contact with Josif. She keeps calling him, but with no response.

Miro aims his AK in the general direction of the attacking KLA. This is the moment of truth. How could Julianna ever forgive him if he kills her people? All those around him are firing on full auto toward the charging KLA.

Miro can't do it. He decides he would rather die than kill a Kosovar. The KLA are almost at the VJ defensive perimeter, some dropping from VJ bullets and grenades. The KLA are upon them; they have pierced the perimeter. Hundreds of men are engaged in a dark, rainy, bloody brawl. The fighting is desperate. The rain falls harder than ever. Lightning strikes all around them, echoing through the hills.

Paralyzed with fear, Miro hugs the ground and pulls two dead men on top of him, feigning death. He listens to others around him fighting for their lives; gouging, punching, jabbing, stabbing, even firing at times. Most terrifying are their screams. Most of the dying call for their mothers.

At one point, Miro hears his name; he recognizes Niko's voice. Miro instinctively pushes the bodies off and looks around. He sees Niko in a struggle with a large, bearded KLA soldier. Interlocked, they fall and roll in the mud, trying to overcome each other with punches and other combative moves. Miro raises his AK, selects single shot, and tries to aim at the KLA soldier just feet away. He is shaking like a leaf. Every time he is about to pull the trigger, they change position, causing Miro to hesitate for fear of hitting Niko.

★★★

Prek's KLA special forces platoon has decimated an entire VJ patrol of about thirty men, but more VJ are heard coming through the woods. Prek and his men run through the dark night as fast as they can to link up with the NATO officers. Prek glances at the prisoners and asks the NATO officers what to do with them. John and Travis are hesitant. They can't take them now, and letting them loose might mean compromising John's and Travis's covert operation in Kosovo. The soaking-wet prisoners on the verge of hypothermia cry for their mothers.

"Prek, take their weapons and just leave them here. No one is going to believe them anyway," John finally orders.

The prisoners are left behind while the rest withdraw back toward the awaiting cars five miles distant. Running at full speed, it doesn't take long to outpace the VJ to their rear. John stops and grabs Travis. "Listen."

"Listen to what?" Travis belts out while breathing hard.

"Exactly. No one is following us any longer."

"Shit, they must be calling artillery . . . *incoming!*"

Whistling artillery rounds land all around them. Huge mounds of mud erupt, followed by exploding fiery flashes that rise high into balls of black smoke. Deadly steel splinters cut through the air. Trees upturn. Two of Prek's men are blown apart by one round.

Miro throws his AK down and jumps on the back of the large, hairy KLA soldier, wrapping his arms around the man's neck and bending his head back. All three are now rolling in the mud. Niko is finally able to break free from the man's grasp and jumps up, looking for a weapon. He grabs an AK from the mud and tells Miro to let loose of the man's head. The huge KLA soldier lies in the mud, exhausted and breathing like there is not enough oxygen to fill his lungs. He looks at Niko, then turns his attention to Miro.

In Albanian, the KLA soldier gasps, "I know you. You're Miroslav Cadikovski, the one who dated Josif Shala's sister. You are also the brother of the murderer Colonel Cadikovski!"

Miro is shocked, looking at the KLA soldier in disbelief. He remembers the mud-caked man as Josif's deputy and friend,

Bekim Mali. Miro kneels down and clutches Mali by the collar, asking in a desperate voice in Albanian, "Is Julianna okay? Where is she?"

The mud-laden Bekim Mali spits in Miro's face.

Miro grabs Niko's AK from his hands. He takes several steps forward and points the AK at Mali's head.

"I will blow your fucking head off right now unless you tell me the truth about Julianna."

Bekim Mali climbs to his feet and walks up close to Miro. In a condescending voice, just inches from Miro's AK, he says, "She is fighting as a hero in our brigade. She will hate you for fighting in the VJ. She is out here somewhere. I am sure she would kill you if given the chance."

He confidently swats Miro's AK aside and slogs through the mud back toward the KLA lines. Miro is stunned. He takes a knee and stares at Niko. With the rain falling hard on his head, Miro collapses in the mud and bawls.

The fighting is now further away, toward the tanks. All around are dead and wounded, both KLA and VJ. Miro, still crying, crawls on all fours toward a body several feet away. It is their squad leader, Vuk, lying faceup with his eyes open. Miro places his muddy hand on Vuk's face and closes his eyes. He knows he is a coward. Had he not feigned death, Vuk might still be alive. Vuk, the one who took care of Miro when he joined the squad. The one who taught him everything he knows about being a soldier. Miro gazes up through his watery eyes and sees Niko standing over Vuk, staring at him with a blank expression.

Niko takes a strong hold of Miro's arm and bellows, "Come on, we need to find Bog and the others. There is still KLA around here. Let's go."

★★★

Travis and John know the only way out of artillery fire is to run. Travis yells as loud as he can for everyone to disperse and rally back at the cars. John, Travis and Julianna run together, this time with Trooper leading the way. Within minutes they are out of the artillery. Eventually they all congregate back at their hidden vehicles. Travis examines everyone; all are nervous, wet, muddy and breathing heavily. Prek accounts for all of his men. Two dead and three wounded. They hurry into the cars and speed away into the darkness. Behind them the battle continues unabated, as if it has a life of its own.

# 16: THE MORNING AFTER

**AFTER THE KLA WITHDREW** late the evening before, Miro and Niko caught a VJ transport truck into Malisheve and collapsed on cots designated as their platoon billets. After just three hours of hard sleep Miro feels someone violently shaking him. At first Miro doesn't even know where he is. After about twenty seconds of being a tossed around like a rag doll he wakes up enough to see a man over him. The sergeant, who Miro doesn't recognize, tells him to eat a quick breakfast and return to the billets to prepare for *the ceremony*.

"The ceremony?"

The sergeant quickly departs without answering. Miro has no idea what the sergeant is talking about, but he has to get his sore body up and move. He prods Niko awake, and they put on their nasty uniforms from the night before and lumber to the mess hall. Neither Miro nor Niko are particularly hungry, but they manage to wade through a long line of servers slapping heaps of steaming-hot food on their metal trays. The mess hall seating is almost at full capacity. They sit where they can, in a corner. Niko starts eating eggs while Miro just stares at his food.

Spitting out pieces of egg Niko asks, "Who's left?"

"I saw Bog come in with us late last night. He seems to be okay. But I haven't seen him since."

"No one else?"

"Not that I know of. I guess that good indoc training helped us survive."

Niko ignores the bad joke. "So, tell me more about Julianna."

Miro jerks his head up, staring at Niko's dirty face. "Why do you need to know more about her?"

"Come on, man, you know—the big ape that you got off my back last night. You and him were talking about her."

"Oh yeah, it's all coming back to me now. Well, you know, she is my wife."

"So, I ask again, who is she?"

"The lady in the car."

"Ah, that's right, I know, you did have a lady in the car with you."

"She is Albanian," Miro whispers across the table.

"And your wife is in the KLA?" Niko blurts out.

"Shhh! Keep it down, man. You want to get us killed after all we have been through?"

"Keep it down? You mean to tell me almost our whole fucking platoon gets wiped out last night by the KLA and you're married to one?"

Miro covers his face with his hands and speaks softly through his fingers. "It's not that simple. We dated before the war. Hell, we have known each other our entire lives."

"No wonder you didn't shoot last night," Niko mused. "At first I just thought you really were a coward."

Miro stands with the tray full of food shaking in his hands. He takes a quick look at Niko.

"I am."

Upon returning to the billets, Miro spots a fresh uniform on his bunk. Niko is just seconds behind him.

"A ceremony. How fucking odd is that?" Miro says loud enough for Niko to hear.

"No uniform on my bunk."

"Who holds a ceremony just hours after a terrible battle?"

Taking his shirt off, Niko responds, "A dictator who wants to show the world what a great victory his army just won . . . even if it wasn't a victory."

Miro snatches up the uniform and heads toward the showers. On the way out of the door he turns around. "All I know is a lot of people died yesterday. Who knows who . . . won. I guess whoever killed more of the other."

Niko is too tired to shower and collapses back in his bunk.

So many soldiers have already showered the hot water is long gone. Miro steps into the stark, cold water anyway, and it wakes him up faster than the mess hall coffee. Washing away the caked-on blood and mud, he still wonders about the ceremony. He towels off, dresses in his new uniform, and opens the lid to a rubbish bin outside the door to toss his old uniform. The stench inside the bin turns him green.

Miro manages to shuffle back to the platoon billet just as the sergeant that shook him awake earlier arrives. He follows the sergeant and a group of other VJ soldiers who are also clothed in fresh VJ uniforms.

Minutes later Miro is standing at attention in front of a large formation. Just above the formation is the rising, torturous morning sun that blinds him and makes his head pound. He already has a headache from dehydration and lack of sleep. Everything on his body hurts—as if he has been through combat.

The blinding sun is eventually blotted out as his brother steps directly in front of him, staring at him with a stone face.

A VJ soldier standing a few meters away announces into a mic, "For heroism on the field of battle, Private Miroslav Cadikovski displayed exemplary courage and dedication in the campaign to free Kosovo. He is now awarded the Serbian Meritorious Medal for Gallantry."

Colonel Cadikovski pins a large colorful medal on Miro's new uniform shirt. He gives Miro a fake smile; his lips are slightly upturned, but nothing else on his face moves. Miro salutes him and his brother salutes back, then turns toward the next soldier in line.

Miro has no idea who the other soldiers are in line, but each one is from a different company in the brigade. The colonel repeats the same process five or six more times. Miro isn't counting. He struggles to remain standing as the sun grows hotter.

At the end of the medal presentation, Colonel Cadikovski gives a patriotic speech that seems to last indefinitely. Miro pays no attention to what his brother is rambling on about, and doesn't care.

"We have defeated the terrorists and the war will soon be won—*blah, blah, blah*. If it were not for these young heroes—*blah, blah, blah*."

Miro just wants the ceremony to be over. Unfortunately, after Colonel Cadikovski is finished, the Malisheve colonel of the secret police makes a boisterous speech about *soldiers doing their duty*. His words are laced with extremist racial views Miro recognizes from the German SS's goal in WWII: extermination of the undesirables. The secret police colonel's shrieking voice only makes the pounding in Miro's head grow worse. His back is also cramping. Bad. Miro bends his knees to just remain upright.

Finally, the ceremony abruptly ends with the secret police speaker slamming his fist on the lectern. A somewhat unenthusiastic cheer arises from the VJ formations, probably because the ceremony is finally over.

Miro relaxes and takes a knee.

"Congratulations, comrade!" Miro gazes up and realizes the compliment is for him. A smiling officer stands erect before him, and many other VJ officers in his brother's brigade are lining up. Miro knows they are shaking his hand only because they desire to ingratiate themselves to his brother.

✹✹✹

Niko is in deep sleep when he is yanked up by his T-shirt. The first thing he sees through his swollen eyes is an old, fat sergeant's ugly face.

"Let's go, Private. You have been handpicked by me!"

"What for, Sergeant?"

"*Body duty*, what else?"

Niko puts his shirt back on, pulls out his AK from under his cot, and limps to a truck outside his barracks. He climbs into the truck's bed with many other discontented VJ soldiers. He takes a seat on the hard wooden slats as the truck lumbers out a side gate of Malisheve. They are on their way back to the previous evening's muddy hell. Along the way Niko observes other details picking up the dead along the route.

A few civilians are among the dead also, but local Kosovars attend to them. Some of those bodies are children used by the VJ as human shields around the Zoos. The sight of disfigured and bloody children floods tears down his face.

The detail heads along the exact route he and Miro took just hours before. When the truck stops, they jump off the back and gather around the sergeant, awaiting instructions.

The old sergeant has all but one stack their AKs. They would rotate being on guard, the *least worst* job of the day. The sergeant reeks of alcohol. For this job, he needs it. He slurs instructions on how to complete the grisly task.

"Gather all weapons and throw them in a pile. Working in two-man teams, pitch the dead KLA in piles to burn later. Put our dead in body bags, and be sure to search them first so you can tag them by unit and name. Bring 'em to the back of the truck, and two of you can stack them from front to rear. Any questions? Good, now get to work. Oh, by the way, the KLA will be out here picking up their wounded and dead. Leave them be and they will leave us alone, I think."

Niko and the other unlucky wretches begin the dreadful work. Each body takes two men to lift, but the VJ dead are more difficult, as they must be bagged and heaved on the bed of the truck. Two soldiers in the truck's bed drag and stack the bodies. When the truck is full, one of them hauls the VJ bodies back to Malisheve with the old sergeant in the passenger's seat. The soldiers are supposed to keep working while the truck is gone but of course rest instead. The truck then returns after delivering its carcasses to men in the penal battalion.

Niko and another soldier meander about searching for the dead. It doesn't take long to find clusters. Some are cut in half, or without limbs or heads. Other bodies, mainly VJ, lie dead without any sign of trauma—just strangely dead. All have the beginnings of rigor mortis. Niko figures they must have died from concussion, as some of them have dried blood in their ears. Often parts of VJ bodies are thrown into one body bag, impossible to determine who they belong to. The penal battalion boys can sort that out. KLA parts are just thrown into a burn pile.

The old sergeant sits on a rock wall smoking cigarettes, occasionally growling at one of the privates for some petty reason. After several hours in the hot summer sun and the growing stench of the dead, Niko and the others are spent. Several have collapsed already.

The sergeant finally gives the men a few minutes to fill their canteens and rest in the shade. The only water available is from a large military leister bag, a large canvas bag of water heated by the sun. After filling his canteen, Niko staggers toward a twisted and broken tree for shade. He falls in the grass. The hot water from his plastic canteen tastes terrible, but it is all he has to keep from becoming too dehydrated. He figures he will likely puke it up, but he drinks it anyway.

Lying on his back and looking at the splintered tree limbs reaching for the sky, Niko is a broken man. His head still pounds, and the putrid smells turn his stomach. Up comes breakfast mixed with hot water.

While struggling to sit up, he hears a few cheers and clapping in the distance. He washes his hands, then pours the remaining water from his plastic canteen on his head. His pulls his wet hair back through his fingers and tries to maintain his balance. It really doesn't matter to him who is cheering or why, but he assumes it is the mysterious ceremony Miro is attending. He lies back down again, and is on the cusp of falling asleep when the sergeant blows a shrill whistle and bellows a string of obscenities at the soldiers to get back to work. Niko rolls over on his side and pulls himself up. First on his knees, then upright. Grabbing a shattered branch to keep his balance, he hobbles back out into the heat to search for more stiffs covered in flies.

✱✱✱

The last person in line to congratulate Miro is a large sergeant who is not there to shake his hand. Instead, he grabs Miro by the collar, a common way VJ sergeants greet privates.

"Let's go, Cadikovski."

The sergeant lets go and turns away. Miro, stunned, follows close behind the sergeant at a brisk pace. The sergeant makes his way through the crowd by pushing soldiers aside. The startled soldiers notice who he is and shy quickly away. Miro tries his best to keep up but simply can't. After several blocks they arrive at the city municipal building, now the brigade headquarters as indicated by the unit flag posted at the front entrance. The sergeant turns around and is irritated he must wait for Miro to catch up.

"You fucking move like pond water!"

"Yes, Sergeant," Miro blurts out, finding enough energy to jog a few steps.

Walking inside Miro recognizes the scene from his brother's headquarters in Skenderaj. Officers shout loudly while radio operators are busy relaying information.

"That's your desk and radio, Corporal."

The sergeant points to the last radio in a long line of radios. The soldier manning the radio wears headphones and hastily takes notes from incoming transmissions. Miro looks at the sergeant.

"That's right, you're a corporal now. Pin 'em on your shoulder straps."

The sergeant tosses corporal insignia on the desk. The radio operator on duty briefly glances at Miro without emotion.

As Miro picks up the insignia the sergeant continues, "You will be doing the same thing that soldier is doing, monitoring the command net. Your duty hours start tomorrow from 0700 to 1900. The battalion commanders will be sending reports for you to write down. You give the reports to me." The sergeant gives Miro a hard stare. "Can you handle that?"

Miro swallows loudly while standing at attention. "Yes, Sergeant, I am a trained signalman."

The sergeant cracks a slight smile and struts away, stopping momentarily to say something to another corporal. That corporal immediately approaches Miro and motions him to follow. They walk out the back of the building toward a large green canvas tent. The corporal flips a canvas flap aside and walks in. Miro, following behind, observes a dozen cots, six on each side.

"This one will be yours. Go get your stuff and bring it over now. You never know when we might deploy."

Miro says nothing as the corporal abruptly turns and

hurriedly leaves. Miro gazes at the cot and around the inside of the tent. He tosses his AK and cap on the cot. *That's my stuff*, he jokes to himself, as all his gear is spread from Skenderaj to Malisheve.

He sits on his cot. "My brother's radioman. Shit."

Miro takes the red-and-white bracelet from his front right trouser pocket. He remembers the spring day when Julianna gave it to him. They hadn't a clue at that time what would happen. Miro's eyes well up as he wonders about what could have been. A life with Julianna, without war. A peaceful life in a comfortable house where they could raise a family and be happy. Because of Bekim Mali, he knows she is with Josif in his brigade—that is, if she survived last night's battle. If alive, Bekim Mali most likely told her he is in the VJ.

He puts the bracelet back in his pocket and goes to find Niko. Maybe he is still asleep in his cot. Since he was not selected to get a fake medal, surely they let him get some rest.

✯✯✯

Niko painfully retraces his steps from the night before. He knows the exact spot where he wrestled Bekim Mali, and the location of most of his dead platoon. First he has more dead to pick up along the way.

Niko thinks it interesting, albeit in a morbid way, how the bodies often lie close together in clumps. Some are even on top of each other, while others lie in rows. It is apparent many wounded have died from their wounds, bleeding out before any medical attention could arrive. Some have a bullet holes while others have been blown apart. Some bodies are burned to a crisp, making identification impossible. One VJ lies on his back with his hands covering his face. Niko pulls the man's stiff hands away, and there is a gaping wound where his eyes once were. He reaches inside the man's pockets and finds pictures of him and his family, along with his required VJ passbook that possesses the necessary information to fill out the tag.

"Come on, grab his arms," bellows Niko's body-duty partner, who is laying out the body bag and about to grab the man's feet. Niko lifts the dead man's rigid, bloody arms. They manage to stuff the corpse into the clear plastic bag. Niko zips it up while his work partner reads the passbook and writes the man's name and unit on a tag. They each take an end of the heavy, limp bag and drag it to the truck. As they struggle to lift the bag onto the bed of the truck, the old sergeant points to a destroyed tank a few hundred meters away.

He mumbles, "See if there are any guys in that tank. Come on, hurry." The sergeant pulls a flask from his back pocket and takes a long swig. "Aaaaahhhh."

Niko turns and examines the steel beast. He and his partner slog in the mud toward the tank, each hoping the other will climb on up and look to see what is inside the turret. Niko notices the driver's hatch in front of the tank is closed. He stumbles to the rear of the beast and painfully climbs on the tank near the left rear sprocket, placing his right foot through a metal loop and grabbing a handle on top of the back deck, pulling himself up. His partner remains on the ground, using a hand to shade his eyes as he studies Niko's movements.

Niko looks down at him with resentment. He despises cowards who hold back and wait for others to do the dirty work. On top of the rear deck Niko cautiously takes a few steps toward the turret and stops. The top hatch is open, and he hopes the crew abandoned the tank to escape attacking aircraft.

The flies circling in and out of the tank commander's hatch is a bad indicator. He dreads to look inside. The situation reminds him of a time he came upon a car accident and forced himself to look inside the crumpled car. What he saw has haunted him for years.

Then the smell hits him. It is worse than the smell of charred bodies. Niko takes a few more steps and gazes into the dark tank. It appears a KLA hand grenade did its deadly work. Niko turns his head and vomits the hot water he just drank. The water runs down the turret onto the ground, near the feet of his partner. His partner gags and runs away.

The sergeant takes another swig and shouts, "Get back there, you fucking pussy, and get them out, damn it!"

Inside the tank it is hot and reeks of decaying flesh. The bodies are blown hollow, with the organs and limbs separated from the torsos. Skin and organs are plastered to the inside of the turret. Large green flies are crawling everywhere. Niko holds his breath but dry heaves as he throws the appendages out of the commander's hatch. His partner squeamishly takes the parts from the ground and throws them inside one of four body bags. Not sure who the limbs and heads belong to, he randomly throws body parts in each bag. He figures as long as there is one head per bag, then it won't really matter.

Niko shouts, "I need you up here to help lift the torsos out."

His partner reluctantly climbs on the tank. Niko, now inside the turret, shoves up through the commander's hatch what is left of the carcasses. His partner throws them to the ground and jumps down as fast as he can. When Niko finally climbs out of the turret, he sits on top of the tank. He is soaked in blood with flies buzzing around and on him. He pulls his canteen out, but it is bone dry. Climbing down, Niko loses his grip and falls onto the ground, landing awkwardly in the bloody mud.

His partner sits him up against a road wheel and pours hot water from his own canteen on Niko's head.

The sergeant watches it all. He bellows, "BREAK," and goes to find cold water for everyone.

The sergeant comes back with several buckets of cold water. The detail refills their canteens and uses the rest to wash their hands and faces. Within minutes they are again slogging through the mud, first checking the dead for signs of life, then going through the routine of recovering the remains.

Niko spots his platoon sergeant, Bog. He is alive and on his knees staring at Vuk Kovac. So many tears are flowing from Bog's eyes he doesn't notice anyone around him. Niko soon finds out seeing people dead you don't know is sobering, but seeing one's dead friends is worse than terrible. Each has ghastly wounds and lies where he died, most next to dead KLA.

Niko notices a KLA body move. At first he thinks he is hallucinating. He splashes through the mud to get a better look. A young KLA soldier lies half buried in the wet mud. He is barely breathing. His eyes are wide open; terror holds him. He opens his mouth to speak, but nothing comes out. He looks at Niko in terror and trembles.

Niko calls his partner and the sergeant over. Niko and his partner use their hands to scoop the mud while the sergeant yanks on the boy's arms and shirt. Once they get the terrified KLA soldier out of the mud, they can't find any serious wounds. The KLA soldier mutters he was smashed last night by a tank. His left arm aches and it is difficult to breathe. He pleads for water. Niko shares his canteen, now full of cold water. The KLA soldier drinks it so fast he coughs some up.

Niko notices the old sergeant has a large revolver on his hip, and fears he might shoot the young man. Instead, the old sergeant helps clean the mud off their wretched prisoner.

As the KLA soldier gulps water, a jeep pulls up, the brakes squeal, and three men in blue uniforms jump out.

"What are you doing with that terrorist?" one of them angrily shouts. "Get out of the way and continue your work."

"The special police," the old sergeant says under his breath to Niko and his partner. "Just ignore them."

Niko, his partner, and the sergeant continue to help the

terrified young KLA soldier. One of the police, apparently the senior one, approaches brandishing a pistol. The other two have machine pistols and stand erect behind him. The policeman aims his pistol at the KLA soldier, and places his finger on the trigger.

The old sergeant steps in front of the prisoner, staring at the policeman pointing the pistol. "I don't kill prisoners. Never have and never will. I have been in the Yugoslav Army for twenty-nine years and I have always upheld what is right, and killing prisoners ain't."

Niko looks at the sergeant with admiration. He really didn't expect the tough old vodka-drinking NCO to be so morally forthright.

"Get out of the way, old man."

The sergeant stands firm.

"In WWII the Serbs fought the Nazis, and you are no Serb. You are a fucking Nazi. *You get the hell out of here.*"

The policeman aims his pistol at the sergeant's face. The sergeant stands perfectly still, not wavering.

Platoon Sergeant Bogdana "Bog" Komazec appears behind the police.

Bog snarls at the three special police, "Turn around and stand over there," pointing his AK toward a line of trees.

Niko grabs an AK from the mud and snaps, "I recommend you listen to my platoon sergeant."

All three special police drop their weapons and stand where Bog instructed.

"You don't remember me," Bog says, "but I remember you. You are Marin's men, the ones who murder innocent men, women and children. One of those innocent men was my platoon leader, Lieutenant Buha."

"Listen, buddy, we never even met Colonel Marin. Sure, he is our boss, but we are the little guys, just like you all. We are all on the same side, remember?"

"I am on Lieutenant Buha's side," Bog slowly states with a damning stare.

"It would be too easy just to shoot them," interrupts the old sergeant.

Bog smiles and nods approval, giving his AK to the older man.

Niko is still holding his AK on the special police.

The old sergeant takes the AK by the end of the barrel and heaves it as far as he can. The weapon lands in the mud with a loud *plop*. He takes out a large knife from his boot and runs his right index finger across the blade.

"Always carry a sharp knife, my father said."

Bog orders the secret police to take off their shoes. Then he instructs Niko and his partner to take out the men's shoelaces and bind them at their wrists and ankles.

"Who wants to go first?" asks the old sergeant with a chilling smile. He reminds Niko of an excited kid on Christmas morning.

Niko runs up to the KLA prisoner, pulls him up by his arms and yells, "Get in the police jeep and get out of here. *Go now!*"

The KLA soldier hurries into the driver's seat, starts it up, jams it into gear, and speeds away.

Bog stares at Niko and his work partner steadfastly. "You guys get out of here. You were never here. *You understand?*"

Both of them don't hesitate. They run through the sucking mud, hoping to melt away in another work detail without detection.

Bog wants to stay for the show but has other business. He grins at the old sergeant and leaves him and his sharp knife with his secret police prisoners. Bog walks away. After about fifty meters Bog hears blood-curdling screams behind him.

The sounds embolden him into action. Bog climbs into the first truck he can find, cranking up the engine. Several VJ soldiers on another body duty detail yell that the truck is only half full. He ignores them and drives back toward the city at full speed. Bog smiles.

Entering the side gate into Malisheve, Bog slows the truck, looking for Marin's special police headquarters. He can't find the headquarters, but he does see a group of special police standing together further down the street.

He kicks the truck into third gear to get a better look. Getting closer, he observes a group of KLA prisoners being lined up by the special police, obviously for execution. Bog steps on the gas. The truck pours black smoke from the exhaust. Forty, forty-five, then fifty kilometers an hour.

The group of six special police look up just as the truck is about ten meters away. Bog slams into them, throwing some aside while running over others. Bog laughs like a madman, having the time of his life. He stomps on the brakes and turns the steering wheel as hard as he can to spin the truck around.

The KLA prisoners scatter while Bog downshifts and floors the gas, running over three more police. One turns around and manages to fire his machine pistol through the truck's windshield before being run over. Glass shatters around the truck's cab, and a single bullet pierces Bogs neck. Thick red blood squirts out like a garden hose turned on full, and Bog loses control of the truck.

It crashes into the side of a brick building. Bricks fall on top of the truck's hood and cab as Bog opens his door using his left hand. His tries to stop the bleeding with his right hand, but with little effect. He knows he is about to die, and he falls out of the truck and onto the hard concrete. Feeling his life slipping away, he feels warm and peaceful. He sees a wonderful bright light; then he is looking down at himself dead on the street.

# 17: WITHDRAWAL FROM SKANDERBEG

**AS THE SUN RISES,** an entourage of cars take back roads and goat trails to return to Skanderbeg. Truckloads of soaked and wounded KLA are also arriving. The barn is a makeshift hospital. Out of one car, Julianna appears, cold and wet. She darts to the barn to help with the wounded. Travis and John, still dripping wet and muddy, slog inside the house looking for Josif.

Loud voices resonate from the plans room. John peeps inside and observes some of Josif's officers engaged in a heated argument, waving their arms and occasionally pointing at a map. One of them notices John, and the man points toward the barn. Travis and John drop their filthy gear on the floor, then slop back outside with their weapons. Trooper is still outside in the light rain. He trots toward the barn, somehow sensing where Travis is heading.

Trooper enters the barn ahead of Travis and John. The dog canters to Julianna, who is trying to hold up a bloody and beleaguered Josif. The NATO officers search him for wounds. All appear somewhat minor, consisting of many hand, face and leg abrasions.

The biggest problem is that Josif is despondent. Julianna cannot hold him any longer, and he sinks against the wall and onto the floor. He mumbles in Albanian as Julianna tries to console him. Travis takes a knee beside them, lifts Josif's head, and gently pours water into his mouth and over his face. Trooper lies by Travis's side while John rambles about looking at the casualties.

John stares as a doctor operates on a KLA soldier's abdomen under a single hanging bulb. Elsewhere, KLA soldiers are doing their best to provide first aid and comfort to the injured. Many lie on the ground moaning in pain, while others are unconscious. Eight VJ prisoners huddle up against a wall, all exhausted and soaked to the bone. They sit or lie on the dirt, some wounded but all miserable. A solemn KLA soldier watches them, holding an AK-47.

The rain finally stops, and throughout the morning KLA soldiers continue to wander in, many carrying wounded comrades. Travis and John each get under one of Josif's arms and walk him back in the house and into the bath. As he comes to, Josif slowly and painfully undresses. Julianna gives him a bath and cleans his wounds. The NATO officers clean up and put on dry uniforms, their only extra set.

Travis dries off Trooper and feeds him, much to the dog's delight.

There is little time for rest. As Josif's cognitive abilities return, he orders a KLA meeting in three hours. Until then, confusion reigns. Nearly half of Josif's brigade has not yet made it back, and from those that have, half are casualties.

Three hours later the meeting takes place in the planning room. There is wide disagreement on the results of the Malisheve battle. Josif, more coherent now and trying to make sense of it all, asks his subordinate commanders about their casualties. More have come back in the last few hours, and now about 70 percent are accounted back; however, only 40 percent are fit to fight.

Josif scans the room. "Anyone know how the Pristina brigade made out?"

"They are about fifty percent combat effective," a liaison who was with the Pristina brigade answers.

"How much damage did the Pristina brigade and our troops do to the VJ?"

No one answers at first. No one really knows.

Bekim finally pipes up. "Well, the VJ didn't have the strength or courage to pursue us or the Pristina brigade after we withdrew."

Travis whispers in John's ear as they walk to the front of the room next to Josif.

"NATO intelligence estimates around thirty tanks, twelve BMPs and two Zoos destroyed."

"And VJ casualties?" Josif asks.

"NATO has no idea, really. That's because the VJ have no idea. NATO signal intelligence has listened in on their brigade's nets, but it is all confusion. They keep talking about some sort of ceremony."

Josif continues as the NATO officers sit in the front row. Trooper lies by Travis.

"Our mission was to destroy the VJ brigade occupying Malisheve. The Pristina brigade was to attack, then suddenly pull out to cause the VJ brigade to pursue them out of the city and into the open. NATO air was to hit them, then we would attack to destroy what was left."

One of Josif's subordinate commanders asks what happened.

"Coming from Skenderaj, Colonel Dragan Cadikovski's Guards Brigade counterattacked. They wanted to trap the Pristina brigade as they attacked Malisheve. Instead of helping the Pristina brigade, we had to strike Cadikovski's brigade with NATO air, then storm their flank."

Travis adds, "Cadikovski's brigade took most of the casualties. The VJ brigade that was coming out of Malisheve retreated when they saw what happened to Cadikovski's guys. They just ran back into town instead of pursuing the Pristina brigade any further."

John stands and faces Josif, then the other occupants of the meeting. "The KLA has not liberated Malisheve, no matter how much damage was done to the VJ. The problem is, Serbia can call on more conscripts, while the KLA can only be reinforced from Albania. Josif, what to do next for your brigade is the big question. Stay and fight in your brigade area, or move south toward the Mount Pastrik area to consolidate with other KLA forces?"

Josif stands in silence, looking down with his hand over his mouth in deep thought. "I am going to radio General Gashi at Mount Pastrik. Take a fifteen-minute break."

Josif radios General Gashi and gives him the rundown on the battle, then asks for guidance. After a long discussion with Gashi, Josif resolves to remain in his area and fight on. Gashi thinks Josif's men will contribute more by continuously attacking the VJ's logistics tail as the enemy moves west and south.

Josif returns to the meeting and issues orders to evacuate his headquarters and break up into smaller platoon-size units of about fifteen to twenty men each.

"Each platoon will be constantly on the move, going from one point to another, and striking whenever they can—as long as they can. The wounded will be carried along, and left at Kosovar homes for further care. Prek's KLA special forces platoon will continue with the NATO officers. All movement will be on foot to avoid VJ checkpoints and controlled roads."

Travis and John feverishly prepare for movement south, stuffing their packs with food and ammunition. Anything that is not absolutely necessary is burned or cast aside. Travis has a difficult time concentrating; he is preoccupied thinking about Julianna. He fears he will never see her again. And worse yet, if she stays with Josif, she might not survive the war.

After a bath, Julianna is again in the barn attending to the wounded. She hears the evacuation orders being passed around amongst the soldiers. While cleaning a wound, she is in a quandary as to who to go with, her brother or Travis. If she stays with Josif, chances are she will never see Travis again. If she goes with Travis, she can make herself useful as an interpreter. Either way, finding Miro seems to be an impossible task.

Travis tells John he will be right back, then hustles toward the barn in search for Julianna. John looks up without saying a word. He knows where Travis is going. Entering the barn, Travis first notices the VJ prisoners are gone. He spots Julianna across the way tending to a KLA soldier. He approaches her by carefully walking around the wounded. She doesn't notice him and he stands behind her, not sure what to say.

"We have to go south now."

Surprised to hear Travis's voice, Julianna hastily turns around, noticing his long, pale face. They affectionately gaze into each other's eyes. Travis is speechless. Julianna calmly turns back to her patient to ensure she has finished wrapping his wound. She puts two more pieces of white adhesive tape on his bandages. She puts her right hand on the man's forehead, wishing him well. The KLA soldier smiles back, then dozes off.

Julianna takes Travis's hand and walks him quickly out the door and behind the barn. Travis embraces her; her fast heartbeat feels like it is thumping inside of him. Both have watery eyes.

"What are we going to do? I don't know if I can leave my brother."

"Listen, Julianna, we must get away from here. Everyone is evacuating, including Josif. This place will be crawling with VJ in hours. *Come with us.*"

Julianna cannot respond. The dilemma is tearing her apart.

Travis urgently pleads, "You know we cannot be apart. You must come with me to the west, and let Josif command guerilla operations here."

"I can't leave my brother again." Tears stream down her face.

AK-47 fire rips through the air, startling them, on the other side of the barn. Julianna waits while Travis grabs his AK leaning against the barn and runs toward the sound.

Bekim Mali is holding an AK-47. Crumpled VJ bodies lie motionless in a pool of blood, their hands and feet bound with rope. Julianna can't wait any longer and follows to see what has happened.

One of the VJ moves slightly. Half of his face is shot off, including his chin and one eye. Begging for mercy while coughing up blood, he looks up at Bekim Mali with his one good eye. Mali pulls out a large knife, eyeing the young VJ prisoner. Travis rushes forward and punches Mali in the face. His large frame hits the ground with a loud thud. Travis takes Mali's AK, and points it at him lying on the ground. Bekim Mali doesn't even look at Travis, but instead notices Julianna run up.

He stares a hole through her, and in Albanian he boastfully states, "I saw your Serb friend Miroslav Cadikovski last night. He is a VJ and a coward. As I was killing other VJ, he hid in the mud playing dead. But don't worry about your Serb friend, my dear, he is okay. You have me to thank because I did not kill him."

Mali laughs as he stands up, spitting at the dying VJ, who is now drowning in his own blood, and walks away.

Julianna is stunned. Bekim Mali is no one to trust, but she suspects there must be some element of truth to his story. She believes he has at least seen Miro. Unable to fully grasp the situation and come to terms with her feelings, she studies the faces of the dead VJ to see if one is Miro.

Travis tries to open the airway of the dying VJ as Trooper checks for any sign of life amongst the other executed prisoners. Julianna, aghast at the terrible sight of brains and blood splattered on the ground, looks away and covers her face with quivering hands. She doesn't know it, but the dying VJ Travis is trying to save is the young VJ who pointed his AK at her but did not shoot as she left the gas station. He had shown mercy in a merciless war.

Travis attempts multiple times to open his airway, but the situation is hopeless. Travis feels the soldier's warm blood soaking his pants and dripping down onto his boots. He gently lays the dead man down, wondering if he has family back in Serbia.

*Why would it matter at this point?* Travis wonders. The Serbs started all of this—the killing, the destruction, the misery. But, after all, chances are he was just a conscript, forced into the VJ, and, like everyone else, just wanting to survive. Travis thinks about looking through the dead man's pockets to find pictures or some type of identification. Maybe he can notify his family, but would it really matter? The man's family will already be notified, just not about the details of his death, and the details are best left alone.

Travis hears someone behind him. He turns his head and spots Prek and some of his soldiers running up; they stop to stare at the bloody scene. Travis looks at Prek without saying a word. Prek says something in Albanian to his soldiers. They immediately chase after Mali and tackle him to the ground. They beat and kick him savagely. Travis recognizes it as a type of KLA justice; he has seen it before when KLA soldiers step out of line. There are no written rules in the KLA, but there are rules, and Bekim Mali has clearly broken them.

Travis puts his arm around Julianna, and they walk slowly toward the house with Trooper close behind. He has no idea what Mali said to Julianna, but he does know he needs to find John and escape Skanderbeg.

Just as they enter the house, Josif runs out. John, close behind, jumps on Josif and grabs his front collar.

"What the hell do you think you are doing? You can't kill prisoners in cold blood!"

Josif pushes John away and shouts, "What do you think we should do with them, leave them here so they can tell their criminal Serb brothers about us? Besides, do you know what they do to us?"

John snaps back, "That does not matter. What matters is that you are becoming just like them. Do you know what will happen if the international community hears about this? NATO could withdraw total support. Then where would you be?"

Grabbing his ruck, John sees Travis and shouts, "Let's get the hell out of here, now!"

Josif takes several steps forward and violently clutches John by the collar this time, pulling him face-to-face. "You don't live here. Your family does not live here. You will someday get to go home to a nice peaceful life with your family in England and forget all about us. About us here left to be slaughtered by the Serbs. But you will still have your NATO book of rules. Rules that state that prisoners should be treated well, fed and comforted."

John tosses Josif aside and they stare coldly at each other. Everyone remains silent for several uncomfortable seconds.

Miles away a NATO bombing run shakes the ground. Almost as if the bombing were a cue, John looks at Travis, taps him on the arm and says, "Let's go."

John whips past Julianna without taking note of her presence. Travis stares at Josif, then back at Julianna, waiting for her response. She stands motionless, unable to speak. Travis grabs his ruck and efficiently tosses it onto his back as he has done hundreds of times before.

Julianna suddenly rips into her brother with unmitigated rage. Travis is thunderstruck, even though he has no idea what she is saying. She slaps Josif on the face, hard, then runs past Josif into the house.

Josif is motionless, his hand touching his face. He turns and gazes at the dead prisoners, then sees Mali still getting the shit kicked out of him by Prek and his men about a hundred meters away.

Before Josif can say anything John yells, "Come on, Prek. That's good enough. We need to get going."

Julianna appears out of the house in her full kit, including pack and AK. The NATO officers, Julianna, and Prek with his platoon move out with Trooper in the lead.

Josif slowly wanders up to Mali groaning on the ground.

"You dumbass, you should have waited until everyone moved out of this place, especially the NATO officers. Why in the hell did you shoot them, anyway? They were all just young conscripts!"

Mali sits up, bleeding from the mouth. "They still would have told everything about us, and I don't know about you, but I'm not taking chances at this point."

"This is the last time I am covering for you. I don't want to be wanted as a war criminal when all this is over."

# 18: INFANTRYMEN NO MORE

**NIKO AND HIS PARTNER** join another work detail without detection. No one cares who the others are; everyone just wants to get the gruesome work over with. The two interlopers continue to tag along with the work crew after the sun goes down, and ride with them back to Malisheve.

Once the men jump off the back of the truck, Niko stands closely behind his partner. He still doesn't know his name. But that is okay, because his partner doesn't know his name either.

"Not a word of what happened today. Nobody. Got it?"

His partner turns, and the two men shake hands and depart. What has happened has happened.

Niko limps to the billets and finds everyone gone, including Miro. He finds only a note from Miro on his cot.

*Meet me at the communications center at brigade headquarters.*

*Miro*

Niko mumbles to himself, "Is this some kind of joke? At the brigade headquarters!"

Hot food and a shower appeal to him more. It is dark, and he shuffles to the mess hall and gets a heaping plate of something that looks like corned beef hash. It is nice and hot. He spoons it down in seconds, then leaves while chewing on a piece of bread.

Niko enters the showers and just stands under lukewarm water with his uniform on. The water on his face feels like ecstasy. Eventually he starts taking pieces of his uniform off until he is nude. He wrings his uniform out, then washes all sorts of putrid smells off his body. Several other soldiers enter but pay him no attention. Niko puts his uniform back on, and with his wet boots squeaking he makes his way back to the platoon billet. Still, no one is there. He undresses and lays his aching body down. Within seconds he is having nightmares.

Miro enters the billet in the middle of the night and finds Niko flailing about in his sleep, yelling something incomprehensible. Miro tries to calm him down by gently holding his left arm. Niko becomes unglued and attacks Miro with a madman's rage. Miro falls backwards but lands on another cot.

Niko comes to his senses. He looks around the dark room, trying to determine where he is.

"Niko, Niko, this is Miro. We're in the billets at Malisheve. Everything is okay . . . for once."

Niko sits on his cot and runs his hands over his head, groaning but saying nothing. Miro sits on the cot next to him.

"Man, where in the hell were you yesterday? I looked everywhere."

Niko raises his head slightly. "I was on body detail."

"What's that?"

"Those of us that were not picked to attend the ceremony were volunteered to pick up dead bodies. I saw the worst shit . . . I saw our platoon . . . dead. Except for Bog, I did see him. He was out there with what was left of his company, which was nothing."

"How did you and Bog survive the fight?"

"I really don't know about Bog, but I was squatting by your side the entire time. Most KLA just ran past me, except for the big ape you got off my back. By the way, what was this big fucking ceremony all about?"

"Some propaganda ploy to draw the press to the ceremony rather than to the battlefield. The ceremony honored those that fought for victory for Malisheve."

"Well, I can tell you there were just as many VJ dead out there as KLA."

"Yes, but the ceremony proved to the press that we are still in control of Malisheve."

"So, why were you tagged to go? Because of your brother?"

"I suppose so." Miro stands and turns on the billet's lights. He pulls a medal out of his pocket and holds it up. "He pinned a medal on my chest for bravery. How fucked up is that? He just wants to show the world his younger brother is a warrior just like him."

Niko stands, stretches, and puts his damp clothes on. "So, where is Bog?"

"Dead."

"I just saw him yesterday afternoon out there by his dead soldiers. Did he off himself?"

"Kinda. He stole a truck meant for hauling bodies and ran over seven secret police who were about to execute KLA prisoners."

"Payback for his lieutenant's murder, I guess."

"Yep, but he was shot and killed."

"Well, so he did commit suicide, just in his own special way. God bless him." Niko sits back on his cot, and once again the two men are facing each other.

"It was bad out there, wasn't it? I mean, out on the battlefield. It must have been terrible."

"The worst day of my life," Niko says slowly as he looks to the floor.

"You are the only one left in the platoon. I have been assigned to the communications center for the headquarters."

"Oh, so that's what your note was about."

"You need to work there with me; otherwise, they will just reassign you to another infantry outfit."

"What exactly do you do?"

"I am a radioman. I take reports and give them to the officers. I only work half a day, from seven to seven. We have our own billet. We get paid and are issued new uniforms."

Miro takes a bottle of vodka from a paper bag. "You see, I got paid!"

"Damn, I need some of that."

Niko and Miro pass the bottle back and forth, discussing what men do when they drink: women. Miro dominates the discussion talking about Julianna. He is more optimistic about his future with her.

"The war will be over soon. We are over halfway to Albania, and the KLA just lost a lot of men. I think Julianna is safe." With a look of panic, he adds, "You didn't see any dead female KLA, did you?"

"No, none. Just men."

Miro smiles in relief and takes another drink.

"I will introduce you to the sergeant after we get some sleep. He is kinda big and mean, but is actually a good guy at heart. He takes care of his soldiers. I will ask him if you can join the gang."

Niko takes another hit of vodka and lies down. Miro does the same.

A couple of hours later the sun rises, and the light wakes Miro. More cautious about waking Niko this time, Miro kicks the cot and jumps back. Niko still slumbers. Miro heads out to the communications center. Outside he sees the sergeant chewing on some soldier that needs to shave. When he is done with the soldier, Miro approaches him.

"Good morning, Sergeant."

"Who says it is?"

"I do."

"Why? What have you done now?"

"I have found a comrade of mine from the last battle. He and I are the only survivors from our platoon. He is an outstanding soldier who we can really use, but we need to grab him now before he is sent to another line platoon."

"What is so fucking outstanding about him? I wanna meet him."

The sergeant walks away looking for more privates to chew on. Miro runs to his billet and takes a clean uniform, boots and toiletries from the supply locker. He runs to wake up Niko. When he enters, Niko is talking in his sleep—something about apologizing to someone. This time Miro kicks the end bed rail as hard as he can.

Niko lifts his head.

"What the fuck?"

Miro throws the uniform and other things from the supply locker on Niko's bed.

"Go clean yourself up. Be sure to shave. I will be back in twenty minutes. I want to introduce you to the sergeant."

Niko rolls off the cot and grumbles. He picks up his AK, pistol, and walks back to the showers. He takes another shower, this time using soap. The water is hot, and he wishes he had more time to just stand under the showerhead. He shaves, dons his new uniform, and walks back to meet Miro.

Miro is already waiting on him, impatiently.

"Come on, let's go. Be sure to sling your AK correctly over your shoulder; the sergeant is pretty picky about small shit."

Miro leads Niko to the communications center. They enter the building and the sergeant is checking radio reports for accuracy.

"Excuse me, Sergeant."

The sergeant stares at Miro with disdain for interrupting.

"This better be important."

"I brought over the soldier I was discussing with you earlier."

The sergeant grunts, throws down the reports and looks around.

"Let's go outside. It's too busy in here."

Niko stands outside at attention. The sergeant approaches him and stares him down from six inches away.

"You know how to read and write?"

"Yes, Sergeant, very well."

"You know how to operate a radio and take reports?"

"Yes, Sergeant, I already know."

"If you come with us, you will need to help with security. How good are you with that AK-47?"

"I qualified expert, Sergeant."

"And that big fucking revolver in your waist belt?"

"I took it off a dead Kosovar, Sergeant."

"A tough guy, huh?"

"Yes, Sergeant."

"Ha! So, tell me why you are so fucking special?"

"I could kick your ass if need be."

Miro has a cow. He closes his eyes waiting for the explosion. The sergeant explodes all right, but into a boisterous laugh. He shakes Niko's hand.

"Welcome aboard. If you do well, you might be a corporal someday like your friend Corporal Cadikovski. He will show you around. A couple of rules first: Do not speak inside the communications center unless spoken to; do not fuck off; and tell me first about anything important."

"Yes, Sergeant!"

"Oh, and by the way, anytime you feel like kicking my ass, just let me know."

The sergeant slaps Niko on the back and goes back inside the communications center, still chuckling.

Miro stands like a statue, stunned.

"Well, aren't you going to show me around?" Niko asks.

Miro snaps out of his trance and guides Niko throughout the center and the billet. It is Miro's time to go on duty, so Niko pulls up a chair and sits next to him. Miro goes over all the reports and shows him how to post the information and report to the officer on duty. Miro is amazed how fast Niko catches on. He is already familiar with all the different communication configurations and can operate the radios like a pro.

Colonel Cadikovski enters the communications center. He notices Niko's presence right away.

"Where have I seen you before?"

Niko jumps to attention. "In Skenderaj, sir. When our American lieutenant was executed by Colonel Marin, I helped Corporal Cadikovski take his body back to our platoon area."

"Oh yes, now I remember. So, you are the only soldier alive from that platoon except Miro."

"Yes sir. I work here in the communications center now."

Colonel Cadikovski picks up the hand microphone and makes a net call to all of his subordinate commanders.

"Commanders, I have an urgent update on our situation. Our scouts tracked the retreating KLA back to the main headquarters of Josif Shala, the KLA 3rd Brigade commander. We raided their headquarters, finding eight murdered VJ comrades. With my authority, our soldiers killed everyone at the KLA headquarters, including Shala and his deputy, Bekim Mali. It appears most of the KLA had already vacated the headquarters before our troops arrived, which tells me they have gone back to operating in small units. Keep your eyes open for ambushes or hit-and-run attacks. That is all, out."

Colonel Cadikovski slowly places the mic down and stares at Miro. Miro is pale and trembling, unable to respond to an incoming radio call.

Niko lightly touches Miro's shoulder. "Take a break. I will take over for now."

Miro runs outside in a panic. The smoke from burning piles of KLA bodies drifts into the city. Bloated bodies filled with gas pop when the fire ignites them.

# 19: NAPALM IN THE NIGHT

**FIVE HOURS AFTER LEAVING** Skanderbeg, Prek holds down the button on his brick handheld radio. He quietly says, "Moving."

Tucking his brick radio away on his belt, he turns and motions with his right arm to move forward. Men appear from behind bushes and the long grass, cautiously taking one step at a time. Each of Prek's men is camouflaged with dark-green face paint and vegetation. It is just getting dark, and they are trying to get close to a large group of men speaking Serbian. Once they come within 200 meters of the voices, Prek has his soldiers low-crawl.

After about twenty minutes, his forward scouts call Prek on the brick. "Militia, looks like Arkan and other militia groups have consolidated. About two hundred."

Prek immediately orders his men to pull back.

Travis feeds Trooper and watches Julianna as she keeps a lookout. He chuckles to himself. Even in camo she is beautiful. He is thrilled she came along with him instead of staying with Josif. He isn't sure why she came. Maybe because she was so appalled with the prisoner executions, or maybe it was because she wanted to be with him. Maybe both.

John is on the radio giving Brigadier Basil Lewis, his SAS commander, a situation report on their plan to link up with the KLA commander, Arsim Gashi, at Mount Pastrik. Unfortunately for John, Lewis is doing most of the talking. At one point John quits listening and covers the mouthpiece on the mic.

"Seems the brigadier isn't too happy with our progress," he says, smiling at Travis.

Travis jokingly responds, "What are they going to do to us, send us to Kosovo?"

Prek makes it back to report to the NATO officers after dark. It has been a long hot day, and finally the temperatures start to slowly drop. A gentle wind begins to blow from the south. Even so, Prek is sweating heavily.

"Arkan's men along with other militias. About two hundred."

Prek pulls out his map and uses a twig and pen flashlight to indicate exactly where the militias are.

Travis gazes at John without saying a word for a few seconds, then states, "Well, now is the opportunity to make your brigadier a little happier."

John takes his cap off and rubs his sweaty face. He waits a few seconds before talking.

"We can either go around them or call in a strike and hope some aircraft are available."

Travis quickly responds, "I am tired of being the prey. It's time to become the predator. Anyway, that's our job, isn't it?"

John is slightly taken aback. He sits motionless for a few minutes thinking over their situation.

Travis surveys Julianna, knowing she has heard the discussion. She looks back at him in the dark and comments, "They are the ones that destroyed my village and murdered innocent people. They are merging with other militias to continue their murderous attacks toward the southwest, probably Peje. They must be stopped."

John is still thinking over their options. "Why is Peje important?"

Prek crawls over when he hears John's question.

"Peje is a small village, but it is the largest route coming in from Albania. It is how the KLA gets supplies and replacements. Otherwise the supplies must be brought through steep mountain passes."

"So you think these militia are going to seize Peje and hold it until the VJ arrive?"

"Yes," Prek and Julianna respond in unison.

Travis picks up the mic and calls for close air support.

"Thunder, this is Razorback, request CAS, over."

"Razorback, this is Thunder, send over."

Travis quickly looks at John in case he has any objections or comments.

"Two hundred troops in the open at . . ." Travis carefully studies the map and sends the coordinates.

All is quiet for about twenty minutes. No one knows for sure if the air support will arrive. Still, no one says a word. Everyone is thinking the same thing. How long to wait?

A few minutes later, everyone jerks when a different voice crackles over the hand mic's earpiece.

"Razorback, this is Grim Reaper, keep your head down, over."

Travis acknowledges and sends word among Prek's men to lie flat on the ground.

The hand mic comes alive again. "Thirty seconds, over."

"Roger," Travis replies.

Travis grasps Julianna's arm and makes her lie on the ground by Trooper. Then he lies on top of them both.

Seconds pass.

Silence. Nothing.

Suddenly two jets scream over them at over 400 miles per hour.

Canisters full of napalm tumble, and the ensuing explosions turn night into day as huge flames envelope the forest where the militias have gathered.

Everyone lying down takes a knee to see the results. Men appear from the firestorm as napalm drips from the trees. Prek's snipers make quick work of them. Down they go, one by one.

Travis picks up the mic. "Target, over."

The heat is intense. John jumps up and gives orders for all of them to move out. Prek gathers his men, and in a matter of a few minutes they resume their movement to the south. Even though all of them are bone tired from humping all day, movement at night is the best for concealment, and survival.

Through the night they move. Within thirty minutes the sound of the fire is gone, and a red glow in the sky is all that remains. Twice they hear air strikes echo in the distance. Someone or something is being bombed.

Trooper constantly snoops about while Travis and Julianna follow Prek and his men in a single file. John, in the rear, keeps an eye out for anyone following. During the first break John reports the air strike to his brigadier, who has to be awakened by a watch officer. John takes delight in reporting the strike, but more so in waking up the brigadier.

At daylight they stop near a swift-running waterway to clean up and get some rest. Prek puts out security while the others remove their boots and jump in the cold, refreshing water. Trooper beats everyone by way of a running belly flop. Travis lies on the bank to wash his face. Before long he is in the water looking for Julianna.

It doesn't take long. He spots her downstream smiling at him. As he rides the current down to her, he notices she is topless while washing her long black hair. Her nipples are just above the waterline. Just as he reaches her, she submerges, then in a few seconds jumps up and kisses Travis passionately. She grabs his trousers and takes them off under the water. Travis embraces her nude body. He gets excited. She kisses and licks him on his face.

Travis suddenly hears laughter, and wakes up to notice Trooper licking his face. He is still on the river's bank, having dosed off. John and Julianna laugh at seeing him sprawled out in the mud. Travis can't turn over. It would be too embarrassing.

Later, Julianna sits by Travis. She studies him, still giggling.

"What were you dreaming about? You were really rolling in the mud."

Travis smiles back. "I can't remember."

"You lie!" Julianna laughs as she takes off everything but her panties and bra, then jumps into the water. After a long night's hot walk, she enjoys the cool running water, dunking her head several times before looking at Travis and shouting, "Come on, jump in. Besides, you're filthy!"

Trooper jumps in after her and Travis follows. It is nothing like his dream, but it is still fun splashing and playing with Julianna and Trooper.

After their swim Travis and Julianna sit in the early-morning sun drying off while John is on the radio reporting their situation. For once things are quiet and peaceful. The birds sing while Trooper snores. They have been up for two days. John thinks about his family. Travis thinks about Julianna. Julianna thinks about Bekim Mali seeing Miro in the VJ.

By midafternoon all are awake and moving about to prepare for another night's movement through the woods. Prek joins them as they eat bread and study the map. John looks up and gazes at everyone with a stern look.

"It will be a difficult hump through hilly and rocky terrain, but if we make good time, Mount Pastrik will be in sight by morning."

Prek goes to brief his men while the NATO officers and Julianna wait for nightfall.

Julianna asks the NATO officers in a serious tone, "Why are

you guys here? Did you volunteer or did some general make you come?"

Travis quickly responds, "*DE OPPRESSO LIBER. To Free the Oppressed.* That's what I do."

Travis and John glance at each other, unsure what else to say. John speaks in a low voice, "We volunteered."

"Why?" Julianna demands.

Travis explains, "We were both in Bosnia before this, but we did different jobs. I was a company commander operating with my soldiers in the woods around Sarajevo. We called in air strikes on hidden Serb artillery. I also had snipers that targeted Serb snipers shooting at civilians in the city. It was serious work, to be sure, and I expected something similar in Kosovo."

John takes a picture out of his shirt pocket and looks at it. He hands it to Julianna. In the photo John has a bright-red dress uniform on, and his wife and three children pose with him in front of a Christmas tree. Julianna loves it, asking their names and where they live. She has never heard of Yorkshire, but that doesn't matter to her. She knows they are waiting and worrying for him.

Julianna focuses on Travis. "And your family?"

Travis has a huge smile on his face. He bear-hugs Trooper.

"This is it. We go everywhere together. No one worries about me, and I am just a number to the Army."

John sarcastically states, "He actually likes this stuff."

"It's all I have ever known," Travis responds, this time without a smile.

"What are you going to do after this?" Julianna queries.

John merely holds up the photo.

Travis is silent. It is an awkward situation for him. To tell the truth, it includes leaving with Julianna back to Germany.

He finally responds, "I don't know. Wherever the Army sends me, I guess."

Julianna and John know he is holding something in.

Darkness arrives and movement begins. Just like the evening before, it is agonizingly slow going. Although rested, everyone is still sore. The straps of their heavy packs dig into their shoulders, and the AKs seem to be heavier than ever. They climb steep rocky hills and cross creeks. The hot sultry night makes them sweat, and mosquitos are everywhere.

A light rain falls at 0130 as they continue their trek toward their final destination: Mount Pastrik. At 0230 they halt to check their position. Travis, John, and Prek get under a poncho with the map and a red-lensed flashlight. Prek knows the area well, and is able to quickly determine their location. They are on course, but still have about three more hours to hump. They take the poncho off and they all sit silently in the rain. Listening. Just several more hours to go.

# 20: SOMEONE IS A TRAITOR

**LIKE A ZOMBIE, MIRO** shuffles to his cot and lies down. The news of Josif's death is bad enough, but chances are that Julianna was with him; Bekim Mali told him so during the Malisheve battle. She was everything to him. His love for her and hope for a happy future with Julianna was what kept him going day to day. Now she is almost certainly gone, probably brutally raped before being killed. She was his wife and his life. Nothing matters anymore. Nothing.

Niko covers for him at the communications center. He receives reports, logs them and updates the map on the wall concerning unit positions. A radio transmission comes in from a VJ patrol concerning a napalm strike on Serbian paramilitary forces. Over 200 dead, some shot but most burned to crisp. Niko gives the information to the sergeant, who immediately hands it to the watch officer. Niko plots the strike location on the map.

The watch officer sends a runner to find Colonel Cadikovski. A few minutes later he dashes in and reads the report and studies the strike location on the map.

"Dammit. What the . . ."

He sits and thinks about it.

"That's impossible. Those guys were supposed to be in tactical mode, dispersed so they had no resemblance to a unit formation. NATO surveillance wouldn't have been able to distinguish them as anything but civilians. Someone on the ground had to call in that strike."

The colonel stands back up and studies the map again.

"They were supposed to arrive at Peje today or tomorrow to hold it until a VJ unit arrives."

Colonel Marin bursts into the room.

"What's this I hear about a napalm strike on our paramilitary? They were to cleanse Peje. Who is responsible for this?"

Colonel Cadikovski ignores Marin's question.

"Someone is a traitor in your unit, Colonel Cadikovski. First one of your platoon sergeants kills my men with a truck. Another three of my men are found skinned alive and their jeep gone. Now this. NATO would not have known their location if someone didn't tip them off . . . from your brigade."

Colonel Cadikovski turns away from the map, facing Marin. His face is red, and veins bulge from his neck.

"The reason the platoon sergeant killed your men is because you executed his platoon leader. Your men were most likely skinned by the KLA, not by our soldiers. The fact that the jeep was stolen sure points to the KLA taking it, not us. Do you see it driving around here anywhere?"

"That still does not explain the napalm strike. It happened in your zone, so someone is relaying sensitive unit locations to NATO. Maybe someone in this communications room."

Marin looks at the radiomen and the officer on duty with a scowl.

"Your job, Colonel Cadikovski, is to weed out this traitor, or traitors. Anyone you suspect, hand them over to me for interrogation. That is an order."

"I'm not handing anyone over to you. Someone last night spotted the paramilitary forces and called in the strike to NATO. It is as simple as that. I wouldn't be surprised if the paramilitary heathens were drunk and loud."

"Like who? The KLA doesn't have the capability to call in strikes from NATO. At least not from there. Maybe from Mount Pastrik, but that is too far away. I still hold you fully accountable."

Marin stomps out of the building. Niko sits in silence, not looking at anyone. He remembers the rules from the sergeant.

"Where is Miro?" Colonel Cadikovski asks no one in particular.

"He is sick, probably on his cot, sir," Niko responds.

"I know why he is sick. That Albanian woman. Well, she is gone now," mutters the colonel to himself.

All radios light up. "FLASH TRAFFIC. FLASH TRAFFIC. A NATO jet has been hit by one of our SA-3s . . . The pilot parachuted before the aircraft crashed . . . Approximate location is . . ."

The captain plots the downed pilot's location and looks on the map for the nearest VJ unit. A scout platoon in three jeeps is within eight kilometers. Colonel Cadikovski radios the platoon leader and gives him instructions to capture and secure the pilot until relieved.

"Let me know when you have him, Lieutenant. And remember, I want him alive."

"Yes, comrade Colonel, moving now."

The colonel looks at his bulky sergeant.

"Go kick Miro out of bed and tell him to get his ass in here to help."

Niko volunteers. "I will get him, Sergeant."

# 21: DOWNED PILOT

**THE NATO OFFICERS AND** Prek sit silently in the rain. Listening. A jet screams past and bombs a target several kilometers away. The deafening noise seems to be right next to them. They watch the aircraft make a wide turn. An anti-aircraft missile is fired from just a few hundred meters away from them. The jet automatically fires hot flares to misguide the heat-seeking missile and makes violent evasive maneuvers, but the missile hits the aircraft's engine, causing a bright explosion against the dark sky.

They see the pilot eject straight upward from the aircraft's canopy. His quiet silhouette slowly parachutes down into the woods. John immediately reports the incident on the radio, while Travis grabs Prek by his shoulder.

"Get your men and let's go."

Luckily the pilot's tracker is operational. John stays in place with Julianna and five of Prek's men, and contacts a command-and-control aircraft. The aircraft receives the pilot's location and sends the coordinates to John, who then relays the site to Travis.

Trooper gallops at Travis's side as they double-time to try and reach the pilot before the enemy. It is the first time Travis and John have split apart, but it is necessary because of the high risk of a pilot rescue. If Travis is killed or captured, at least John will still be able to support the mission.

Sprinting through the dark forest, gripping an AK, and listening to John on the radio is not an easy task. Travis must stop several times to get his bearing on the map. The risk of running into VJ or militia forces is high, as he knows they will also be pursuing the pilot.

After half an hour Travis slows down. He hears loud voices and sees bright headlights from four vehicles. Inching closer he spots roving flashlights and loud radio transmissions. Travis looks through his starlight scope on his AK and observes what he fears the most: A VJ unit has captured the pilot and is throwing him in a vehicle.

Travis must make a decision: to take direct action against the VJ and risk getting the pilot killed, or try and determine where they are taking the pilot. He chooses the second option, betting that the VJ will likely take their prisoner to a close location and wait for their superiors.

As the jeeps depart, Travis and Prek's men run as fast as they can, but the jeeps are soon out of sight. Their only chance is to continue down the road to try and spot the location for the inevitable VJ linkup. If senior VJ authorities apprehend the pilot, then all bets are off.

Travis's hunch pays off. Within ten minutes they come upon a small building with the four jeeps parked outside. He calls the location to John, who sets up the rescue mission. To secure the site, Travis places Prek and his men around the building. Apparently there is no VJ security outside, at least not yet. He sits behind a tree with Prek and Trooper with the handset to his ear.

Within a few minutes John relays that the rescue bird is inbound with an ETA of fourteen minutes. Two VJ walk outside of the building to stand guard. The guards don't seem to be too worried, as they light cigarettes and joke loudly just outside the front door. That still complicates things.

Travis and Prek devise a quick plan. Once ETA is two minutes, Prek's snipers will take out the guards while Travis kicks the door open. Trooper will go in first, and attack the most dangerous man. Travis will then enter behind Trooper, closely followed by Prek and six men.

They sit in the stillness of the night and wait. The guards have quieted down but are still not paying attention. They casually walk around the small structure. John's voice breaks the silence.

"Five minutes out."

None of Prek's men report any approaching vehicles. Travis takes a deep breath. The tranquil night will soon be shattered with extreme violence.

"Four minutes out."

Travis grabs his AK tightly and starts to breathe deep. Anxiety racks his brain. He will have to think clearly when the time comes, and it's coming fast. More people are going to die.

"Three minutes out."

Travis says a silent prayer and rises to his feet. He, Trooper and Prek, followed by the rest of his men, walk slowly to the front of the house. Miraculously, both guards are in back of the building, probably drinking. Travis walks straight up to the front door.

"Two minutes out."

Travis twists the doorknob very slowly, and it turns. Trooper is hyper alert by his side, his nose touching the door. Prek and his men are crammed together.

A crack in the night rings out. Everyone jumps.

Travis assumes one of Prek's snipers has shot a guard walking toward the front. Chopper blades suddenly cut through the air.

Another shot from one of Prek's snipers indicates the other guard has met the same fate as the first.

Travis slings the door open, and Trooper bolts past him,

lunging at a VJ soldier pointing a pistol at the doorway. Trooper bites deeply into the man's right arm, causing him to drop the weapon.

Travis spots the pilot sitting on the floor and screams, "*Lay down!*"

He and Prek's men pile into the room packed with men and cigarette smoke. Travis sees terrified faces. Faces about to meet their doom, an image imprinted in his brain forever.

The sound of AKs on full automatic is deafening. The flashes from the guns' muzzles light up the room. Within seconds the VJ soldiers lie in pools of steaming blood.

The man Trooper attacked is dead. He was able to grab his boot knife with his left hand and stab Trooper through his tactical vest several times before he bled out through his right brachial artery.

Blood is splattered everywhere, on the floor and the walls. Travis, operating on pure adrenaline, glides through slippery blood and on top of bodies to reach the pilot, who is still lying prostrate on the floor. Travis quickly checks him for injuries.

The pilot just stares at Travis, unable to respond. Travis gets behind him and lifts him up under his arms. He drags the pilot over dead bodies and out the front door.

Outside a Blackhawk is landing, and men in black jump from the sides. Travis passes the pilot to the first man, then turns around to get Trooper. Within seconds he picks Trooper up and carries him to the chopper, where he kisses his snout and hands him to a man in the chopper.

Travis screams, "My dog needs emergency medical care now! He has stab wounds."

One of the men in black runs up to Travis and yells in his ear, "Higher orders you and Lieutenant Colonel Phillips to leave with us. They say it is just too dangerous for you guys to stay any longer."

Travis wasn't expecting this, and responds, "Phillips isn't here and I'm not going anywhere with you guys. I have a mission to complete here."

"Sir, it's an order. I am sorry."

Travis looks at the US Air Force special operator and says, "Tell the general I will see him in a couple of days."

The last words Travis hears spoken from the rescue team is, "You're going to be in deep shit, sir."

The helicopter leaves as fast as it landed. Within seconds all sight and sound of the aircraft has vanished. Silence returns to the night.

While Prek gets accountability of his men, Travis quickly calls John to report success. Prek gives Travis a thumbs-up, then points to Travis's neck. Travis didn't notice the wound on the left side of his neck, most likely from a ricochet inside the building. Prek slaps a white gauze bandage on him and wraps it with medical tape. Suddenly the noise of approaching vehicles is heard, and headlights beam through the trees. No order needs to be given; Travis and Prek's men run back toward John's location.

Travis spots John sitting on the ground and talking on the radio.

Julianna immediately notices Travis's bloody neck bandage and scurries to gather medical supplies from her pack. One of Prek's soldiers holds a flashlight while Julianna cleans Travis's wound with cold water and mild soap. She holds gauze tightly to his neck, but it is instantly saturated. The wound is still bleeding. She pours more water over his neck, pats it dry, then firmly presses a fresh bandage.

She gazes at Travis with sorrowful eyes. "It's not too bad, just a flesh wound. It looks like a bullet grazed you."

Travis feels her warm body against his as she tends to his wound. There is something comforting about her presence, her tenderness, and that she really cares about him.

After John is off the radio he crawls over to Travis, looking closely at his wound while Julianna continues to tightly hold the gauze.

"What happened, Trav?"

Travis nonchalantly says, "Oh, it's just a scratch. I'll be okay."

"Okay enough to continue tonight?"

"Sure, I can make it. We need to get the hell out of here before the VJ find us. They're gonna be *pissed* after the mess we left them back there."

John, confused, looks at Travis, thinking, *Why would the VJ get drunk after seeing the mess?*

# 22: NIKO

**NIKO FINDS MIRO PACING** back and forth inside their billet. His eyes have a scary, glossy look, and he is repeating something to himself that Niko can't understand.

"Sit down, Miro."

Miro hasn't even realized Niko is in the room. He keeps pacing and simmering in a petrified trance. Niko glowers and slaps Miro in the face. Miro plops on a cot holding his face with both hands.

"Listen to me, Miro. We don't have much time."

"What the fuck do you want? Julianna is gone. Do you not understand I have nothing now?"

"You have me, and a war to win."

"A war to win. Fuck off, Niko."

"Seriously, listen to me, Miro. Julianna wouldn't want you to quit. We have some serious business."

"What are you fucking talking about? What business?"

"I am an American, Miro."

Miro looks up at Niko. "What are you trying to say?"

"I am CIA."

Miro stands, finally taking stock of what Niko is saying. "This is no time for jokes, Niko."

Niko speaks in perfect English to Miro. "I am from Virginia. I grew up in Prizren, Kosovo, back in Yugoslavian times. My parents moved to America while I was in high school. I am a CIA field agent and was collecting information but waited too long to depart Kosovo. Well, you saw what happened to me when I tried to fake my way across the border into Montenegro."

Miro asks, "So you made it this far without the secret police figuring out who you are?

"Yep. Thank God. But Marin smells a rat, and it's me."

"So you killed the KLA during the battle? The very people you are here to support?"

"No, I haven't killed any KLA. I was just trying to get that big ape off me when you helped."

"What did you do during the battle then? You were shooting at someone. I could hear it."

Niko took the revolver out of his belt. "I shot six."

"Who, what six?"

"Of our platoon, including Vuk."

"You killed our comrades, our friends?"

"I had to do it."

Miro backs away from Niko. He grabs his AK leaning against his cot and points it at Niko. Shaking. Tearful. Terrified.

Niko points his pistol at Miro's face. Steady. Stern. Unafraid.

"Whose side are you on, Miro?

# 23: MOUNT PASTRIK

**JOHN SLOWLY RISES. "OKAY,** let's go. I'll tell Prek."

All night they weave through the dense forest, careful to stay away from roads. Travis's neck throbs, but his mind isn't on the pain. Losing Trooper is a gut punch. He silently cries, so much he can't wear night vision goggles. He uses his sleeve to dry his face.

The stakes are high. Travis could have left it all behind by jumping aboard the chopper with Trooper. But that isn't him, not at this point when the future of Kosovo will most likely be determined in a few days. Besides, he can't leave Julianna, nor John for that matter.

By daylight Mount Pastrik is in view. They gaze in wonder at the huge mountain. It is like a big mound of dirt that was dumped there long ago. It is mainly open rocky terrain with areas of dense trees. Erosion has caused deep crevices, or fissures, in places. A dirt road haphazardly spirals around the mound.

John kneels beside Travis while Julianna sits on the other side checking his neck wound. Artillery rounds land randomly on the mountain, shaking the ground and throwing dirt and rock in the air.

"Harassing fires—there isn't a VJ forward observer, at least not yet," John says. He continues in a matter-of-fact manner, "That was General Gashi I was speaking to last night when you came back to camp. I told him I would give him a ring once we were in sight of the mountain. He said he would send some scouts to guide us up."

"I guess that will be okay," Travis responds nonchalantly, preoccupied with Julianna as she examines his wound. She puts her hand on his once she is finished. Their eyes meet.

John picks up the hand mic and calls General Gashi. Within an hour, twenty KLA special forces suddenly arrive from a large mountain fissure. They are from a different platoon but the same company as Prek's platoon. Prek and his men are exultant. It has been months since they were together. Some are brought to tears, hugging their special forces brothers.

Once greetings are exchanged, they jog across open terrain to the base of the mountain. With KLA scouts leading the way, they move into a large crevice. John, Julianna and Travis are in the middle of the column as they negotiate the twisting and turning crevice, past hair-raising drop-offs and at times climbing almost vertical rock formations.

Artillery intensifies, pounding the mountain viciously. One round screams in and explodes right above the deep crevice. Dirt and rocks shower the column; everyone takes shelter the best they can.

They continue on, observing KLA soldiers in trenches and preparing fighting positions. Most of the positions are completed, including an overhead cover of logs and camouflage. Travis notices the positions are correctly emplaced. Each position covers the ground in front along with supplementary firing positions to provide interlocking fires with adjacent units.

The column continues at a snail's pace, climbing up difficult terrain. Sucking thin air. Legs cramping. AKs, RPGs and ammo heavy as hell.

Artillery suddenly stops. For a reason. The deep, rhythmic sound of chopper blades cuts through the air. Within seconds two huge heavily armed Yugoslavian Hind-D helicopters fly just above them. They travel at 140 miles per hour, so fast that it is nearly impossible to aim and fire before the flying tanks disappear at tree-top level. Machine guns, rockets and bombs annihilate KLA positions. The choppers are gone in minutes, flying to the other side of the mountain.

John screams to Prek, "Get me an RPG!"

Prek takes an RPG from one of his men and hands it to John. John grabs it, slings it over his back, and starts climbing out of the crevice. Prek takes an RPG and follows. John, with his tall and lean athletic body, easily climbs up the steep rocky slope. He reaches the top and looks for a good RPG ambush position. Prek points toward a couple of large boulders. They sprint to hide behind the massive rocks as the intense noise of chopper blades once again breaks the air.

The Hind-Ds are within sight, crushing KLA positions with bombs and machine guns. A few brave soldiers climb out of their firing positions to aim RPGs. The RPGs miss and explode near KLA positions further down the hill. The helicopters' tremendous speed evades everything except small arms fire, but the bullets merely bounce off the Hind-D's armor.

John turns toward Prek. "We must either get a flanking shot or a shot from above."

One Hind-D flies low while the other covers it by flying above and behind. They both make a long turning arc around the hill, looking for targets.

Travis is still in the crevice with Julianna and the rest of the KLA special forces soldiers. He calls Pine Tree, desperate for tactical air support. NATO won't send any type of fire support because the Hind-Ds are too close to friendly troops. The only friendly attack helicopters are with the American task force in

Albania, sitting idle without approval to engage the Hind-Ds.

The Hind-D pilots spot Travis and others in the crevice. The lower chopper flies into the crevice just above the ground. The other helicopter provides overwatch from behind. The Hind-D in the crevice begins to fire machine guns.

Just as the chopper passes, Prek runs from behind the boulder and fires his RPG broadside into the helicopter. The body of the craft explodes. The Hind-D falls directly into the crevice floor, burning. Prek smiles.

John aims his RPG into the flank of the second Hind-D. The round hits the tail boom, and the helicopter spins out of control, twirling around until exploding into a fireball further up the mountain.

John and Prek rush to the side of the crevice but cannot see anything below. Dirt, dust and debris fill the crevice from the Hind-D's enormous prop blasts. They climb down and into the dirty abyss. John and Prek feel their way, listening for voices, or moans. VJ artillery resumes with greater intensity. The sides of the crevice start to cave in.

# 24: CODE

**MIRO THROWS HIS AK-47** on his cot.

Niko stuffs his revolver in his belt and comments, "Okay, we need to work fast. Just listen for now. Get the keys to the communications truck and meet me there. While I am inside, lock me in until I tap the door. Keep the van in sight and tap on the door three times if they are coming to the van. We will be moving out before long, and the sergeant or another radioman may want to get it ready. So, again, three taps. Got it?"

"Yeah, I got it," Miro grumbles.

"Don't let me down, Miro. This is more important than you think."

Miro slings his AK and tries his best to gain his composure as he goes to check out the keys to the communications truck. He walks into the communications center and notices the sergeant is already moving some radios to put in the truck. He has the keys in his left hand.

"Let me take those keys, Sergeant, and I will open up for us."

"Thanks, Corporal." He throws the keys to Miro.

Miro casually walks out of the building but sprints to the truck.

"The sergeant is on his way to load some radios."

"Damn. Well, open up and let me in. Hurry."

Miro fumbles about trying to unlock the padlock. Once open, Niko climbs into the dark van, turns on the lights and fires up the large AM radio in the back corner. He tunes in to a specific frequency.

"Pine Tree, this is 404, over. Pine Tree, this is 404, come in, over."

A loud squeal blasts from the small speaker on the side of the radio, then, "This is Pine Tree, over."

"Pine Tree, prepare to copy, over."

"Send it, over."

Miro taps three times, sticks his head in the door and squawks, "The sergeant is coming."

"Let him in."

The sergeant climbs the three steps to get into the van and places a heavy radio down on the counter, then proceeds to hook it up. He hears something.

"What is that noise?"

Niko yells from the back, "I am testing the AM, Sergeant."

"Ah, good idea. We haven't used it yet and we may have to if we get out of range from division headquarters."

The sergeant steps back out of the van. Niko uses the hand mic to break squelch in a specific sequence. Because the transmission is in the clear, Niko sends a predetermined code. To anyone else listening, it would just sound like a bunch of squelching. He sits in his chair for almost fifteen minutes, concentrating on his code squelches.

"Okay, done."

Niko stands, sweating through his uniform. He looks at Miro with a smile.

"AM works like a charm at night. The reflection of AM waves from the ionosphere—skywave propagation—can reach for hundreds of miles."

Niko changes the channel on the AM and turns it off. Miro doesn't ask anything. He doesn't want to know in case he is questioned by the secret police.

"So, my business is done. I've got to run before Marin fingers me. Coming along?"

"*Where are you going?*" Miro asks in desperation.

"Mount Pastrik, where else?" Niko casually states.

"I have nowhere to go. The KLA would kill me if I go to Pastrik."

Niko glances at Miro as he puts on his gear. "Yep, you're probably right. They will find out who I am, and they will know who you are."

The sergeant walks back into the van, carrying bundles of electronic gear. He notices Niko with his combat gear on.

"Where you going?"

"I have gate guard duty for a few hours."

"Okay, but come back here to help us load once you are done."

"Of course, Sergeant, where else would I go?"

Niko walks out of the van, AK in hand. Miro is shaking, speechless.

The sergeant leans out of the back door as Niko walks into the night.

"By the way, you are lucky you have guard duty. The colonel and Marin are pretty lit up about the American pilot getting away. It is not very fun being around them right now." The sergeant chuckles and slaps the outside of the van.

Niko gets his ruck from the billets and walks casually to the special police headquarters. He spots Colonel Marin's armored jeep with dark side windows. He wanders around to the front of the vehicle and looks through the front windshield to make sure no one is in the jeep. No one is, so he calmly opens the driver's door, hops in and notices that the keys are in the ignition. He starts up the engine, backs up and coolly drives to the front gate.

The sergeant on duty at the gate is the one who was in charge of the body detail, the one that dealt with the three special police with a knife. Niko pulls up to the sergeant and rolls down his window. The sergeant is dumbfounded to see Niko in the jeep. He pokes his head inside to see if anyone else is in the vehicle. He puts his hands on his knees and lets out a full belly laugh.

"Man, you got balls. If I were you, I would get the hell out of here as fast as you can."

Niko smiles. He stomps on the gas and the jeep lurches forward, never to be seen again by Marin. Within the hour his jeep will be at the bottom of a deep mossy lake.

# 25: LINKUP

**DIRT SWIRLS INSIDE THE** crevice as John and Prek listen for voices. The dirty air finally starts to dissipate, revealing people crouching down by the crevice's walls. Some begin to move, while others are in the fetal position with their hands over their faces. Above the noise of artillery, the first sound John and Prek can distinguish is coughing.

Everyone in the crevice is completely covered in dirt, hacking out mouthfuls of the grime. They drink water and douse themselves over their heads with canteens. Faces become recognizable. Julianna shakes her long ponytail, but dirt just covers her shoulders and head again.

"Anyone hurt?" yells John with his hands cupped over his mouth.

As they check themselves and each other, miraculously there are only minor cuts and abrasions. When the helicopters attacked, they hugged the walls of the crevice as the machine-gun strafing chewed up dirt down the middle.

"Okay, let's move. No time to rest here; it's too dangerous," John bellows, and the column reforms. They sling their AKs and stumble up the mountain one step at a time, coughing and blowing brown and red mucus out of their mouths and noses.

They reach the wreckage of the Hind-D Prek shot, still burning red hot with a long plume of black smoke drifting into the wind.

There is no way around the wreckage. One of the KLA soldiers that greeted them at the bottom of the mountain climbs out of the crevice. He waves to the nearest KLA in a trench about fifty meters up the mountain. Several wave back. Within minutes they arrive with a rope to help everyone up and out.

Climbing up the rope tests arm and leg muscles. The strain is almost unbearable for some, and others on top help by pulling them up. Eventually all make it to the top. They run in the open to the top trench line where they are greeted by several curious KLA soldiers. Prek tells them about the NATO officers and their mission to provide air support. The KLA soldiers can't contain themselves. They are excited, sending word down the trench to make way for the important column.

The NATO officers take note of the trench construction; reminiscent of the First World War on the Western Front, the trench zigzags to prevent someone from shooting straight down the trench line, and to limit artillery or grenade blasts.

KLA soldiers give them cold water as they pass them by. The cold water is a blessing. They drink plenty and pour it over their sweaty, filthy heads.

At a large wooden bunker, Travis and John both set up their Satcoms. Travis calls for close air support to knock out VJ artillery while John updates Pine Tree.

"Request CAS on artillery positions surrounding Mount Pastrik, over."

"Sorry, but we cannot hit enemy artillery until we destroy all the SA-3s, over."

"How long is that going to take? The mountain is getting pounded, over."

"Expect one to two hours, over."

"You're no use to me. Let me know soonest, out."

John isn't having any better luck with Pine Tree than Travis has with CAS support.

John yells in Travis's ear, "Pine Tree doesn't believe this is going to be the VJ's main effort. They think it will be at Peje where the main pass is into Albania. If the VJ can plug that up, then they can starve out the KLA on Pastrik."

Travis stares at John with a long face. "The VJ *want* this mountain. Time is not on the VJ's side to wait out the KLA on Pastrik."

"I think you're spot on, mate; let's go find Gashi."

The KLA scouts lead the column around the exterior trench line, constantly rotating around in the zigzag design. KLA man positions in the trench, pointing their weapons into kill zones, awaiting the VJ attack. KLA and VJ snipers play cat and mouse.

Artillery pounds the mountain without letup.

They shuffle to General Gashi's underground bunker. The NATO officers set up their antennas on top of the bunker and enter the concrete cave. Despite the situation, General Gashi is still smiling and optimistic. On his wall is a map of the mountain with all the KLA positions, including mortars and mined areas.

He greets everyone, and is so happy to see the NATO officers he pours some scotch in small glasses.

Right when he is about to take a drink Gashi stares at Julianna, who looks more like a dirt clod than herself. He walks up to her, examining her closely.

"You are Julianna Shala?"

Julianna is surprised General Gashi knows who she is, and wonders why he is asking her. She comes to the position of attention.

"Yes sir, that is I."

"Someone is here that very badly wants to see you again."

Julianna is stunned. It must be Josif. Her eyes swell with moisture. She feels guilty about how she treated him the last time she saw him. She realizes now that it was Bekim, not her brother, that murdered the VJ prisoners.

General Gashi whispers in a KLA soldier's ear. The soldier quickly departs.

John's radio crackles. "Pine Tree to Razorback, over."

John grabs the mic while everyone listens.

"This is Razorback, over."

"Change in plans. New coded information just deciphered. You're right, enemy's main effort is to capture and hold Mount Pastrik. Supporting effort is to attack the VJ at Peje trying to block KLA reinforcements from Albania, over."

"Good lord, what other information did you get?"

"Every position the enemy will occupy before they assault Mount Pastrik. We are pre-planning the targets for air strikes, over."

"Can you send that information to Gashi? We are with him now."

"WILCO, out."

General Gashi raises his glass. "To an independent Kosovo."

The NATO officers are suddenly full of energy and vigor.

"To an independent Kosovo!"

Julianna isn't interested in toasting. She hears footsteps coming down the wooden stairs. Her hands tight over her mouth, she feels her heart throbbing out of her chest.

The curtains open. The person walks into the room. Julianna is smitten. The NATO officers are so stunned they forget to drink their toast to Kosovo.

Julianna embraces Deidra so hard neither can fully breathe. Tears rain down their cheeks. The NATO officers are also overcome with emotion. They gently pull Deidra from Julianna's arms and hold her tightly. It seems to be a miracle.

"NATO didn't bomb my bus. The Serbs made us get off the bus, and they blew it up with demolitions in front of Serbian news crews. The whole thing was a Serb propaganda stunt to discredit NATO. Shabin and I walked for three days to get to Macedonia. We found a ride that took us all the way to your parents. Shabin is still there, and in good health. I obtained American BDUs and came back to fight. By the time I made it to Skanderbeg, the VJ were there, so I headed to where all KLA are going, here at Pastrik."

"So, Shabin is safe with my parents?" Julianna asks, tears and mucus mixing on her face.

"Yes, and your parents love him like he is their own!"

# 26: ATTACK POSITION

**MIRO BOUNCES AROUND IN** the back of the communications truck as it makes its way along a long column of VJ combat vehicles moving south. The once-paved roads are now nothing more than a series of potholes. Between the potholes and bomb craters, vehicles have to constantly weave around them, making the long convoy look like a sluggish slithering snake.

The sergeant drives the truck, but the passenger's side is empty because of Niko's desertion. A sore point. The communications equipment, along with Miro, another operator and a VJ captain, are in the back of the truck. It is nothing more than a large, green-painted aluminum box with two small windows on each side.

Drenched in sweat, Miro tries to keep his balance on a chair while monitoring the brigade command net. The heat from the radios and amplifiers only make the hot, stuffy box worse. Every few minutes the radio operators pour water on a towel draping each radio to keep them from overheating. As the radio operators receive reports and unit positions, the captain places the information on a large map that hangs on the wall opposite the three radios.

Miro is nauseated while trying to ward off the sweat. Meanwhile, he must keep up with an endless stream of reports blasting over the radio. Between the heat and movement of the truck Miro vomits on the floor. The VJ officer curses Miro, smacks him on the head and kicks his chair over. Miro scrambles to clean up the mess with the wet towel from the top of his radio. The smell inside the van is so wretched that the officer opens the back door of the van, letting in fresh but dirty air.

For security reasons, the door is not supposed to be open. After all, this is a command-and-control node, a precise target for NATO and the KLA. It is a dangerous job. Receiving reports is not too dangerous, but transmitting begs for trouble from NATO electronic warfare assets.

An RPG from an ambush could come ripping through the side, or an aircraft's precision missile could turn the truck into an instant fireball. Opening the back door only makes it riskier by inviting snipers. After a few minutes the officer has Miro close the door. When he does so, a large cloud of dust and dirt billows inside.

To help mitigate the risk from ambushes and aircraft, the VJ have placed civilian cars in front of and behind the truck. The cars are stolen from Kosovars and driven by VJ soldiers wearing civilian clothes. With over twenty civilian cars in the convoy, the VJ can transport about 100 soldiers under the guise of innocent civilians.

Miro drinks hot water from his plastic canteen and pours the remainder over his head. His head is still spinning and pounding. Sorrow overtakes his thoughts. Again, the captain hits him over the head, this time for not paying attention to the radio transmissions. Miro somewhat regains his composure, although every minute is miserable throughout the long day. The officer has forbidden Miro and the others from eating rations. It is fortunate that the other radio operator has brought a large container of water. It smells like plastic and is hot but at least wet.

In the early evening the convoy stops for fuel. The sergeant pours five large cans into the gas tank. Miro and the other radio operator take turns pissing in the woods. Relieved to be outside of the truck and away from the loud crackling radios, Miro sits on a log and pours more water over his head and face. What a day. He raises his throbbing head and sees the last images of the setting sun.

Miro's brief peace is shattered when he hears and feels NATO aircraft bombing. The ground rumbles, and other soldiers go about their duties with a sense of urgency. In minutes he is back in the van. He spends the rest of the night trying to keep up with incoming reports of unit positions as they move around Mount Pastrik. It is frustrating work as units get lost in the dark and send inaccurate locations. The officer placing their positions on the map is livid, calling units back and ripping their asses.

Miro's fear of suddenly dying from a NATO air strike makes him a nervous wreck. There is a reason why senior officers, including his brother, are not in the communications vehicle. Although the radio transmissions have the latest technology, with frequency-hopping capabilities to avoid NATO interception, Miro knows NATO aircraft will eventually detect and target command-and-control vehicles like his. The civilian cars purposely placed around his vehicle are most likely the only reason he is still alive. With every violent detonation during the night, Miro wonders if his vehicle will be next.

By morning's light most movement is finally over. The hour before was a slow movement into a heavily forested area. Miro hears branches swiping the outside walls of the van. Explosions continue to pound the ground. The sergeant driving the truck, in his struggle to drive between the larger trees, often has problems with the clutch, forcing the vehicle to lunge awkwardly forward and stall at times.

Finally, they stop, and the operations officer opens the back door. A rush of cool morning air flows into the van. Miro turns around to see where they are on the map. He is surprised how far south they are, between Mount Pastrik and the Albanian border. Even more surprising is the enormity of the VJ forces surrounding Mount Pastrik. On the map is an army-level operation consisting of almost all the VJ forces in Kosovo.

The sergeant sticks his head in the door and directs Miro to assist in setting up a large radio antenna. Miro, sore after sitting in the metal chair all night, jumps out the back door onto the soft forest ground.

Fast-movers scream by in the sky. Serbian Migs and NATO aircraft of all types are fighting for the air. VJ artillery unleashes a hell-storm of high-explosive rounds on Pastrik. Miro's brother's armored car pulls up around the van. Colonels Cadikovski and Marin appear from the back seats and enter the communications truck.

The sergeant supervises soldiers as they camouflage the truck with tree limbs and set up perimeter security. The operations officer takes over Miro's radio: the largest and final battle of the Kosovo war is about to begin. The radio crackles while Miro's brother orders an immediate attack on Pastrik. His Guards Brigade joins most of the Serb Army to seize and hold the last KLA stronghold in Kosovo.

# 27: FINAL FIRES

**DRESSED IN FULL VJ** combat gear, Niko walks at double time through various VJ formations as they prepare for their assault on the northern side of Mount Pastrik. No one knows who he is and no one cares. No one really even notices him. He is just another soldier amongst thousands.

The VJ assault begins. Over 30,000 men are attacking a mountain containing 15,000 KLA. MiGs scream past trying to gain air superiority long enough for the VJ troops to seize the mountain.

The VJ advance up the hill behind a creeping wall of artillery. Smoke fills the air. Men scream as they step on antipersonnel mines or trip claymores. The KLA blow preset demolitions, and mortars pound the VJ just before they arrive at the KLA forward positions. Hand-to-hand combat ensues: stabbing, shooting, screaming. The first KLA positions are overwhelmed within minutes.

VJ penal battalion soldiers are forced to clear minefields by running ahead of regular VJ troops. They bypass KLA positions and step on tripwires, blowing their legs off. VJ battalions attack past the penal battalion soldiers, who are thrashing in pain. Behind the VJ formations are the special police, shooting any man who takes cover instead of attacking.

General Gashi states loudly, "NATO has air superiority now. They are striking all the unit positions that Pine Tree has targeted."

Two US B-1B high-altitude bombers drop over sixty bombs on the second echelon of the attacking VJ, causing large gaps in their formations. The lead VJ echelon at the base of the hill is eventually decimated by a crescendo of automatic weapons from KLA positions.

Niko occupies a KLA trench that was overrun. It is stuffed with dead bleeding bodies. Two KLA and four VJ. It was a scout position, and he spots a half-buried radio. He yanks it out of the loose dirt and keys the mic. It still works. He makes contact with KLA on top of the mountain, but they think he is a VJ soldier.

Niko laughs to himself. He actually *is* a VJ soldier.

He finally gets connected with one of General Gashi's officers. Niko calls in a fire mission on the VJ second and third attack echelons just behind him in the woods. The officer plots it, and Albanian artillery whistles over his head, devastating the VJ formations before they can attack.

KLA scouts crawl to Niko's position and guide him up the hill through minefields and numerous tripwires. Wearing a VJ uniform, he gets odd looks from KLA soldiers in their fighting positions. Most assume he is a prisoner. Niko gets tired of being spit on and drops his ruck and takes off his uniform.

He pulls out blue jeans and instantly becomes a KLA soldier.

General Gashi transitions into the warrior mode. "It's time to do our duty!" He sprints out the door. John and Travis follow. They run up and out of the bunker and across the mountaintop to a reinforced command position.

Prek greets them and has already set up their radios. Their view is spectacular. They can see all of the southern slope of the mountain, across the open plains below and into the thick woods close to the Albanian border.

General Gashi leaves to check on his men. He is a commander on the move, circulating amongst his men to encourage them while also assessing the situation.

Julianna and Deidra remain in the bunker for now. Holding each other, they are still overwhelmed by their reunion. Julianna cannot stop crying she is so happy. The bombing outside does not faze them, at least not yet.

Niko finds the concrete command bunker and runs down the steps, opens the curtain and sees the map on the wall. He quickly walks up to it, examining the VJ positions he encoded to Pine Tree to ensure they are accurate. Niko smiles. He knows the aerial strikes are bombarding each of the positions. He turns to run outside, glancing at the two women hugging and crying. He doesn't know that Julianna, Miro's wife, is one of them.

From the NATO officers' command position, they can clearly observe thousands of VJ sprinting across the open toward the mountain. The good news is that the air strikes are hitting all the positions, but on the flip side, 30,000 VJ are rushing the mountain at the same time.

VJ artillery lets up on the hill because NATO aircraft make quick work of their positions. However, the mass of men continues almost unabated toward the mountain.

"Razorback, this is Godzilla, over."

Travis and John crane their necks and spot sixteen air streams high in the sky. Two B-52s are at 10,000 feet.

"This is Razorback, over."

"Roger, Razorback. Just wanted to let you know we are going to bomb a brigade headquarters and VJ troops to the south of the mountain in the woods close to Albania, over."

"Roger, over. Good luck."

The NATO officers and Prek follow the B-52s as they fly out of sight.

"I thought they were going to drop bombs?" asks Prek.

"Hold on to your teeth," John yells.

Several thousand yards of woods light up in an incredible fireball.

Miro is outside the communications van on security detail. He is glad that they are well hidden in the woods instead of in the open with other VJ soldiers on their attack. Marin is gone also, driving the VJ soldiers to their duty, herding them like sheep for the slaughter. Miro is still shaky. He knows just about anything can happen. He knows from his experience in the Malisheve battle. He is right.

Cluster bombs fall from the sky by the hundreds, blowing up as they hit anything: trees, ground, the truck. He instinctively crawls underneath a BMP. The oxygen is sucked out of the air. Fire licks under the BMP and burns his entire body. It fucking hurts. He does what he must—crawl back out from underneath the armored infantry carrier and try to make it into the open.

Miro crawls like a madman and starts to run on pure adrenaline. He sees his brother, on fire, fall out of the communications van. Miro runs up to him, but it is too late. He watches in horror as his brother's skin melts. Miro looks for the sergeant but does not see him. All he sees is smoke and fire. He runs the best he can into the open field and rolls over and over to extinguish his burning uniform.

Niko runs to trenches overlooking the B-52 strike. He knows Miro is in the strike zone, and he starts running down the mountain. The KLA in their fighting positions think Niko has gone mad and tackle him.

Julianna and Deidra climb out of the bunker and occupy the nearest fighting positions. They have no idea where the NATO officers are, so they join several KLA soldiers raking fire down on the attacking VJ. Because of Miro, Julianna is hesitant to fire, so she aims in front of the VJ to make them go to ground. Sometimes it works, but most of the time the VJ speed up.

Deidra fires for vengeance. She has waited a long time for this moment. She leans dangerously over the parapet and fires her AK on full automatic, killing dozens of attacking VJ. She only stops momentarily to slap in a new magazine.

Over 100 VJ tanks and BMPs are crossing the open fields. They will reach the mountain within minutes, many coming up the huge crevices. Travis calls for tank killers, and six A-10s, working in pairs, whistle in, firing both their guns and Maverick missiles.

About a third of the armored vehicles are already deep in the crevices by the time the aircraft arrive. A platoon of three tanks grinds up a deep winding crevice without being detected by NATO air. The squeaky metal tracks slip and slide on loose dirt and stones.

KLA soldiers spot the black smoke plumes and clouds of dirt rising from the crevice. Six soldiers set up an RPG ambush at the top and wait. The first beast appears. The antennas, front glacis and main gun poke out of the dirty air. An overly zealous KLA soldier runs toward the front of the tank, takes a knee, aims his RPG—and waits. The tank's gun sights are pointed too high to see the soldier, who is just feet away.

The tank continues over the ridgeline. The underbelly is exposed for just a few seconds. The KLA soldier steadies himself and squeezes the trigger. His rocket penetrates right under the driver's position and explodes. All hatches blow off simultaneously. Leaping flames burn red hot from the holes. Seconds later the ammunition ignites, and the entire tank blows sky high. The soldier is vaporized.

The two remaining tanks attack past the burning tank. They spin their turrets with machine guns blazing. Dozens of KLA are instantly killed. Tank gunners snug inside the turrets fire the 125 mm main gun, obliterating the heavily fortified sandbag bunkers. Five KLA soldiers belly-crawl toward the rear of the tanks and destroy both with RPGs.

The tanks still in the open and climbing up other crevices become victims of hungry A-10s. Each will eventually explode, their turrets popping off high into the air and landing upside down on the ground. VJ soldiers following behind the tanks quickly learn to move away or be blown to bits. The BMPs stop and spew infantry out the back. The infantry continues on foot up the mountain.

Niko explains to the KLA preventing him from running down the mountain that he is going to save a friend, and they let him go.

Miro lies in the open field almost nude. He has torn off his uniform and has severe burns. His eyes hurt the most. He gets on his knees, then his feet, and staggers toward the base of the mountain to look for cover under the large rocks. Bullets whiz past him, but from behind. Marin is chasing him, firing his pistol. Miro's left hand is hit. Two fingers are gone. He drops to the ground and looks around. Marin is still running toward him.

One of Prek's snipers scans the fields with his scope, looking for high-value targets—officers and senior sergeants. He spots a man with a tattered uniform staggering across the field until he drops. Chasing the man is what every sniper in the KLA dreams of: a colonel in the Serbian Secret Police.

Miro looks at Marin's pistol, aimed at him from just feet away. He looks at Marin's face rather than the pistol. The colonel's eyes bulge with a special kind of hate.

"I knew you and your friend Niko Radic were the traitors!"

A hole appears in Marin's chest. He drops his pistol and falls backwards.

Niko runs full speed across the open field toward the half-naked man in the grass. He witnesses Marin being shot and assumes the man on the ground might be Miro. When he reaches Miro he barely recognizes him.

Marin starts to move, trying to reach his pistol. Niko pulls out his revolver and dispatches Marin. Blood spouts from his mouth. Niko throws the revolver as far as he can in the open field. Niko notices Miro has third-degree burns on most of his body. His left hand is mangled and bleeding profusely. Worst of all are Miro's eyes. His lids are completely burned off, and he is starting to go into shock.

Niko jabs Miro with a shot of morphine, then pours water over a clean bandana and ties it around Miro's head, covering his eyes. He then places a tourniquet around Miro's left wrist.

"Hang in there, buddy. I've got you now."

Niko lies on the ground, rolls to Miro and stands up with him on his shoulder. He starts running back to the mountain while KLA on the mountain cover his movement.

Travis and John are worried. Thousands of VJ infantry and many tanks continue up the mountain unabated. Travis gets on the horn.

"Broken Arrow. I repeat, Broken Arrow."

NATO pilots in Kosovo know what *Broken Arrow* means. It is a holdover term from the Vietnam War. Friendly forces are about to be overrun.

Every pilot, no matter their current mission, scrambles toward Mount Pastrik.

The NATO officers and Prek watch in amazement. Aircraft are stacked high over the battlefield as a command-and-control aircraft controls bombing runs from over ten NATO countries.

Combat deaths on this scale in the Balkans have been unprecedented since World War II. Tanks explode and roll down the mountain, crushing dozens. Other VJ infantry are killed by flying tank debris, such as road wheels and broken track. Still, the VJ infantry continue.

KLA around the mountain rake fire on VJ that escape the aerial bombings. Many VJ still reach the KLA fighting positions and engage once more in close combat. The battle rages for hours, seesawing back and forth. Trenches are overrun, then retaken numerous times. The battle seems to be out of anyone's control. No one is safe.

Niko drops to his knees and places Miro down carefully. He checks Miro's pulse. He is still alive. Bombing runs burst all around them. He lies down over Miro and waits. Dirt is so thick in the air that visibility is near zero. Shrapnel slices past just inches above Niko. The ground rumbles.

General Gashi appears at the NATO officers' position. The three of them huddle close together. They are losing the battle, even with all of the airpower and hard fighting. A VJ hand grenade lands in their position. Prek throws it back just in time. He exits with his AK and starts killing waves of VJ getting closer to General Gashi and the NATO officers.

Travis grabs the mic. "Request immediate napalm around entire mountain. Final protective fires, over."

Within two minutes a transmission is returned. "Keep your heads down, for God's sake."

John goes ballistic. "You're going to kill a lot of friendly, maybe even us. You can't do that. It is against the Geneva Convention to knowingly kill allied forces. Call them back and cancel it, now!"

General Gashi disagrees. "Do not cancel the fire mission. We must win no matter the costs."

He then runs outside and screams for all KLA to withdraw to their final positions on top of the hill. He sprints around the mountain making sure they all know about the order. Some cannot run because they are engaged in close combat. Others are shot in the back trying to get to the top trenches, but most run like hell and make it. Julianna, Deidra and other KLA withdraw just a few dozen yards to the top trench.

John is on the radio trying to call off the strikes. Travis sucker punches him in the face, knocking John down into the mud. He bounces right back, picks up Travis and throws him like a rag doll to the opposite wall. John picks up the mic. Travis crawls up and grabs John's legs, yanking as hard as he can. John drops the mic, falls, but jumps back up.

A burst of machine-gun fire erupts inside their position. Shards of hot metal cut into John's arms just as he grabs the mic to call off the napalm. John's ears are ringing. He can't hear anything, but he tries talking on the mic. He sees that the hand-mic cord is cut and the radios are shattered. He turns around. Gashi is holding a smoking AK-47. He has just destroyed the radios. It is impossible to call off the final fires.

Three KLA who prevented Niko from running down the mountain rush to help. They scream to Niko about the napalm strike. Two KLA take Miro under their arms while Niko lifts his feet in the front. Niko is in muscle failure but pushes himself over the limit, moving his body beyond what he has ever done before. He barely maintains carrying Miro as they struggle to reach the mountaintop.

Two US Navy Tomcats fly low and fast just in front of the NATO officers' position. They let loose canisters of napalm down the side of the mountain, engulfing VJ and some KLA soldiers in a firestorm. KLA soldiers hear the screams of men burning to death. They will all have PTSD.

More napalm is dropped around the mountain, which now resembles a volcano spewing black smoke. Secret police shoot any VJ soldiers running back, but this time the VJ survivors overwhelm them and kill all the secret police.

The battle is over. The war is over.

John and Travis creep outside and watch as hundreds of VJ soldiers and dozens of tanks withdraw north. In a few minutes Prek joins the NATO officers. They survey the battlefield. The destruction is complete. Fires burn vehicles and dead corpses.

The stench is unbearable. Everyone coughs and pukes. Some put bandanas over their mouths and noses. KLA soldiers search for the wounded, either VJ or KLA.

The NATO officers shake Prek's hand. John offers his hand to Travis. Travis returns the shake in silence. He leaves to look for Julianna while John speaks with General Gashi.

Travis finds Julianna and Deidra still huddling in the top trench. He jumps down and places a hand on each one. They look up at him with their eyes wide.

"It's over. Finally, over. Come on out."

Once out of the trench the three embrace each other. After a few minutes Deidra silently breaks away to help with the wounded. Julianna and Travis are together. Julianna puts her head on his chest and takes comfort in holding him tight. She wonders about Miro. He is exactly twenty-one feet away, still alive.

# 28: RETURN TO LANGLEY

**NIKO EXITS KOSOVO BY** car and flies out of the Skopje airport to Frankfurt. After a five-hour wait he catches a flight to Dulles. His boss meets him at the airport. They say nothing to each other until they are in a government car at the curbside. Once inside Niko receives a hearty handshake. Still, no words are exchanged.

They arrive at CIA headquarters and are dropped off at a side door. Niko's boss enters first. Niko doesn't know what to expect, but he assumes it won't be pretty. They take an elevator to the CIA director's office. Niko stinks and is unshaven. As he sits in the director's outer office, he worries why the director wants to see him. He has never met the man before.

The director's personal assistant receives a buzz. "Yes sir, they will be right in." Niko's boss rises and motions for Niko to follow. As they enter a large room, they see the director pacing back and forth. He makes no eye contacts but speaks while he continues to walk fast behind his large wooden desk.

"Bad judgment, very bad judgment. You should have egressed out of Kosovo before the VJ manned the border crossing into

Montenegro. One day, just one freaking day, and you missed the last opportunity out. We sure could have used all the information you had gathered, but instead we had nothing to go on. Did they ever suspect you . . . interrogate you?

"Yes sir, no sir."

The director stares through Niko, waiting for a better answer.

"The Serb Special Police knew there was an insider, but as far as I know, they never knew it was me until too late."

"Too late for what?"

"I stole a special police colonel's jeep and linked up with the KLA on Mount Pastrik. That was at the beginning of the battle."

"So, no interrogation?"

"No sir."

"Did you tell anyone anything?"

"Yes sir."

"Well, who? Why?"

"I told a Serb man named Miroslav Cadikovski I am in the CIA. I had to do it so I could get on the AM radio in the VJ communications truck. He was my lookout."

"What happened to this Cadikovski guy?"

"He is in an American military hospital at Landstuhl. He might be flown to the States for skin grafts if he survives."

"Ah, a good Serb?"

"Yes sir, my closest buddy in the VJ. He was forced in like myself. We had no option."

"Did you kill any KLA?"

"No sir, none."

"Do you have any idea how important those codes were you sent before the battle, uh—what's your real name, son?"

"Divid Petrovic, but everyone calls me David. Uh, no sir, I don't."

The CIA director steps directly in front of David and holds out his hand. David is surprised. He tightly grasps the director's hand.

"David, you may have won this battle. Your VJ positions were exactly on target. We were able to hit those targets a little later than we wanted, but we destroyed plenty of VJ, all their headquarters along with their logistics. I'm proud of you, son."

"Thank you, sir."

"Have a seat, David. There is something wrong; what is it?"

"I had to kill men I didn't want to kill."

"Like who?"

"My friends in the VJ. The guys I was with for months. They were good guys and helped me whenever they could. They trusted me. I murdered them."

The director wants to say something stupid, something like field agents should always emotionally distance themselves, blah, blah, blah. He catches himself and asks something else.

"Are you suicidal, David?"

"I don't know, sir."

# 29: WHAT COULD
# HAVE BEEN

**TRAVIS SIPS ON HIS** favorite scotch as he sits in his recliner watching American football on the Armed Forces Network. He also goes through his mail, throwing out most in a box for shredding. Trooper leans against the side of Travis's chair with his full weight, then uses his snout to lift Travis's leg for attention. It works. Trooper has trained Travis to automatically scratch behind his ears.

"Ah, a letter from John!"

Travis opens the letter and anxiously reads it several times. John is on the full colonel list. He has also been presented with a shiny medal for his time in Kosovo. His last comment is, "By the way, fellow, I seriously recommend you not fall in love again in a combat zone. Cheers, John."

A picture of John with his family is included. All smiling.

Travis puts his scotch down and picks up a piece of paper from a side table. *LETTER OF REPRIMAND to Lieutenant Colonel Travis S. Savage, United States Army*, for refusing a direct order to depart a combat zone. Travis is upset, but he understands his boss had to do something about disobeying his order, even if in the end his disobedience proved worthwhile. The letter of reprimand means Travis will never make full colonel, and will not be qualified to receive any awards for his mission in Kosovo, or even a purple heart. His neck wound while rescuing the downed pilot cannot be proven to have come from the enemy, thus no purple heart.

Travis doesn't really care about medals or any recognition. His mission was classified, and what he did in Kosovo will not be made public for many years. He picks up his scotch and listens to the Armed Forces Network. The game is over, and some US Air Force general who he has never heard of is blabbing about how decisive airpower is, and how his pilots alone saved Kosovo from Serbian tyranny.

"Airpower alone can be decisive, as Kosovo has proved. The Army just needs to hold the ground afterwards."

Somehow the general forgets to mention anything about the KLA.

Travis wads up his letter of reprimand and throws it to the other side of the room. Trooper unhesitatingly fetches it and tears it up.

"Now I know why I adopted you."

He gets up, takes a knee, and hugs Trooper tight, kissing him on top of his head.

At night when Travis turns out the lights he sees shadows and hears men scream in agony. If he falls asleep, the horrors of war burn through his soul. Sweating through his sheets, he eventually wakes up screaming. Some nights he finds himself in a different room after he runs into a wall.

That night, like so many other nights since he returned to Germany, he lies in bed listening to Trooper snore. He gets up and looks through the window at the beautiful lights of Stuttgart. He thinks of Julianna. He has a lump in his throat. For what could have been, but will never be.

# 30: A BEAUTIFUL DAY
# IN DRENICA

**THE LARGE BANNER READS** *Dita e Veres 2000.* Cars slowly make their way through a British KFOR checkpoint into the festival. A Welsh soldier in a jeep stands behind a machine gun, overwatching his sergeant check each vehicle.

The sergeant is slightly taken aback when he observes the next car pull up. It is a dirty white two-door Crvena Zastava. The driver is smiling but has a knob for a left hand. Skin grafts cover much of his arms. His face has the most grafts, particularly around his eyes. His right hand is on the steering wheel. Around the wrist is a red-and-white braided bracelet.

The sergeant peeks inside the car and is surprised to see two beautiful women in the back seat. Each has a child. The woman on the left is dressed in a traditional Kosovar dress and has a three-month-old boy on her lap. The woman's smile is penetrating, and in perfect English she thanks the sergeant and NATO for saving Kosovo. The woman on the right is ecstatic, pointing out the window with her young son.

"Look, Shabin, do you see all the dancers?"

The sergeant smiles back and motions them through.

The car pulls into a large crowd and parks. Thousands of people are attending, including KFOR and former KLA soldiers providing security. General Gashi mills about the crowd shaking hands. Within minutes he is mobbed by Kosovars wanting to meet him. He will be the future commander of the Kosovo Army and prime minister of Kosovo . . . a new country.

Prek walks up to welcome Julianna and Deidra. He embraces them and meets the children, little Miro and Shabin. He finally meets Miro for the first time. Prek has heard much about him, mainly from Niko, who is now back in the States.

They sit with Julianna's mother, Mirjeta. Her father, Agim Shala, is near the stage preparing to play his flute with the rest of the musicians. Julianna kisses Mirjeta, then hands the baby to Miro and joins the dancers. Above the stage are large banners with the faces of KLA heroes who lost their lives in the war. Josif's is front and center, flapping in the wind.

Prek sits by Deidra and holds Shabin on his knee. Deidra peeks at Prek. She thinks he is very handsome.

Once more it is a beautiful day in Drenica. Everyone is smiling.

CPSIA information can be obtained
at www.ICGtesting.com
Printed in the USA
LVHW040501121120
671367LV00007B/171

9 781646 631872